VEDBÆK

KLAMPENBORG

LYNGBY

ALLERUP

RØDOVRE

RØNDBY

HVIDOVRE

BISPEBJERG

VESTERBRO

AMAGER

ØRESUND

COPENHAGEN

N

THE GIRL IN
THE PHOTO

THE GIRL IN THE PHOTO

Heidi Amsinck

MUSWELL
PRESS

First published by Muswell Press in 2022
Copyright © Heidi Amsinck 2022
Map copyright © Frederik Walkden

Typeset in Bembo by M Rules
Printed and bound by CPI Group (UK) Ltd, Croydon CR0 4YY

A CIP catalogue record for this book
is available from the British Library

ISBN: 9781739879419
eISBN: 9781739879426

Muswell Press
London N6 5HQ
www.muswell-press.co.uk

To my sister Helene

March

1

Monday 11:23

Detective Inspector Henrik Jungersen waited under his umbrella
as the uniformed officer who had been first on the scene pulled
himself upright next to the flower bed.

'Where?' he said, when the man had finished spitting and
wiping his mouth on his sleeve.

'First-floor landing.'

Henrik glanced up wearily at the red villa fronted by an
immaculate lawn and ornamental pines.

It was too big, too quiet.

More vehicles were arriving up the gravel drive, blue blinks
intermittently illuminating the tall conifers that shielded the
property from the road. He had told forensics to wait outside,
so that he could have a moment alone with the corpse, and had
already donned his white, hooded coverall, but he didn't feel
like going in.

Not yet.

He walked across to the Alsatian cowering by the squad car.
It had belonged to the victim and, by all accounts, had been
locked in the back garden for days. The partner of the officer

who had just been reacquainted with his breakfast was trying to make the dog drink from a plastic bottle. No interest. Plenty of puddles it could have quenched its thirst from, Henrik guessed.

He stroked the dog behind the ears and on the silky golden patch on its forehead. It whimpered restlessly. Probably wondering what had happened to the hand that usually fed it. 'Where did you find it?'

'In the back garden,' said the officer. 'Crap everywhere. It was the barking made the woman next door call the police. Complaint wasn't taken seriously at first, apparently.'

'Next door where?' said Henrik.

The officer pointed to the property to the right of the villa. Looking up, Henrik caught the movement of a curtain dropping back into place. Typical of leafy Klampenborg for a curtain twitcher to call the police about a dog making a racket. Where he came from, you would have popped over, had a word, tried to establish the facts before involving the authorities.

Anything before involving the authorities.

'Did she say anything?'

'Couldn't shut her up,' said the officer, twirling his index finger at his temple to suggest the mental state of the neighbour. 'Nothing of use, though.'

Stupid woman, thought Henrik, feeling indignation rising in his throat. If she had only walked over and pressed the doorbell when she first suspected something was up, they might not be in this mess. He would pay her a visit afterwards, give her a piece of his mind.

The Alsatian would hopefully recover. Henrik would gladly have taken it himself until a new owner could be found, but he respected animals and their needs enough to know that his was no life for a dog.

Not lately.

Not since Jensen had exploded back into his life.

Where was she now?

It was a dangerous thought. He tried to dismiss it. Of all the women in Copenhagen, Jensen was the last one he needed to concern himself with.

He sighed, blowing steam into the cold, damp air. Bloody rain, pissing it down for weeks on end. Grey on grey. Much like his mood. Wasn't spring supposed to start in March?

He closed his umbrella, tossed it in the front seat of his car and jogged up the steps to the villa, feeling the eyes of the officers on him.

A wodge of mail was stuck under the front door, circulars mostly. He put on his latex gloves and face mask and bent down to retrieve one of the few proper letters.

Mrs Irene Valborg

There wasn't a postmark on the envelope. When had postmarks stopped being a thing? He opened the letter and found it dated over two weeks ago, a reminder from the dentist. Not a good sign, as if the stench coming from deep inside the house hadn't already told him all he needed to know.

Once on a hot day during his early years as a police officer, he and a colleague had forced open the door to a flat in Valby after neighbours had complained about a stink in the stairwell. He had found the resident, a man in his eighties, seated on the sofa with his eyes wide open, his dinner tray on his lap and the TV blaring.

Dead for a month.

Crawling with flies.

Ever since, Henrik had been wary of them, these loners decomposing like fruit rotting in a bowl. It was the real reason he had asked for a moment on his own with the corpse under the pretext of reading the crime scene. Whatever he was about to find, he would rather there were no audience.

He had seen more than his fair share of death during his many years on the force. Why should he find these bodies in advanced stages of decay, these discarded human husks, so abhorrent and unnatural? It was inexplicable even to himself. A corpse was a corpse, after all.

He wanted to turn around and run back out, but he couldn't. Not now.

Not with everyone out there watching.

The front-door lock looked new and of decent quality. It hadn't been forced, but that meant nothing. Burglars had methods of sweet-talking their way into the homes of the elderly. There was also a sophisticated-looking alarm system, though Henrik guessed this had been switched off when the killer had gained entry to the property, or Irene might still be alive.

He took a picture of the sticker with the name of the alarm firm, making a mental note to check when the system had been installed.

The house was neat and tidy, no signs of a disturbance. It was full of antiques, faded old stuff, as though time had stood still here for a century. There was a spiral-bound address book next to the telephone, tradespeople mostly, their names written in scratchy blue ink. Not much in the way of family and friends, as far as he could tell.

It didn't look like anything was missing, but burglars were after cash, or valuables that could be handled and sold fast. Somewhere in the big, silent house there would be a handbag with an empty wallet, a jewellery box ripped open and plundered.

As he made for the stairs, a low humming noise told him he was nearing the remains of what had once been a talking, walking, breathing human being. His tread grew slow and reluctant on the steps. Before he reached the landing, he stopped and peered over the top, feeling his mouth widen in an involuntary grimace as he did so.

Irene was lying on her side, just inside a sliding security grille that separated the landing from the first-floor bedrooms. It was partially closed. Had the old woman realised what was happening and attempted to close the grille behind her, but been caught short by the burglar? She was a tiny little thing, like a bird, stick-thin limbs looking ready to snap.

Why kill her when she could have easily been shoved aside? The Persian rug on the landing had soaked up her blood, adopting it into its intricate pattern.

He forced himself to think like a police officer. While distressing to him, he knew that the flies and larvae, which had developed in abundance in the centrally heated house, would help them establish the time of death.

A bronze statue of an elephant, set on a marble plinth, was lying next to the body with bits of hair and skin stuck to it. It looked like the burglar had acted on impulse, grabbing the nearest heavy object he could find. Perhaps he had panicked. Perhaps Irene had been screaming and he had wanted to shut her up. Seeing as her neighbours worried more about barking dogs than the welfare of humans, he needn't have bothered.

Slowly, Henrik leaned over the body, his palms tingling. Part of Irene's skull was missing. Her dentures had come loose and were halfway out of her mouth, like comedy teeth.

In his youth, violence had been par for the course. The Friday night street fights with broken bottles, the perpetual low-level threat of the biker gangs. Someone in his street had been stabbed to death in a robbery. No need to romanticise the past, but to his mind the violence had become more callous and extreme in recent years.

Irene Valborg looked way into her eighties. Even if the perpetrator had wanted to kill her (which seemed unnecessary), why do it with such ferocious force?

Henrik was starting to feel queasy. He had the kind of concentrated headache that heralded vomiting. Saliva was running in his mouth, making him want to spit.

As he turned to go, he was distracted by a small movement around Irene Valborg's face. Transfixed, he watched as a fly made its leisurely way from her mouth into her nose.

He didn't look left or right as he bounded back down the stairs two steps at a time, through the gloomy hallway and out into the open, glad for once of the rain that meant no one lingered after his signal that they were free to enter the house and begin the investigation proper.

2

'I'll take it,' said Jensen.

Having scaled the spiral staircase to the flat's mezzanine deck, she had made straight for the rain-splattered dormer window. The advertised view of the Church of Our Saviour didn't disappoint. Its brown and gold helter-skelter spire rose above the red-tile roofs of Christianshavn's old apartment buildings like something out of a fairy tale. Far below, squashed in the uneven space between abutting red and yellow housing blocks was a tiny courtyard filled with bicycles and prams and a wooden picnic table surrounded by shrubs in terracotta pots.

'You're sure?' said the agent, sounding surprised.

She was a heavily perfumed woman who, judging by her wheezing, ought not to spend her days climbing stairs.

'I'm sure,' said Jensen.

There was a chest of drawers and small futon in the crawling space under the eaves. Downstairs, a tiny sofa, a dining table and two chairs.

'It may be small but it's perfectly adequate for one person. Cosy, don't you think?' said the agent, as Jensen looked around.

Small was an understatement. The flat was arranged vertically, the clearance below the exposed oak rafters too low in most places for an adult to stand upright. But, in weeks of looking, it was the only place Jensen had seen that she could imagine herself living in. The rent was reasonable, and the view of her favourite Copenhagen church had clinched it.

The flat's postage-stamp size with its awkward nooks and crannies explained why it had been on the market for longer than the few hours it usually took for Copenhagen rentals to be snapped up.

By the time she had aborted her flight to London in January, the container with her belongings had already travelled halfway back to England. Secretly, she was relieved. The possessions she had accumulated through fifteen years as a foreign correspondent would have reminded her of the life she used to have, before Margrethe had decided to close the London office. She couldn't imagine them in the Copenhagen flat, the books she had bought on happy Saturday afternoons drifting through the West End, the assortment of novelty mugs.

The estate agent was looking at her with open curiosity, clearly wondering how someone in their thirties had wound up without much in the way of belongings, prepared to rent a flat without seeing it properly. 'May I ask what you do?' she said.

It was an excellent question, and one Jensen didn't have an answer for. She was no longer an employee of *Dagbladet*, despite the editor-in-chief Margrethe Skov's heavy hints that she was happy to let bygones be bygones.

'If I come back, I want it to be as an investigative reporter. I pick the stories, you take me off the daily grind,' Jensen had said, pushing her luck.

'Very funny, Jensen, but, as you well know, that's a luxury *Dagbladet* can no longer afford,' Margrethe had responded with genuine regret in her voice.

They had agreed on a compromise: if Jensen found a good story, Margrethe would buy her articles on freelance terms.

Of course, others had made advances after Jensen's piece on the Magstræde murder had hit *Dagbladet*'s front page, including the TV news of the Danish broadcasting corporation. 'You're exactly what we're after,' the editor had said.

Jensen had told her she needed time to think it over.

Margrethe would dismiss her as a traitor if she said yes, especially seeing as Jensen had spent the past two months in her spare room, while Margrethe had gone to work every day to keep *Dagbladet* afloat. Jensen had recovered relatively quickly from the physical injury she had sustained in Magstræde, but it had taken longer to sleep through the night, and she was still more jittery than she liked to admit whenever she left the safety of the Østerbro flat. Lately, though, she had been getting restless. Her stuff at Margrethe's, what little there was, would fit into a taxi; she would be able to move in and unpack in under half an hour. Gustav could give her a hand.

'I'm a journalist,' she said to the estate agent, tracing a raindrop down the Velux windowpane with one finger.

Whatever else happened, that much was always true. She never just talked to other people, she *interviewed* them. Always hoping to discover something, looking for an angle, writing headlines in her head.

'Who owns this place?' she asked.

'Kristoffer Bro,' said the estate agent, adding when Jensen's face remained blank: 'He is an entrepreneur. IT. Very successful, very well known.'

'Not by me,' said Jensen. 'But then I've been away for a few years.'

The estate agent nodded as if this made perfect sense. 'His girlfriend is an actress – she is on TV a lot,' she said, reeling off an unfamiliar name. 'Stunning. Kristoffer lives with her in a big place out in Nordhavn now.'

Of course he did. Who would live in a flat the size of a broom cupboard once they had made it? A place like this was for dreamers.

Losers.

'So who do you work for?' said the agent.

'Myself, for the time being,' said Jensen, clapping her hands free of dust from the windowsill, before the agent got a chance to ask the next question forming on her cerise-coloured lips.

'When can I move in?'

'Well, let's see,' said the agent, smiling while fishing an inhaler out of her handbag and taking a puff. Her lipstick left a dark pink mark around the mouthpiece. 'There's paperwork. I shall need two months' rent up front. And of course, Kristoffer would have to agree,' she said.

Jensen nodded, beginning her descent to the main living area, followed by the agent, whose heavy tread made the steps creak alarmingly.

Jensen walked over to the short wall of kitchen units at one end of the living room and looked out. A young man was playing the double bass in a flat across the courtyard with a look of intense concentration.

'And I'll have to see proof of income,' said the agent.

'Ah,' said Jensen, turning around and leaning against the sink. 'That might be a problem.'

'I see,' said the woman.

'But I promise you, I am good for the rent.'

Jensen smiled but the agent was having none of it. The mirth on her face had vanished like the sun slipping behind clouds. 'In that case, I shall have to ask you for six months' rent up front,' she said.

Jensen paused. In the silence, she could hear the patter of rain on the windowpane, the traffic on the street below, the creak of the old timbers. She could see herself in the flat, she liked it; it felt as right as any place was going to be and the liveliness of Christianshavn felt comforting.

Besides, she got the feeling from the agent's set jaw that the woman wasn't the negotiating type.

'Not a problem,' she said, finally. 'But in that case, I want to move in tonight.'

The sun lit up the woman's face again. 'I'll see what I can do. You are obviously in a rush,' she laughed.

Jensen thought about it. Was she? 'In a rush' implied that you had some sort of plan, which she didn't.

All the same, she felt impatience rising in her gut as she headed for the door. She had dithered long enough. 'Once my mind is made up, I don't like waiting.'

3

'For Christ's sake, who'd do something like that to an innocent little old lady?'

The booming voice of Mogens Hansen, known to all as 'Monsen', gave Henrik a violent start. He had been brooding over the crime scene photos from Irene Valborg's villa in Klampenborg, staring at them for so long that his mind had wandered off to other matters. His team had gone home, on his orders. Mark Søndergreen and Lisbeth Quist, his trusted lieutenants, had stayed behind, but he had finally persuaded them to leave. Nobody was going to make any progress overnight.

'Not all little old ladies are innocent,' he said, recovering his composure enough to hide his surprise at seeing the famously work-shy Chief Superintendent in the office so close to midnight.

Monsen's breath was sour with red wine and cigars which meant he had been to one of his dinners with Copenhagen movers and shakers. He jabbed a finger at Henrik, a slight slurring of his thunderous voice. 'Are you saying she deserved to have her skull bashed in?'

14

'Of course not, but we shouldn't assume that the old are all sweetness and light. If anything, it is patronising,' said Henrik, feeling himself sliding towards one of the Chief Super's lectures on how society was going to hell in a handcart.

Luckily, Monsen was distracted by his own epic yawn. 'You speak in riddles, Jungersen. What are you doing here so late anyway?'

'I could ask you the same.'

Monsen stared at him red-eyed. 'In the doghouse with Mrs Jungersen again, are we?' Monsen poked Henrik's side with his elbow.

'Just wanted time to think. Sometimes you have to wait till it's quiet around here,' said Henrik.

Monsen chuckled. 'Don't kid a kidder.'

Denial was futile. Monsen had known him for years and recognised a Jungersen domestic crisis when he saw one, Henrik's reluctance to leave the office being a major clue. There had been many such crises over the years, though this was the first time his wife had not let him back in the house after a couple of days.

'If I told you once, I told you a thousand times, it's not worth letting work come between us and our spouses,' said Monsen.

No danger of that in your case, thought Henrik.

It was true that, over the years, Henrik had used work as a means of avoiding a chilly atmosphere at home, usually self-inflicted. But how could he begin to tell Monsen that it was Jensen, a woman with dark blue eyes and an infuriating habit of sticking her nose in his business, that had brought his marriage to its knees?

Taking Henrik's silence as confirmation that he had hit the bullseye, Monsen patted him on the shoulder. Henrik knew that the Chief Super would be mindful of the role he had played in the Magstræde case, firing a single shot with his Heckler & Koch as Jensen's life hung in the balance.

Since he had stepped out in uniform for the first time more

than two decades ago, Henrik had carried a gun. Twice a year, he had been tested for proficiency at an army shooting range, and many a time had he drawn his gun, but not until that night had he ever fired it on active duty.

There had been an aftermath, a tiresome bureaucratic process in which he had had to justify himself over and over. His immediate boss, Superintendent Jens Wiese, who headed up Special Investigations, had also insisted on him seeing a psychologist, something Henrik considered unnecessary.

('Ha! Enough material in you for a bloody textbook,' he heard his wife say.)

Monsen and Henrik stood for a while side by side, looking at the pictures of Irene Valborg taken from various angles. Henrik knew that Wiese disliked these little tête-a-têtes of his with Monsen, envious of their easy rapport and feeling bypassed, but Monsen did as he damn well pleased and, for that, Henrik liked him immensely.

'So, what *are* you thinking?' said the big man, loosening his tie and undoing the top two buttons of his white shirt. He belched quietly under his breath, releasing a faint odour of garlic.

'A couple of things,' said Henrik, taking a step back. 'One: why does an old lady all of a sudden buy an Alsatian and turn her villa into Klampenborg's answer to Fort Knox?'

Monsen stared at him in astonishment. 'Do you need to ask? Old people are living in fear of crime. I am only grateful that my own mother isn't alive to see the state of society today, may God rest her soul.'

'But why now, why not three years ago, or ten?'

'The old dear probably read something in the papers that frightened her. Looks through the ads in the Sunday supplements and calls in an alarm firm with an over-enthusiastic salesperson. Next?'

'Why use such force on her?'

16

'Fear of detection? Make sure she is well and truly dead so she can't shoot her mouth off? Or just a general societal decline in decency and self-control? Take your pick.'

Henrik shook his head. 'It wasn't necessary to kill her.'

'Necessary? When is it ever? Look at that chap who was killed a month ago on the allotment out at Amager.'

Henrik remembered the case. 'Vagn Holdved.'

'That's the one. Almost got his head torn off, for Christ's sake. And for what? A few quid in his wallet and some prescription meds?'

'No leads yet?'

'Nada.'

'Why not?'

'Ask Lotte. Her case.'

I don't mind if I do, thought Henrik, recalling his colleague's whip-straight blonde ponytail and runner's physique.

('Now?' he heard his wife say. 'You're seriously thinking of sex now?')

His wife still wasn't answering his calls. What more did he have to do to get her to listen, prostrate himself naked on the doorstep of their family home with 'sorry' tattooed on his forehead?

'You look rough, Henrik, if you don't mind me saying so. Buy your wife some flowers and go home,' said Monsen, walking away with a heavy paw lifted in farewell.

Henrik suppressed a cynical laugh. How nice it must be to live inside Monsen's head, in a world where a bouquet of roses was enough to stem a woman's fury. Monsen had never met Henrik's wife. Just as well. He didn't fancy the Chief Super's chances in head-to-head combat.

'Just five more minutes, and then I am out of here,' he lied.

When Monsen had left, and Henrik was certain he was alone, he went to his office and shut the door behind him, then pulled down the blinds and switched off the lights.

He was too tired to bother unrolling the sleeping bag that he kept in his locker. He knew he couldn't go on like this, but he had to cut down on his hotel bills, and staying with his father, now that his stepmother's Alzheimer's had got worse, was unbearable.

He sat on the settee, undid the laces of his old Timberlands and thought of Jensen. He had no idea where she was these days. Bar a couple of lacklustre articles, which suggested she was still in Denmark, there had been nothing under her by-line for quite a while now, not since the Magstræde case that he had to admit Jensen had outsmarted him on.

He couldn't text her. To stand a chance of getting back into his wife's good books, he would need to be on his best behaviour from now on.

Zero tolerance.

One strike and you're out.

Still, it would have been nice, if Jensen had thought to give him a sign of life. Most likely, she was still cross with him.

His wife and Jensen.

You would have to search for years to find women with longer memories or a more maddening predisposition for carrying a grudge. How had he managed to fall out with them both at once? This seemed a spectacular feat of recklessness, even for him.

He sighed deeply, lay down on the sofa and covered himself with his leather jacket, praying for the sleep that he knew would not come for hours, if at all.

4

Tuesday 11:47

Christina Vangede lit up the wet car park opposite Gentofte Church like a human neon sign with her platinum-blonde hair, pink coat and orange tan. Her make-up was dissolving in tears, which was odd as none of the other mourners now beating a hasty retreat to their cars seemed badly marked by the occasion. Jensen guessed they were mostly business acquaintances. Carsten Vangede had been respected, maybe even liked, but not loved, she decided. Except by his sister.

The coroner had decided that Carsten had hanged himself after going bankrupt, but Deep Throat, the anonymous source who had told Jensen how he and Carsten had both been defrauded by their accountants, had suggested otherwise. Carsten had bought a flight to Thailand hours before he died, and what kind of suicidal man did that? Jensen had decided to stay in Denmark to find out, but the story had turned out less than straightforward.

To her relief, Deep Throat had not been among the mourners at Carsten's funeral. He would be appalled at the meagre

19

outcome of her investigation, and she didn't feel like disappointing him.

Plenty of time for that yet.

The problem was that no one was interested in suicides of bankrupt, alcoholic, unmarried Danish males in their fifties, let alone the police. 'So he bought a plane ticket before he topped himself. Who gives a shit?' one exasperated detective had told her before hanging up.

What would Henrik make of it? He was keeping his distance. She supposed he was feeling guilty that he hadn't turned up to drive her to the airport as he had promised.

Too right.

She felt in her bag for the spectacle case that had belonged to Vangede's fraudulent accountant and closed her hand around the cold, smooth, oblong shape. It was now the only link to the man who had used the name Bjarne Pedersen to syphon cash from Carsten's operation.

Carsten had given her the case.

It had to matter.

Printed inside the lid in gold letters was the name and address of an optician in Randers: a trail which went nowhere, according to Vangede, but Jensen still wanted to speak to the optician himself. She and Gustav had left multiple messages that had so far gone unanswered.

The vicar had rattled through the funeral service with a single spirited church singer dragging the mumbling congregation through Danish hymns that Jensen remembered from school.

Gustav was keen to join the wake at a nearby bistro, but Jensen sensed they would be better off speaking to Christina before she got the chance to get drunk or mawkish, whichever came first.

The woman was no way near her dead brother in appearance, and thankfully a lot chattier, but her ravaged face and raspy voice suggested the siblings had shared a fondness for partying. 'I feel so bad,' she said, lighting up under her leopard-spotted umbrella and blowing the smoke out of one side of her mouth. 'I should have been there for him, but I had no idea how bad he'd got.'

'When did you last see him?' said Jensen.

Christina shrugged. 'Before Christmas last year, I think.'

'And how did he seem?'

'Not good. Depressed. Sort of withdrawn. But we didn't talk for long. He dropped by when we were sorting Mum's house. She died last year, and Carsten came and picked up a few keepsakes. Of course, he didn't lift a finger to help. I mean, don't get me wrong, I loved my big brother, but he could be a right arsehole sometimes.'

She closed her eyes, dragged deeply on the cigarette and shook her head as if dispelling bad memories.

'How do you mean?' said Jensen.

'Just fucking unreliable. Selfish. He used to help me out now and again, with the kids and all that, and then suddenly it was like drawing blood from a stone.'

'You mean he used to give you money?'

'Yes, until suddenly he didn't. He was loaded from those bars he ran while I could barely make ends meet.'

'Actually, he was bankrupt,' said Jensen.

'Really?' said Christina, her caterpillar eyebrows meeting in the middle as she frowned. 'Who told you that?'

Jensen decided not to reply. Christina would find out soon enough that her brother had nothing left. If she was hoping to inherit, she was in for a big disappointment.

'I'd try and ask him about it, but he'd just tear my head off. That's why I stopped seeing him. Stopped taking the kids to him, too. Frankly, he was being a bad influence.'

Gustav and Jensen exchanged a glance. From the look of the three adolescent tearaways now squabbling on the backseat of Christina's Kia, that particular horse had bolted long ago.

21

Christina was nearly down to the filter on her cigarette. Jensen knew they didn't have long. 'Did it surprise you that your brother killed himself?' she said.

'Surprise me? Had the shock of my life when the police came around. Thought it was one of my boys at first, nearly had a heart attack.'

'I mean, was it out of character for Carsten?'

Christina took one last hefty drag and dropped the cigarette butt onto the tarmac, squashing it with her brown suede boot. 'It's always out of character, isn't it? Until someone goes ahead and does it. The stupid sod.'

'Look,' said Jensen, scribbling her mobile number on a crumpled business card from *Dagbladet*. 'I don't suppose we could come and have a look at Carsten's house? Not now, I mean, but perhaps you could think about it, give me a call?'

Christina studied the card. 'So you'll be writing about my brother?' she said, her grief momentarily forgotten.

'Yes,' said Gustav. 'We're investigating whether—'

Jensen cut him off. 'Researching. What Gustav here means to say is that we're researching male suicide for a feature for the paper. I met your brother once, so when . . . well, it got me interested.'

'Oh?' said Christina. 'When was that?'

'January?'

'And?'

'He was pretty drunk, to be honest.'

'Yep,' said Christina, pocketing Jensen's business card and getting into her Kia. 'Sounds like my brother, all right.'

5

Regitse Lindegaard was almost half an hour late by the time she rolled up the drive to her mother's villa in her tank-sized grey Volvo. Not that she was minded to apologise. Having run from the car to the front door in the pouring rain with her trench coat pulled up over her head, she seemed irritated rather than contrite to see Henrik and Mark already waiting in the hall. In her late fifties and made up to the hilt, she was not bad looking, if you liked a woman who had grabbed every intervention going to stay youthful. Henrik wasn't partial himself and Regitse's lateness was doing little to warm him towards her. He made a show of checking his watch, waiting in overbearing silence until she had finished brushing the rain off her coat sleeves and moaning about the state of Copenhagen traffic. Her perfume clung to the stale air like an unwelcome guest.

'Detective Inspector Henrik Jungersen,' he said. 'And this is my colleague, Mark Søndergreen.'

Her hand was bony and cold with a sizeable diamond that dug into his flesh. 'Regitse,' she said.

Unlike most bereaved relatives, she had not asked to be taken to see her mother's body first, but requested they meet at the villa. There had been no tears, no anxious questions about how her mother had met her end. On the face of it, this was suspicious, but in Henrik's experience, an offender would, at the very least, have tried to conceal their indifference with some kind of act.

'I am sorry for your loss,' Henrik said, watching her face closely for a reaction.

Any reaction.

With the exception of a nerve twitching by the woman's left eye as she stepped past them into the house, there was nothing there. Henrik got the impression that even if Regitse were experiencing some form of grief, which he doubted, she wouldn't cry in front of them in a million years.

'We still don't have a motive for your mother's murder. Anything you can tell us would be helpful,' he said, as he and Mark caught her up in the living room.

'I thought you said it was burglary?'

Her clipped accent betrayed her posh North Copenhagen roots which many years in a suburb of Aarhus had done little to soften.

'Burglary is one option. We were hoping you could tell us if anything's missing,' said Henrik.

Regitse was already doing a tour of the ornaments, frowning at each painting in turn, opening boxes and lifting porcelain figurines. To Henrik's surprise, Irene Valborg's handbag had been found by her bed, with 3,000 kroner in her wallet. There had been no jewellery to be seen, though, except the rings on the old woman's fingers. The killer had not bothered with those.

'Well?' he said.

'Everything seems to be here.'

'How long since you last visited?' he said, wondering how she could be so sure, but Regitse ignored the question.

'Did you check her safe?' she said.

24

'Safe? What safe?'

Regitse made for the stairs, muttering under her breath. 'Bloody amateurs.'

'Wait. You might get a bit of a shock,' said Mark, ever considerate.

Too late.

They found Regitse looking down at the dark stain on the landing. The oriental carpet where her mother died had been removed by forensics.

'So, this is where he got her,' she said, her hard exterior showing momentary signs of cracking.

'Yes, we think she may have been trying to get to safety, closing the grille behind her when the killer struck her from behind,' said Mark.

Slowly, Regitse recovered her composure and began to look around, more solemnly now. There were remnants of red powder left on the walls, furniture and ornaments that had been checked for fingerprints. 'There used to be a statue of an elephant there, a bronze,' she said, pointing to the low bookshelf on the landing where a lighter-coloured rectangle marked the shape of the plinth.

'It has been taken away as evidence. We believe it was the murder weapon,' said Mark.

Regitse nodded, tiptoed around the stain and made for her mother's bedroom. The bed had been made. The room was neat with no clothes or effects lying around. No signs that Irene Valborg had been about to go to bed when she had been disturbed, nor had she only just got up by the look of things. It wasn't unheard of for burglars to be working in the middle of the day, especially not in a quiet area like this. Still, it wouldn't have been someone's first choice. Did that mean the perpetrator hadn't been a burglar after all?

Regitse aimed straight for an oil painting on the far wall, one of many gold-framed Danish landscapes adorning the walls of her mother's bedroom. She lifted the painting off the wall and began to examine something behind it.

Henrik saw to his astonishment that it was the metal door to a safe that had been cemented into the wall cavity. No one on his team had spotted it. The door was unlocked.

'It's empty,' Regitse said, feeling inside. 'I thought as much. There used to be a few million kroners' worth of diamond necklace in there. There's your motive, inspector.'

'Detective inspector,' said Henrik. 'Let's not get ahead of ourselves. Who is to say your mother didn't sell her necklace?'

'Sell it? Ha! You obviously have no idea what my mother was like.'

'I get the feeling the two of you weren't close.'

'What's that got to do with anything?' she snapped.

'If she'd done something with the necklace, you might not have been the first to know,' said Henrik.

'Believe me, it was her pride and joy. Her *only* pride and joy. More important to her, certainly, than her nearest and dearest.'

'An heirloom?' asked Mark, diligently taking notes.

'No.'

'What then?' said Henrik.

'She bought it not long after I left home. Came into an inheritance.'

'Who did she inherit from?' said Mark.

'Some relative, what do I know. We never saw any of my mother's family.'

'And did she ever wear the necklace?' continued Mark.

'Oh no, far too expensive for *that*,' said Regitse in a mocking voice.

She had moved on to her mother's bedside table, rummaging amongst the trinkets in the drawer. Henrik felt his patience running out. 'How come you knew exactly where the safe was?' he said.

26

'Because she showed me. She was very proud of how clever she had been to get it.'

So, she had been security conscious all along, taking no chances, and yet a short while ago, she had tightened the ring of steel around her house by another couple of notches, effectively barricading herself inside.

'My father's gold watch is missing,' said Regitse.

'Are you sure?' said Mark.

'For God's sake, yes, I am sure,' said Regitse. 'My mother kept it in this drawer ever since my father died.'

'Expensive?'

'Wouldn't have thought so. My father wasn't a materialist.'

Unlike you and your mother, thought Henrik. 'Anything else?' he said.

Regitse looked around. 'I don't believe so.'

Henrik was no expert, but there were several other valuable-looking items in the room, including paintings and silverware. The necklace could have been stolen to order, but why grab an old watch when there were other things worth more?

'Would you know why she had new locks fitted? Or the alarm system?' said Henrik.

Regitse shrugged. 'No idea, but I can't say I'm surprised. She was always paranoid about somebody taking that necklace from her. Wouldn't even allow me to touch it.'

'And the dog?'

Regitse Lindegaard frowned. 'What dog?'

While Mark explained about the Alsatian, Henrik touched his temples with the tips of his fingers and closed his eyes. Nothing added up. If the necklace really had been stolen, despite Irene's paranoia, how had the killer known it was there? And more importantly, how had he got into the safe without need to resort to an angle grinder? Could she have opened it for some other reason? Or had it been open already?

David Goldschmidt at the Forensic Institute would tell him

27

for certain, but Henrik was pretty certain the old woman hadn't been tortured to reveal the code.

'Can you think of anyone in her circle who might have done it?'

'Circle? My mother was eighty-six. There was a cleaner, but she sacked *her* just before Christmas.'

'Oh?' said Henrik, perking up. 'How do you know that?'

'Because Minna rang me to complain. Been working for my mother for years and suddenly it's "Thanks very much, here's what I owe you, jog on."'

Mark moved in with his notepad. 'Can you give me Minna's full name, please, and a number, if you have it?'

Regitse begrudgingly obliged. 'But I am telling you, Minna didn't do this. The woman doesn't have it in her, and her husband's practically an invalid.'

'Then who did?' said Henrik, suddenly thinking of something. 'Is there a gardener?'

'Troels, yes. She hasn't sacked *him*, by the looks of the lawn and driveway, but then my mother always was very much about keeping up appearances. No matter that the core is rotten, if the apple is shiny and red on the outside.'

A description equally befitting you, thought Henrik, while Mark diligently noted down the details on the gardener who would have to be interviewed along with the cleaner.

'I doubt very much that he or Minna even knew about the safe. Perhaps my mother made a mistake and told a stranger about it. Perhaps whatever cowboys sold her the security gear.'

Possible, thought Henrik, but that still didn't explain the open safe. Nor why Irene Valborg had had to die in the process. And those were not the only things about this case that were hard to fathom. 'How do we know that it wasn't you who took the necklace? You could easily have got the code then pretended there had been a burglary,' he said. 'Perhaps *you* killed her.'

'And why would I kill my own mother?'

Henrik looked around at the house. 'Big pile like this, got to be worth a few bob. I assume you're the only beneficiary of your mother's will?'

'If I had wanted to kill her in order to inherit, why steal the necklace?'

'Perhaps you didn't intend to, but your mother got in the way. Or perhaps you made the necklace up to mislead us. Or you killed her, without thinking of the necklace, and you have only just discovered that it's missing, to your obvious annoyance.'

He could feel Mark looking at him; he was going too far.

Regitse responded with admirable cool under the circumstances. 'Too right I'm annoyed, but I didn't kill her. You're wasting your time while the real killer is out there, getting away with it.'

Was she telling the truth? If it was money she was after, she surely wouldn't have needed to wait long for her mother to die of natural causes. Unless she was desperate?

'What I don't understand,' he said, 'is why you wouldn't visit your mother more often?'

'I am busy. My husband has an extremely demanding job,' said Regitse, rummaging through yet another box of trinkets.

'Still, the odd phone call to make sure she was all right? Wouldn't have taken you more than a few minutes.'

Regitse snapped the lid to the box shut and walked over to Henrik, standing so close to him that he could see the powder that had caught in the fine hairs on her upper lip, the mascara that had smudged in the rain and caught like black tears at the corners of her eyes. Her gaze was unflinching.

'Your job is to find who did this and retrieve the necklace. You got that?' she said, pushing out her chin.

Henrik folded his arms across his chest, standing four-square and looking her in the eye.

Caught in the middle, Mark's gaze darted nervously between them.

'Well,' said Regitse. 'What are you waiting for?'

Henrik felt heat spread from his abdomen to his chest. He had had it with being everyone's whipping boy.

His wife's.

Jensen's.

Keeping it together on two hours' sleep only to be spat at by the likes of Regitse Lindegaard. Well, she had picked the wrong day for it. 'I don't care who you are, or what your husband does. You don't get to call the shots round here,' he said, jabbing a finger at her. 'This is my investigation.'

Regitse laughed, as Mark attempted unsuccessfully to lower Henrik's arm. 'You pathetic man. I am staying in Copenhagen overnight. Tell me when there's a development.'

She made for the door.

'There is a development right now,' said Henrik in a loud voice, stopping her in her tracks. 'You are coming with us.'

'Why?' said Regitse, the smile finally wiped off her face.

'We're going to need everything you just told us written down. I'm sure you'd want to assist our investigation as much as possible. It might take some time, though. Mark here is not the fastest of typists with his two sausage fingers, and he is very thorough, so I'd cancel my plans for the afternoon, if I were you.'

6

Tuesday 17:14

Gustav staggered over the threshold to Jensen's new flat, dropped the box he was carrying on top of the already sizeable stack in the living room and threw himself on the floor, rolling onto his back. 'Never again,' he cried.

Jensen would have joined him, had she felt sure that she would be able to get up again. She headed for the kitchen tap, letting the cold water run straight into her mouth and swallowing in greedy gulps.

After the funeral they had gone to IKEA in Gentofte and it had been hell. What were those hundreds of people doing there, hoarding flatpack furniture on a rainy Tuesday in March? Gustav's price for fetching and carrying had been a plate of *Köttbullar* in the cafeteria, which he had insisted on having before they start. She had watched in disgust, nursing a bottle of water as he wolfed down the meatballs, mashed potato and gravy.

'What?' he had said, in between mouthfuls. 'It's tradition. You wouldn't have Christmas Eve without ris à l'amande and cherry sauce, would you?'

'Actually, I would,' she said, shivering at the thought of the cold rice pudding with almonds that followed the roast bird on Christmas dinner tables across Denmark. 'I hate ris à l'amande.'

'You know what your problem is?' Gustav had said, pointing at her with a speared meatball. 'You've been away from Denmark too long. Even your accent's gone funny.'

'My accent?'

'Yeah,' said Gustav, launching into a mocking rendition of Danish with a British accent.

She had bashed his arm with her water bottle, and he had laughed with his mouth full of half-chewed meat. Even he had flagged, though, on the tortuous trail around the warehouse, echoing with screaming kids and domestic arguments.

'How much stuff do you need?' he complained as she loaded the shopping trolley with bedding, towels, a clothes rail and lampshades. She also bought crockery, cutlery and pots and pans, glasses, cushions, a rug, a cafetiere, a kettle, dishtowels and a clock.

They had been queuing to pay along with dozens of other weary shoppers when Jensen's phone had trembled into life. She recognised the Randers phone number: the optician who had once sold a pair of metal-framed spectacles to Vangede's fraudulent accountant.

Finally.

He sounded angry. 'Jensen?'

'Speaking.'

'You have left twenty-five messages on my voicemail. I don't know who you are, but I want it to stop. Right now.'

'I am a reporter. I am writing a story about the death of Carsten Vangede. Are you—'

'Don't,' said the optician. 'I don't know anything about those glasses. I sell hundreds of pairs every year.'

'So Vangede already came to see you?'

'I don't want to talk to you.'

'But you must have a record of the prescription. The man I

am looking for went by the name of Bjarne Pedersen. He might have—'

'Shut up,' said the optician, almost screaming the words.

Then he hung up.

Gustav stared at her questioningly. 'Well?'

'That was the optician. He sounded weird,' said Jensen.

'Weird how?'

'Like he was scared.'

It had been their turn at the till then, and they had got preoccupied with lugging heavy boxes of furniture and household items from the store to the car park.

Jensen thought about it now. Had the optician been warned off by someone? If so, who?

'Wouldn't it have been a hell of a lot easier if you'd just got the container with your stuff shipped back to Copenhagen?' said Gustav from the floor.

'Perhaps. But I prefer it this way: new things, new start. Besides, I haven't decided yet if I am staying for good.'

Gustav gestured at the boxes. 'Looks like it to me.'

Jensen didn't bother explaining. He wouldn't understand that this felt like a smarter way to try out living in Copenhagen. If by the autumn she had decided it wasn't for her, she could leave the flat to the next tenant and take off back to London.

The flat was perfect. Almost. The washing machine was broken, and she was running out of clean clothes. Quickly, she composed a message to the asthmatic estate agent (*about time she earned her fee*), then threw a cushion at Gustav. 'Get up, you have work to do.'

'Oh what?' whined Gustav. 'You never said.'

'You weren't going to leave me to unpack all this stuff by myself, were you? And I thought you wanted to be my apprentice.'

'Yes, your *journalism* apprentice, not your personal handyman. Speaking of which, are you going to return to *Dagbladet* now?'

'Sorry, Gustav, but the answer is still no. I thought I might try out working for myself for a while.'

'You haven't done very well so far.'

'Says who?'

'Margrethe, for one.'

'Well, it takes time to organise everything.'

'Organise what?'

'My office, for starters.'

Gustav hoisted himself up on his elbows and stared at her, suddenly interested. 'And where is that?'

'You're looking at it. Now get up. There's a takeaway in the offing. I know a really nice Korean not far from here. They do bubble tea. Work first, eat second.'

Now she had his full attention. In twenty minutes, he had put the kitchen stuff away while she had made the bed and hung up the clock. The flat was beginning to look like a home.

'Can we have a break now?' Gustav said, flopping onto the sofa. He took out tobacco and papers for a roll-up, having recently graduated from his vape. Jensen suspected he thought smoking was cool.

'You're not smoking that in here,' she said.

'Right you are, Mum,' he said without looking up.

She was going to have to persuade him to stop smoking altogether. Later, when she had more energy for a fight.

Her phone rang, the switchboard at *Dagbladet*. Could be Margrethe wanting to know where Gustav was. She hadn't stopped watching his every move after the assault he had suffered in January. He had only just had his front tooth implant done and could smile again without looking like an extra from Oliver Twist.

'Jensen,' she said.

It was Markus, the receptionist whose frosty welcomes at the newspaper could always be relied upon, especially now Jensen no longer held any sway as a paid employee.

She had given Markus a wide berth since he left her homeless two months ago when he had demanded his sublet flat back with only a few days' notice. 'What do you want?' she said, warily.

'I've got someone here who is refusing to leave before she's seen you.'

'Who?'

'Won't say her name. Posh bird. Rude as hell.'

'She *does* know I don't work there anymore?'

'Told her as much. Didn't make a blind bit of difference.'

'OK, there in twenty,' she said, ending the call and turning to Gustav, nudging him to get him to take off his headphones.

'You got your wish,' she said. 'We're taking a break. Someone at *Dagbladet* I've got to see.'

Gustav made a move to get up.

'No, not you,' she said, grabbing her coat. 'Stay here and chill. I'll be back with supper before you know it. Set the table, will you?'

She was out the door and it had slammed behind her before Gustav could protest. Being seventeen years of age, and the nephew of Denmark's gobbiest newspaper editor, it was something he was particularly good at.

7

Tuesday 18:31

Jensen was soaked when the glass doors slid open to admit her into *Dagbladet*'s high-ceilinged lobby with the bronze bust of the newspaper's nineteenth-century founder. She suspected he would be turning in his grave at the state of Denmark's newspaper industry.

Markus, receptionist with an attitude, waved her over to his desk. 'I am not your bloody personal assistant,' he hissed under his breath.

'Never asked you to be,' she said cheerily.

She nodded at the heavily made-up woman seated in one of the lobby's two leather armchairs and reading a free copy of *Dagbladet*. 'That her?'

'Yes,' said Markus.

'Never seen her before in my life.'

'Not my problem. She won't leave until she has talked to you.'

Jensen walked warily across the marble floor, conscious of the trail of rainwater she was leaving in her wake. The woman looked pissed off. Perhaps she was unhappy with something Jensen had written? Not many articles to choose from lately. 'Believe you wanted to see me?'

36

The woman lowered the newspaper and looked her up and down, frowning. '*You* are Jensen?'

'You expected a man?'

'Yes, frankly. Or someone bigger, taller.'

'Sorry to disappoint,' said Jensen.

Belatedly, the woman beamed and stretched out her hand, flashing a large gemstone on her on her finger. 'Regitse Lindegaard. Is there somewhere we can talk? Somewhere a little more private?' She glanced meaningfully in the direction of Markus who, having feigned disinterest a minute ago, was now straining to hear their every word.

'Of course,' said Jensen, leading Regitse towards the sliding doors while giving Markus the finger behind her back.

The café around the corner where Jensen had sometimes eaten lunch during her time at the newspaper was nearly empty and would be closing in twenty-five minutes, according to the exhausted-looking barista.

Excellent, thought Jensen: a hard stop to whatever heart-to-heart her guest was planning on.

She ordered tea for herself and offered Regitse coffee or water, both of which the woman declined with an impatient sweep of her bejewelled hand. Jensen chose a seat by the window for the two of them. Outside, Copenhagen was winding down for the day, the last of the rush-hour traffic passing by in a watery blur.

Regitse glared at her for a while with open curiosity. Her smile didn't quite reach her eyes. It looked like she had had work done to her face.

Lots of work.

'So, you're the famous Jensen,' she said at long last.

'Not sure about famous, but that's my name,' said Jensen, squirming.

'Come, come,' said Regitse. 'What's with the false modesty? You were all over the papers not two months ago after you

37

solved that Magstræde case. With considerable danger to your own life, I gather.'

'Just a flesh wound,' Jensen said, automatically touching one hand to her shoulder.

Occasionally, she still felt pain where she had been stabbed. There was just a pale red scar there now. 'How can I help you?' she said.

'You're direct, I like that,' said Regitse, smiling. 'Cards on the table then. I need your help. My mother was killed.'

'Gosh,' said Jensen, covering her mouth with one hand. 'That's terrible.'

Regitse didn't look as if she shared the sentiment.

'What happened?'

'Burglar bashed her over the head. Happened a couple of weeks ago, though my mother's body was only discovered yesterday. Irene Valborg.'

Jensen remembered reading the story online. She had had a half-baked idea to write a feature on violent crime against the elderly, something which seemed to be happening more frequently of late. 'Look,' she said, relieved, 'if that's what you want to talk about, Frank Buhl is *Dagbladet*'s crime reporter ... I'd be happy to introduce you?'

'No,' said Regitse, a sudden note of steel in her voice. 'Not him. It's you I want.'

Regitse looked about her in the almost empty café, staring for a moment at the yawning barista to make sure he wasn't listening. He couldn't have looked less interested. She lowered her voice and leant across the table. 'My mother owned a priceless diamond necklace. I went to Klampenborg this morning and it was gone.'

'You think it was taken by the killer?'

Regitse looked at Jensen as though she was an idiot. 'Who else would have taken it?' she said.

'I don't know.'

38

'My mother is killed by a burglar and her necklace is missing. You think the two aren't connected? Then you are not as smart as I have been led to believe.'

'Did someone break in? Was the door forced?'

'No, but my mother was eighty-six. It would hardly be beyond the wit of someone nasty to trick their way into her house.'

'Or maybe it was someone she knew? Someone she didn't think could possibly want to harm her?' said Jensen.

Regitse didn't respond, but Jensen could see the cogs turning behind her chemically smooth forehead as she tried to work out if she was being accused of something. Jensen used the brief pause to get her own question in. 'If you don't mind me saying so, you don't seem particularly upset by your mother's murder. Sounds like it was brutal, so why are we sitting here talking about a missing necklace?'

Regitse held Jensen's gaze, her face, botoxed to within an inch of its life, betraying no emotion. 'My mother and I . . . To tell you the truth, I am not sorry the witch is dead.'

'What was she like?'

Regitse snorted. 'Let's just say that she would have given the Ice Queen a run for her money.'

Like mother, like daughter, thought Jensen.

'And your father?'

'Weak. She made his life hell. He was on his knees trying to make ends meet for her. They should never have got the Klampenborg house. Far too much for him on a civil servant's salary, but that was my mother for you. Nothing was ever good enough. Dad was dead less than a year after his retirement, chased into an early grave by her incessant nagging.'

'There was the necklace, though. There must have been money for that. Was it a present from your father?'

Regitse laughed bitterly. 'If Dad had worked until he was a hundred, he'd never have had that kind of money. No, she bought it herself with an unexpected inheritance. Her way of taunting him with what he couldn't buy her, I suppose.'

'Did she ever wear it?'

'Not to my knowledge.'

'Was it insured?'

A new hardness entered Regitse's gaze: 'No. Turns out my mother only had regular contents insurance.'

Jensen whistled quietly. 'But why not, when she took such careful steps to protect it from being stolen? Doesn't make sense to me.'

'My mother was suspicious of everybody. I wouldn't put it past her worrying about being robbed by someone at the insurance company. And the hefty premium would have put her off anyway.'

Jensen reckoned Regitse looked like someone who could buy herself pretty much what she wanted. Perhaps she had outdone her mother and married a rich man. As though she could read her thoughts, Regitse absentmindedly began to twirl the enormous diamond ring on her left hand. 'I want you to find it. Quickly,' she said.

'I am sure the police will—'

'You don't get it,' said Regitse, looking straight into Jensen's eyes. 'The police are too slow. The detective I saw this morning was a real arsehole. Made me hang around for hours to make a statement.'

'DI Henrik Jungersen? Bald guy, leather jacket, rough face?'

'You know him?'

You could say that, thought Jensen. 'He was in charge of the Magstræde case.'

'From what the papers wrote, it was you who solved it, though. Doesn't say much for his detective powers.'

'Actually, he saved my life,' said Jensen, instantly regretting it. It was somehow too intimate, too personal, for her to be telling Regitse this.

Although the mention of Henrik had made her a lot more interested in the case than she had been a minute ago, she felt no warmth for the woman opposite her. Why would someone this wealthy be so hellbent on getting her mother's necklace back, even if it *was* worth a lot of money? There was something desperate about Regitse, something that made Jensen wonder if she was being entirely honest. Besides, she wouldn't have a clue where to start. If the necklace really had been stolen, it was probably halfway across Europe by now, the diamonds wrenched from their pronged settings. Writing Irene's story could be interesting, but she suspected Frank Buhl would go ballistic if she offered *Dagbladet* her own angle on the murder and selling the story to any other newspaper would feel like a betrayal.

But then again, there was Henrik.

He wouldn't like it if she began working for Regitse on *his* case.

Not one bit.

She shifted in her seat.

'I am not sure,' she said, sipping slowly from her tepid camomile tea.

'About what?'

'Not sure I'm the right person,' said Jensen. 'Aren't there professionals for this kind of thing? A private detective maybe?'

'If I thought there was someone better, I wouldn't be here,' said Regitse. 'You have initiative and I can see that you're not exactly busy. Look, I'll pay you fifty thousand kroner now, and another fifty on delivery.'

'Seventy-five,' said a familiar voice.

Gustav had appeared out of nowhere, making directly for their table with a plastic bottle of Coke in one hand and an unlit roll-up in the other. He had taken off his over-ear headphones and was looking expectantly from Regitse to Jensen.

'What are *you* doing here?' said Jensen.

41

'Markus told me you'd gone somewhere quieter. Didn't take Sherlock Holmes to work out where.'

Regitse looked in disgust at his dirty black jeans and Converse trainers, the greasy, dark hair falling into his eyes. 'This is a private conversation,' she said, waving him off like someone shooing away a dog.

'Actually,' said Jensen, surprised at the firmness in her voice. 'Gustav is my assistant. Where I go, he goes.'

Gustav smiled triumphantly. Regitse looked him up and down, then glared at Jensen with a look that was both over-bearing and pitying. 'Suit yourself.'

She got up from her chair and drew herself up to full height. In her stiletto boots, she was several inches taller than Gustav, something Jensen got the distinct feeling Regitse was rather enjoying.

'This is my number,' said Regitse, throwing a card across the table. 'I will be staying in town tonight and heading back to Aarhus around six tomorrow evening. Think it over. If you're interested, I expect to hear from you by then.'

8

Wednesday 10:43

The allotments at Kløvermarken were desolate in the driving
rain, and none more so than the one that had once been tended
by the late Vagn Holdved. Henrik cursed as he skidded and
slipped on the muddy ground, dirtying his boots.

Holdved's plot was more modest than its neighbours. It had
a small, red-painted cabin in its centre, next to a pole with a
Danish flag that had been beaten into sodden submission by
the weather. You were meant to lower the flag before sunset,
Henrik remembered someone telling him when he was a boy.
Obviously, no one had thought to do the honours since Holdved
had taken a fatal blow to his skull.

Once you were behind the brown beech hedge, which
sheltered Holdved's allotment from the narrow track that
ran alongside it, it was hard to imagine that the centre of
Copenhagen was only a few kilometres away.

Henrik was no gardener but noticed a couple of apple trees
and raspberry bushes. The vegetable beds had been turned over,
ready for a spring that Holdved himself would be missing.

Lotte Nielsen had been only too happy to chew over the case

43

when Henrik had stopped by her office with two lattes from the canteen. Quickly, he had got the distinct impression that she was getting nowhere. Holdved had been killed on his few square metres of lawn with his own spade. One of many strokes to his head and neck had almost decapitated him.

According to his son, who had checked the cabin, nothing other than his prescription sleeping tablets appeared to be missing, aside from cash which he claimed Holdved always kept plenty of in his wallet.

'Didn't do plastic cards, apparently,' Lotte had said, handing Henrik the evidence bag so he could take a look for himself.

The brown leather wallet was rounded from the old man's buttocks and shiny from years of wear. It made Henrik think of his own father. Holdved's bus pass was still there, along with a receipt from a supermarket where he had bought milk.

The absence of cash in his wallet, and the missing sleeping pills, did not amount to proof that Holdved had been the victim of robbery. A retired bank manager, who had been on a waiting list for his allotment for years, he was a widower who kept himself to himself, preferring the wooden cabin in Kløvermarken to his two-bedroom apartment in Emdrup. He had had no debts, no obvious enemies, and little contact with his son and daughter, showing almost no interest in his five grandchildren according to his son, who had told Lotte this with some bitterness.

'Witnesses? CCTV? Prints?' Henrik had asked Lotte.

'None of the above. No cameras anywhere near and on a freezing Tuesday in February, you're at little risk of being spotted by passers-by out there.'

'Still, doesn't seem like your average opportunistic addict, does it? Thinking ahead to wear gloves and clean up after himself? And all that for a few thousand kroner and some sleeping tablets?'

'Not impossible.'

'And the gloves?'

Lotte shrugged. 'It was cold.'

More to the point, how had the killer managed to travel away from the area without being spotted by a single soul, given he would have to be covered in blood himself? He might just have managed if he had come by car.

'Why all the questions?' asked Lotte, frowning. 'Do you have a theory?'

'No,' admitted Henrik, rubbing his calloused hand over his bald head. 'It was just something Monsen said. About the brutality of the crimes we're seeing these days.'

She laughed. 'That old chestnut. What got him started on that, the Irene Valborg murder?'

'Yep,' said Henrik.

He had thought about it. Even by today's standards, both murders *did* seem extraordinarily violent, given that the victims were old and weak and would hardly have put up a fight.

'You don't think they're connected, do you?' said Lotte. 'With all due respect, I don't see it.'

'No,' Henrik had said. 'You're probably right.'

Regardless, he had got straight into his car and driven to Kløvermarken on the island of Amager. He didn't always understand why he did things, but now, up to his ankles in mud and with rainwater running down his neck, he was seriously starting to wonder if he was losing his touch.

There was no purchase for his thoughts on the allotment, nothing to see but the sad saturated earth where an old man going quietly about his business had breathed his last.

Henrik walked over to the wooden cabin and stood on tiptoes looking through the window. Staying overnight at these particular allotments was permitted, and Holdved had kitted out the place nicely with a bed, a stove and bookshelves.

Henrik carefully lifted the police tape and used his lockpick to open the door. It was freezing and damp inside. The furnishings were fit for the scrapheap. Either Vagn Holdved had been struggling to make ends meet, or he preferred to slum it. Whichever it was, there had been nothing here to steal. Henrik had seen far more lavish plots on his way in. Of all the allotment owners, if you wanted to rob someone, Holdved would have been last choice.

Lotte's problem, he thought. Perhaps Monsen had a point and Danish society had hardened. More violent criminals, less respect for the elderly. He thought of his father again and made a note to take a look at his locks, give him the talk about not opening the door to strangers, even when they looked like nice people or wore a uniform.

He was about to leave when his eyes caught on something by the bed: the tiniest dark speck on the edge of the white pillow. He moved closer, noticing that it was the corner of a photograph that had dropped down between the pillow and the headboard. He put on his latex gloves and retrieved it carefully, getting out his reading glasses to take a proper look. It was a school photo of a teenage girl, taken some years ago judging by the state of it. There was a tiny hole in it from a pin and a faint slug-like trail of glue on the back, suggesting it had been ripped out of a photo album. Did anyone still glue photos into albums? He bent down and retrieved the pin from under the bed. There was a patch of missing plaster on the wall above the headboard.

He assumed the girl was Vagn Holdved's daughter. Henrik looked around but there were no other photos in the cabin. He recalled that there had been none in the old man's wallet.

He frowned. Wasn't Vagn Holdved supposed to have had little contact with his children? Perhaps he had felt bad about that, wistful for the time that had passed and wanting a second chance? Henrik knew only too well what that meant.

Still, why would Holdved only keep a photo of his daughter and not his son? He would have to ask Lotte next time he bumped into her.

46

It wasn't unheard of that parents loved one child more.
('Tell me about it!' he heard his wife say.)

Henrik knew he had a soft spot for his youngest son Oliver, but there was a straightforward explanation for that: at seven, Oliver still thought his father was funny, cool, all-knowing. His older siblings had long since clocked that this was far from true.

He dropped the photo of the girl into an evidence bag and put it in his pocket, before heading for the door, his mind already on the nice single-shot latte he was going to pick up from Baresso on his way back to the office.

9

Wednesday 12:54

Having taken one look at the weather, Jensen and Gustav had jumped on the S-train from the Central Station to Ordrup and continued from there to Irene Valborg's villa. Jensen was on her bicycle and Gustav on a new e-scooter bought for him by Margrethe with the seemingly limitless generosity she reserved for her nephew. Before Jensen had even mounted her bike, Gustav had sped towards the horizon like an exclamation mark in his black jeans, jacket and helmet.

Despite the short distance to the house, they were both wet and cold when they arrived. The driveway was barred with tape and a police sign warning them not to enter.

'What I don't understand,' said Gustav, wiping rain off his face, 'is why you don't just accept that woman's offer.'

'Come on, Gustav, I wouldn't have a cat's chance in hell of finding that necklace.'

'No matter, we take the seventy-five grand. Have a half-decent stab at it, and then tell her, "Sorry, we can't do it."'

'*We?*'

48

'Yes. We'll go halves, won't we? Thirty-seven and a half grand each?' He grinned.

Gustav might have dropped out of school, but there was nothing wrong with his maths.

'In your dreams,' Jensen said.

She could do with the money, though. The upfront payment for the Christianshavn flat had swallowed most of her liquid funds. 'Let's just have a look first. I haven't made up my mind yet,' she said.

She moved one of the bollards with police tape attached to it and began to push her bicycle up the drive. 'Are you coming?'

Gustav smiled broadly.

Jensen was surprised to find no police officer on guard at what was still a major crime scene. All the better to get a good look around.

Gustav whistled. 'And she lived here by herself? You could fit three families in here, four even.'

'Do you see that?' said Jensen, pointing to the front door.

'What, "Beware of the dog"?'

'That, but also the lock. It's new, a fairly hefty one too.'

'Looks like she wasn't too keen on uninvited guests. But then again, she would have to be loaded to live around here.'

'But why change the lock now?'

Gustav shrugged and put on his trusted headphones, traipsing onto the lawn for a tour around the house. He walked up to one of the windows, cupped his hands against the glass and looked inside. Jensen walked up beside him and did the same.

'And to think she was lying in there for two weeks before her body was discovered,' said Gustav, his voice too loud.

She gestured at him to take his headphones off. 'Might have been longer, if it hadn't been for her dog. Apparently, the neighbours complained about it barking all the time.'

The living room was cluttered with antique furniture and paintings.

49

'It's like a museum,' said Gustav, shuddering. 'Do you really think her necklace was stolen?'

'I don't know,' said Jensen.

'But you're interested, aren't you?'

When she didn't respond, Gustav took it as affirmation. 'Yes!' he exclaimed.

She shushed him, still not sure that taking money from Regitse Lindegaard was the right thing to do. She could see all sorts of issues with it, and press ethics were just the start of it.

Her guess that Regitse had married a rich man had been spot on. According to her Google search, Tim Lindegaard was the CEO of a manufacturing company near Aarhus that he had inherited from his father. Fifteen years older than Regitse. No kids. The Lindegaards lived by the beach in Risskov, an affluent suburb of Aarhus, in a modern concrete villa that looked to Jensen like a bunker but had won several architectural awards. Which made it even harder to explain Regitse's keen interest in the whereabouts of her mother's diamond necklace. What was it to her if it had been stolen? What was the rush?

Gustav and Jensen both turned at the sound of a car speeding up the drive.

Too late to run.

'Shit,' said Gustav.

'Let me handle this,' said Jensen under her breath as she walked smilingly across to the car from which a big and broad uniformed officer was emerging.

'Ah, I was wondering where you'd got to,' she said, noticing the takeaway coffee and crumpled pastry bag on the passenger's seat.

The officer towered above her. Jensen suspected his anger had a lot more to do with his guilty conscience than their presence at the house. She and Gustav hardly looked like criminals intending to tamper with a crime scene.

50

'Can't you read?' said the officer, gesturing at the bottom of the drive.

Jensen held up her hands. 'We come in peace. We're journalists.'

The officer took out his notepad, licking his thumb before turning the page. 'Who do you work for?'

'We're freelancers.'

'Show me your press cards.'

She dug out hers.

'And yours?' said the officer, turning to Gustav.

'He doesn't have one, he is my assistant,' said Jensen.

'Can't he speak?' the officer snapped, keeping his gaze on Gustav.

'I don't have one, I am her assistant,' said Gustav, all wide-eyed innocence.

The officer glared at them. He made them both write down their name, address and phone number, before begrudgingly letting them go. 'This isn't the last you'll hear of this,' he said.

'What did he mean by that?' said Gustav when they were out of earshot. 'Are we in trouble?'

He sounded like he found the prospect exciting, which made Jensen wonder (again) what kind of misdemeanour had got him kicked out of school. Margrethe had been at her wits' end when she had brought him to *Dagbladet* and forced Jensen to take him on as an unpaid trainee.

'I doubt it,' said Jensen, looking around at the quiet residential street, imagining dozens of pairs of eyes staring at them from behind the blank windows.

The houses were different shapes and colours, but all huge, set back on large plots and hidden by mature trees. Øresund, the strait separating Denmark from Sweden, was not far away. Some of the people here would have yachts moored at one of the several marinas that dotted the coast. Gustav donned his hood and got on his e-scooter, stopping after a few yards when he sensed that Jensen wasn't following. 'Are we going back or what?'

'Sure. Right after we pay the neighbour a visit,' she said, nodding in the direction of the enormous white villa to the right of Irene's red one.

'Why?'

'I want to know what they were thinking when they heard the dog barking in the garden for days on end. They must have wondered why Irene didn't let it in. Why didn't they just walk over and ring the doorbell?'

Gustav turned his e-scooter around. 'OK, we'll see the neighbour. But after that we're going. And then you can tell that upper-class woman with the rock on her finger that we'd be only too happy to take her money.'

'After that we're going,' Jensen laughed. 'The rest I have yet to decide.'

10

Next door's front garden was as neat and tidy as Irene Valborg's. The drive was lined on either side with daffodils nodding their yellow bonnets in the rain, the lawn a soft green carpet.

The neighbour opened the door seconds after they rang the bell. 'Who are you?' she said, in a loud school-mistressy voice, her beady eye peeking through the gap left by the chain. Before they got a chance to answer, she pointed a gnarled finger with a shiny red nail at Irene Valborg's house. 'I saw you, over there. The policeman sent you away. What do you want?'

No pulling the wool over the eyes of this one, thought Jensen, but she could tell that the woman wanted to talk. Without that human instinct where would journalism be?

'My name is Jensen. I am a reporter, and this is Gustav, my trainee.'

'Which newspaper?'

'Freelance, but I used to work for *Dagbladet*.'

'Don't read that muck,' she said, shaking her head. Jensen nodded. Klampenborg was the die-hard stronghold of *Dagbladet*'s conservative competitor.

'I suppose you're here about the murder,' said the woman. 'Terrible business. We're not safe anywhere these days, not even in our own homes.'

'It must have been an awful shock,' said Jensen. 'Look, I don't suppose we could come in and talk to you for a few minutes? You might have vital information.'

The chain stayed put, but Jensen felt the woman softening. 'That's what I said to that policeman yesterday, but he just wasn't interested. Very rude man, if you ask me. He looked like someone from one of those motorcycle gangs. If it hadn't been for his badge ... Wait a minute, I have his card right here.'

No need, thought Jensen.

The woman disappeared behind the door. 'Detective Inspector Henrik Jungersen,' she read. 'Far too young to be in charge of a case like this.'

'I know him,' said Jensen. 'He is in his forties, I believe. A very experienced police detective.'

'Pah. He even had the audacity to insinuate that I should have spoken to Irene myself.'

Jensen could see the disappointment. Life alone in the big villa had to be very tedious. And when, finally, something dramatic had happened about which the woman had plenty to say, she had found the recipient uninterested and impatient.

'But we'd be only too glad to listen, wouldn't we Gustav?' said Jensen.

Gustav made a face to the contrary, but quickly rearranged his features into those of a geeky young man. This was one of his two personas, the other being teenage delinquent. Jensen hadn't decided yet which was the real Gustav. 'Have you had many journalists visiting then, Mrs ...?' she said.

'Holm. A couple of photographers came. But no reporters. No one cares what an old woman has to say. I must have called the police dozens of times about that dog and two weeks later they turn up. That's not my fault, is it? I mean how can it be my fault?'

'Of course not,' said Jensen. 'How about we come in to dry ourselves off for a bit, and you can tell us all about it? You have my word that we won't quote you for anything, unless you want us to?'

Mrs Holm paused for a moment. Then she stepped back and slammed the door. Jensen began to prepare herself for a wet trip back to Copenhagen with nothing to show for it. Then she heard the rattle of the chain being pulled back.

'To tell you the truth, I would be glad of a little company. To think that something like this has happened right next door to me,' said Mrs Holm, pressing a handkerchief to her prominent nose.

A stale air escaped from the house, a scent of hairspray and, very faintly, cigars. As Jensen stepped inside followed by Gustav, she waited for Mrs Holm to add something to suggest that she felt sorry for her neighbour, but nothing came. Irene Valborg didn't seem to have inspired affection in anyone.

'Shoes off,' said Mrs Holm, shutting the heavy front door behind them. 'You too young man.' Big-boned and straight-backed with neatly coiffured white hair, she looked like someone used to giving orders. Her house was a carbon copy of what Gustav and Jensen had managed to see through the windows next door. Antique furniture, table lamps with pleated silk shades, oil paintings of pastoral Danish scenes. An old clock on top of a mahogany tallboy ticked away loudly. No other sound was audible, no birdsong, no traffic noises from the road.

'I will make some tea,' said Mrs Holm disappearing into the kitchen.

'I don't like tea,' said Gustav when she had gone.

'You do now,' said Jensen.

Gustav made a tour of the lounge. He picked up a large Chinese vase and pretended to be about to drop it on the parquet floor, laughing when Jensen shot him an angry look. She bent down to study a row of silver frames with old photos in them, family portraits mostly.

Mrs Holm approached with a rattling tea tray, brusquely refusing Gustav's offer of help. 'That was taken in the 1950s, just after we bought the house,' she said, nodding at the photo in Jensen's hand. 'Irene had moved in with her husband Ove a couple of years before us. Do sit down.'

She gestured at an arrangement of armchairs and sofas set around a coffee table topped with green leather.

She handed them both a delicate bone china cup and offered up a silver dish of shop-bought vanilla cookies. Gustav took three. Jensen kicked him under the table.

The tea was delicious, loose leaf, poured through a silver strainer. Jensen warmed her hands on the cup. 'Did you and Irene see much of each other? Back then, I mean?' she said.

'Now and again, but if you mean were we friends, no, we weren't. Irene was never a warm woman, and I am sorry to say that she didn't exactly improve with age. I was widowed before her. When her Ove passed away, I thought things would change. We could have been companions, the two of us, rattling around as we were on our own in these big houses, our children busy with their own lives.'

She shook her head as if trying to rid herself of a bad memory. Unsuccessfully, it seemed.

'May I ask what happened?' said Jensen.

'There was a, shall we say . . . unpleasant incident. I had tried to telephone Irene a few times after Ove died to offer my con- dolences, but she never answered the telephone, though I knew she was home. I thought she must be grieving terribly. I know I was when my husband died. So, I cooked a casserole for her and went over and rang her doorbell.'

'And?'

'Well, she *did* come to the door, but she was absolutely furi- ous. Snatched the glass dish out of my hand and smashed it to pieces right there on her front step. Told me to . . . to . . .'

'To what?'

'To piss off and mind my own business.' Mrs Holm pressed her handkerchief to her eyes.

Irene Valborg had had a point, thought Jensen: Mrs Holm *did* seem rather nosy. She could well imagine Henrik making short shrift of interviewing her.

'You see that's why when that infernal dog started barking night and day, I didn't go over there, because she had made it perfectly clear that she wanted to be left alone.'

'Had she always had a dog?'

'No, she got it last year, just before Christmas. What old ladies like us need a big dog like that for, I don't know. Of course, it was too much for her. Never took it for a walk, just let it out in the garden to do its business until it barked to be let back in.'

'And one day, the barking carried on all night?'

'Yes. Made a terrible racket, impossible to get any sleep.'

'Of course, that would have been because your neighbour was lying dead on the floor inside her house and couldn't let it in,' said Gustav, unable to keep the reproach out of his voice. 'Didn't you think that something might have happened to her?'

Steady on, Gustav.

Jensen kicked him under the table again, and he sat back angrily in the sofa, his arms folded across his chest.

Mrs Holm looked outraged at the suggestion that she had been remiss in some way. 'I couldn't very well have conceived that she had actually been *murdered*, could I?'

'Of course not. Everyone can see why you wouldn't have jumped to that conclusion,' said Jensen.

'I just assumed that she could no longer manage the dog inside the house and had decided it should now live outdoors permanently. So, I rang the police and complained.'

'And what did they say?'

'They told me to hang up. The number was for emergencies only, and I was to go to the local police station and make a complaint.'

57

'And did you?'

Mrs Holm nodded. 'Several times.'

'And no one did anything?'

'No, not for two weeks. Then all hell broke loose.'

There was a pause while the three of them listened to the rain tapping against the windows.

'Who do you think did it?' said Mrs Holm conspiratorially, but before Jensen could reply, the doorbell rang.

Mrs Holm looked perplexedly at Jensen and Gustav, before getting up from her chair and making her way into the entrance hall. 'I am not expecting anyone,' she said.

Jensen heard the chain go on, the door opening. 'Oh, it's you,' said Mrs Holm, grumpily.

Then Jensen recognised the voice she had first heard in London, fifteen years ago, across the dinner table at the Danish Ambassador's residence: rough, with the West Copenhagen accent that made him sound as much like a criminal as a policeman.

A voice like no other.

Henrik.

Livid.

'Get your guests and tell them to come out here now!'

11

'You're doing it again,' said Henrik, slamming his hands hard against the steering wheel.

They were parked in the road outside Irene Valborg's house. He was wearing his black leather jacket with his usual black jeans and white shirt. Jensen noticed that his boots were caked in fresh mud. The car was in a state, littered with takeaway paper cups and sweet wrappers.

Mrs Holm had protested in the strongest possible terms at being bossed around by a policeman young enough to be her grandson. A stand-off had ensued, which Jensen had broken by promising Mrs Holm that she and Gustav would come back another day. Jensen had asked Gustav to return to Copenhagen without her. She would have to speak to him about his temper. It wasn't like him to have got so worked up. What was the matter with him?

'Lovely to see you again, too,' she said to Henrik.

'You were supposed to leave Copenhagen. That's what you said.'

'Guess I changed my mind.'

He turned and looked at her, fury in his eyes. 'I know. I saw you.'

Jensen was astonished. 'You did?'

'I went to wave you off, only to see you stomping out of the terminal in the direction of the nearest taxi.'

'You were supposed to take me to the airport. I waited for you for ages at the hotel.'

'I was late, but I was going to make up for it.'

'Sure.'

'Believe what you want. Why did you stay?'

Jensen shrugged. 'Unfinished business.'

'I hope you don't mean me. I can't see you anymore.'

'Like you're not seeing me now, you mean?'

Henrik turned to her with an aggressive stare. 'It's not funny, Jensen. She threw me out. That Sunday night when I got back, my stuff had been packed and left in a bag on the doorstep, new locks fitted, the works.'

She. Her.

'I didn't tell her about us, if that's what you think. I never told anybody,' said Jensen.

This wasn't strictly speaking true. There were quite a few people who knew of the presence of 'the cop' in her life: Liron, the Israeli street barista, for starters. And Esben, her friend the MP, his driver Aziz and Gustav. Margrethe had probably worked it out, too. But none of them would have had any interest in telling on her and Henrik, would they?

Henrik sighed and rubbed his face hard as though he was trying to scrub a stain from it. 'She read the articles you wrote for *Dagbladet* in the paper that Sunday and put two and two together.'

'Ah. The coverage said a policeman had come to my rescue.'

'Quite.'

Henrik hit the steering wheel again, swearing loudly. '*Pis!*'

'Have you tried talking to her?'

'She won't answer my calls.'

60

'She can't know for certain that anything physical happened between us. Besides, you've not exactly been stalking me these past few weeks,' said Jensen.

What are you doing?

Not her job to persuade Henrik that his marriage was fine or condoning his radio silence.

He shot her an intense look. 'It wasn't just physical though, was it?'

Jensen shrugged and looked out at the rain. He was right. She felt his fingers stroking hers probingly, sending a jolt of heat through her body, then being abruptly withdrawn.

'For fuck's sake, what are you doing to me, Jensen?'

She held up her hands. 'Not guilty, your Honour.'

'And more to the point, what in God's name are you doing here?'

'Just going about my business. The Irene Valborg murder is interesting,' she said. 'Not your straightforward burglary, I would have thought. What do you make of—'?

'No.' Henrik interrupted her. 'We are not going to have this conversation, Jensen.'

He leaned across her lap to open the passenger door. 'I wish you well. You will always have my heart, but you're going to get on your bike now and return to Copenhagen. Leave the Irene Valborg murder story to your friend Frank Buhl.'

'Why?'

'Because if I see you, or even talk to you, I am going to do something stupid again, and if I do, my wife will never take me back. Please go now and stay out of my way.'

'No,' said Jensen.

'What, you want me to beg?'

'It won't help.'

'Why not?'

'Because Irene's daughter has asked me to investigate what happened to her mother's necklace and I am going to accept.'

'The bitch,' said Henrik under his breath. 'You can't.'

'Why not?'

'Because it's unethical. Because it interferes with an official investigation. Because that woman is a money-grabbing monster. Want me to go on?'

'My choice,' said Jensen. 'Last time I checked I was old enough to decide for myself.'

'I will make an official complaint to Margrethe Skov.'

'You can do that, of course, but I never returned to *Dagbladet*. I am freelancing.'

'Since when?'

'Since January.' She turned to look at him, but he refused to meet her eyes.

'If you don't mind me saying so, Henrik, you're the one who's married. I never asked you to cheat on your wife, let alone leave her for me.'

She had hoped it perhaps, long ago, but she knew deep down it was never going to happen. Somehow, she had always thought this made Henrik's infidelity less objectionable.

He said nothing. Despite herself, she felt sad. There had been times in the past fifteen years when she wished they had never met, and this was one of them.

'I hope you and your wife manage to figure it out,' she said as she got out and slammed the car door.

He sped off, his tyres skidding on the tarmac.

'And Foxtrot Yankee to you too,' Jensen said as she walked across to her bicycle and began the ride back to Ordrup station.

12

When the call came through about a violent assault at a care home in Lyngby, Henrik was almost grateful for the distraction. He would rather work, preferring the absorption of tasks immediately in front of him to the endless churning of thoughts about his fucked-up life.

He just wanted everything to return to the way it had been.

Before Jensen had turned up in his life again.

Before he had lost all control.

Was that too much to ask?

He knew that blaming Jensen for what had happened was wrong and felt guilty for the way he had spoken to her earlier, but not guilty enough not to wish her gone from Copenhagen.

Dispatching Mark to the care home, he sped through the city with his blue light plonked on the roof of his car. Ulla Olsen, the eighty-one-year-old victim, had been taken by ambulance to the national hospital better known as Riget (The Kingdom). One of the officers first on the scene in Lyngby had described the attack as 'frenzied'. There had been no updates since, but if there was a chance of a statement from her, Henrik didn't want to miss it.

He heard the ear-piercing wail as soon as he stepped inside the Accident & Emergency reception area, flashing his police badge. Ulla Olsen had been whisked away already.

'You wouldn't have got anything out of her anyway,' said one of the paramedics, a blonde woman with a pasty face and dark rings under her eyes. 'She was well gone.'

The paramedic nodded at a middle-aged woman in a red coat who had sunk to her knees in the middle of the floor, howling. 'That's the daughter. It was her who called it in.'

'And the victim?'

'Severe bleeding from several blows to the head. She has dementia but is strong as an ox. Touch and go, I'd say.'

Henrik nodded his thanks and approached the woman on the floor. Her hands were dark red with blood. She was smearing the linoleum with it. A couple of nurses were trying to calm her down, repeating her name over and over. 'Anette. Anette. Listen. Anette.'

Henrik gestured at them gently to back off. He knelt down in front of the woman and held her tight until her body relaxed and her screaming became a protracted moan, then heavy sobs. She clung to him.

'I know,' he said. 'I know.'

To the nurses, he said: 'Could you get us a blanket?'

He managed to manoeuvre the woman into a seat, leaving the bloody mess behind on the floor.

It was another ten minutes before Anette had finished crying. Henrik waited patiently, ignoring the curious glances from passers-by. Never rush people in shock, bitter experience had taught him.

'I am Detective Inspector Henrik Jungersen, Copenhagen Police,' he said when she had fallen silent.

'They wouldn't let me go in with her,' she said, sniffling.

'She is in the best place possible. They are looking after her now.'

'I want to see her.'

'You will. But first, let's talk a little.'

'Is she going to die?'

Henrik said nothing. That was another thing he had learned. Never promise anyone a happy ending.

One of the nurses returned with the blanket he had asked for. He put it around Anette. As she began to cry again, he watched a cleaner wipe away the blood stains on the floor. The old hospital would have seen far worse.

Life went on.

'Tell me what happened,' Henrik said when they were alone again. 'From the beginning.'

'I came after work, like I do most weekdays,' she said.

'What do you do, Anette?' said Henrik, knowing he had to try to calm her down a little more.

'I am a teacher. Primary school just down the road, so it's easy for me to visit.'

'That's nice for you.'

'Not really. Mum doesn't know who I am anymore.'

'Alzheimer's?'

'Vascular dementia.' Anette swallowed back sobs. 'Mum was sitting in her armchair, like she always did. I thought she was wearing a new red top. But it was blood, all the way down the front of her white blouse. She was slumped forwards.'

Henrik nodded, letting her continue in her own time.

'I screamed for help, and the staff came and rang for an ambulance.' Anette got up from her chair and began to pace up and down, the blanket falling to the floor. 'I've got to phone the family to let them know what's happened.'

'Plenty of time for that,' said Henrik.

'My car,' said Anette, stopping in her tracks. 'It's still in Lyngby. I've got food shopping in the back.'

Henrik had seen this reaction plenty of times in people struggling to come to terms with sudden violence and death. Useless thoughts crowding in when the reality in front of you was too much to bear.

One of the nurses came up to them and addressed herself to Anette. 'Your mother is being treated for her injuries. She will be placed into a coma.'

'I want to see her,' Anette cried.

'It will be a little while yet before they have settled her,' said the nurse. 'Maybe in an hour or so?'

'Meanwhile, why don't I take you back to Lyngby to get your car? We can talk a little more on the way, and if there's time, you can show me where you found your mother,' said Henrik.

'You'd do that?'

'I need to go anyway.'

Anette sat in silence for most of the journey to Lyngby, watching the traffic passing by in the rain. 'I suppose you've seen it all, being in the police and everything,' she said, biting her lower lip. A heavy tear rolled down her cheek.

'I've seen a lot, but you never get used to it,' said Henrik, thinking of Irene Valborg's scrawny body.

'Who'd attack an old woman who can barely remember her own name?'

'I don't know,' said Henrik. 'But I can assure you that we'll be doing everything we can to find them. Is there anyone else who visits her regularly?'

'Who would that be? She only has me.'

'Anyone at the care home she is friendly with?'

'I don't think so. I mean, she enjoys the activities they put on, the keep fit, the crafts, but she's too far gone to form actual relationships. She is under observation pretty much around the clock.'

Not quite, thought Henrik. *Not if someone can come into her room and bash her over the head.*

'Has your mother suffered from dementia for long?'

66

'A few years. Wasn't too bad in the beginning, but she went downhill quickly. We couldn't keep her at home anymore. She kept running off, forgetting where she was. Turned up at Ordrup station once.'

'Ordrup?' said Henrik, turning to face Anette. 'Did she live nearby?'

'No, Bispebjerg,' said Anette. 'I don't even know how she managed to get there. First thing I knew about it was when the police called me. She was so distressed when I got there. Can you imagine how terrifying it must be, not knowing who or where you are?'

Henrik nodded. His stepmother was getting to that stage now, but of course his dad refused to see that he could no longer care for her. Henrik and his wife, while things were still tolerable between them, had checked out a few care homes and left the brochures discreetly on his dad's hallway table – where they had done nothing but gather dust, to Henrik's immense frustration. 'Your father still alive?' he asked Anette.

She shook her head. 'Long gone. Mum and Dad divorced about thirty years ago. He remarried but passed away in 2002 from a stroke. Forty-a-day man.'

'What did your mother do? For work, I mean?'

'She was a cleaner. Private homes, mostly. Bought a small flat in Bispebjerg after the divorce, so presumably my father gave her some money. In which case, it would have been about the only thing the bastard ever did for her. She loved that flat, her little balcony full of flowers. Couldn't stop crying when we sold it.'

Henrik was consulting his sat nav, lost in Lyngby. Monsen lived nearby somewhere, but in the perpetual rain all the streets looked the same.

'Turn left here,' said Anette, putting him back on the right track.

The blue blinks soon came into view, eliminating the need

67

for further map reading. Anette's eyes widened at the sight of the police vehicles parked outside the care home. She shrank back into her seat.

'They will be looking for clues. Anything at all that might help us catch who did this. Fingerprints, foreign fibres, DNA,' said Henrik, speaking slowly and deliberately. 'Would you take me to your mother's room and tell me if anything is missing?'

'Why?'

'If anything was stolen, that might help explain what happened.'

'Well, she always has her handbag with her.'

'Shall we go and look for it?'

He led her down the corridor, supporting her arm. Mark was approaching them from the other direction, trying to catch Henrik's attention. Henrik shook his head at him.

Not now, Mark.

'Can we have a few minutes?' Henrik said to the scene-of-crime officer in charge.

They were given gloves, overshoes and masks and shown where to walk. A white-suited photographer from forensics had the presence of mind to step in front of the bloodied armchair, shielding it from view as they passed. Anette walked across to a small closet next to the bed. The handbag was inside. A black patent number with a gold clasp.

Henrik watched her open it. 'Her purse is here, comb, lipstick, pill dispenser.'

'Everything where it should be?' said Henrik.

'Seems so.'

'Good. Any other possessions someone might have taken?'

Anette shook her head. 'We got rid of everything when Mum moved here. As her doctor said at the time, it was a one-way ticket. But she didn't own anything anyway. Just old stuff of no value.'

Not a simple burglary then. Maybe one of the other residents at the home? Someone who thought Ulla Olsen was evil, or possessed, or some other crazy nonsense?

Had the offender meant to kill her and been disturbed, or struck randomly and fled when the bleeding had started? He thought of Vagn Holdved and Irene Valborg. Both had been killed pretty decisively. Three extreme acts of violence against elderly, defenceless people in a couple of weeks amounted to a lot, but it wasn't necessarily a pattern. The attack on Ulla Olsen didn't fit. 'Come,' he said to Anette, turning towards the door. 'I'll walk you to your car.'

'Wait a minute,' she said. She had opened the drawer in her mother's bedside table and retrieved a photo from inside.

A photo taken some years ago, of a girl of school age, smiling red-eyed into the camera at a party.

'Who the hell is this?'

13

'OK, so where do we start?' said Gustav.

He was lying on Jensen's sofa, his torso draped across the seat and his skinny legs dangling over the armrest. Takeaway paper bags and the remains of bao buns were strewn across the coffee table. You could hear the eternal rain on the Velux window upstairs, the ebb of the evening traffic on Torvegade.

'We write a list of all the questions we need answers to,' said Jensen, noisily sucking up the last of her iced green tea through a straw.

She rummaged through the plastic bag of office supplies that Gustav had borrowed from *Dagbladet*, picking up a pen and a pack of neon-coloured post-its and throwing them to him. Earlier in the evening, they had been to Margrethe's office, so Gustav could ask for permission to continue to work with Jensen, though, in Margrethe's words, she had 'no fucking clue' what she was doing freelancing. 'It's tough out there on your own. You'll be on your knees, begging to come back.'

Between them, Jensen and Gustav had decided not to

70

mention the job they had agreed to do for Regitse Lindegaard, who had already paid the first instalment of their fee.

Margrethe, imposing behind her desk, with her eyes boring into them from behind her thick glasses, had reluctantly consented to the arrangement. 'But if anyone touches as much as a hair on Gustav's head, I will hold you accountable, and this time I *will* kill you,' she had said to Jensen, before addressing her nephew, softening her tone. 'Keeps you out of mischief for now. But I want you back at school after Easter. This was only ever going to be a temporary arrangement. I spoke to the head at Holger Hansen's High School after our visit. They have a place for you and I've said yes to it.'

At this news Gustav had turned a bluish shade of white. It had taken a Vietnamese takeaway for Jensen to restore the colour to his cheeks, though he refused to answer any of her questions about what had happened.

He peeled off a lurid pink post–it and glanced at her expectantly. 'Shoot.'

'OK. Why did Irene buy a necklace she never wore?'

Gustav looked up. 'Who cares? It happened thirty years ago. We only want to know who took it.'

'Hear me out,' said Jensen. 'If you came into an unexpected inheritance, what would you do with it?'

'Dunno. Travel the world, use it as a down payment on my own place, buy a car?'

'Precisely,' said Jensen. 'You'd spend it on something fun, not a diamond necklace to keep in a safe.'

Gustav wrote in capital letters on the post–it and stuck it to the wall above the sofa. 'So how do we find out what the reason was?' he said.

Jensen bit her lip. 'Well, we could ask Regitse.'

'You already did, remember? She was clueless.'

'Or perhaps the jeweller Irene bought the necklace from? There must be a receipt somewhere.'

'OK,' said Gustav. 'Next?'

'How could the burglar have known the code to the safe?'

'Perhaps she was stupid enough to write it down somewhere, or it was her date of birth or something.'

'So, an eighty-six-year-old woman who is canny enough to get a new alarm system, a prison-style security grille and an Alsatian, makes life that easy for a burglar?'

'Perhaps the safe happened to be open when the burglar broke into the house?'

'Unlikely coincidence.'

'Next?' said Gustav with a note of irritation in his voice.

'OK. What made her get all that security? Had someone threatened her, perhaps? We can ask the security firm. Maybe she told them?'

Gustav had already slammed the post-it on the wall and was ready for her next question. 'Caught your drift five minutes ago,' he said.

Where was it coming from, this sudden short fuse of his? Jensen continued. 'Seeing as there was no sign of a break-in, it seems likely that whoever did it was someone Irene knew or expected or both,' she said.

'Who? Everyone hated her guts.'

'Still. Who was it?'

'Done,' said Gustav slamming the third post-it against the wall.

'Let's say instead that Irene didn't know the burglar and that he managed to talk his way into the house by pretending to be a policeman. And let's say that she gave him the code to the safe for whatever reason . . . then where would someone go to sell a necklace worth that much?'

Another post-it went up with a slam.

'She could have hidden the necklace somewhere in the house,' said Jensen.

'Why would she do that, if she was so scared someone would take it? You just said she was canny.'

'Well, somewhere else then.'

Gustav added a green post-it to the wall. It said *Necklace hidden?* in big angry letters.

'Gustav, what's wrong?'

'Nothing's wrong,' he said, but he wouldn't meet her eyes.

'You've been snappy since you got here. Is it because of what Margrethe said?'

'What of it?' he snapped.

'When she said you had to go back to school you went white as a sheet. Does it have anything to do with why you were expelled from that school in Aalborg?'

Gustav sat up abruptly and for a brief moment it was Margrethe's fiery eyes glaring back at her. She had never seen him so angry. 'None of your fucking business,' he said, looking for his rucksack and coat. 'I wish you'd all just leave me the fuck alone.'

Before she could say anything, he had walked the few steps to the door and slammed it so hard behind him that Jensen's newly acquired IKEA clock fell off the wall and broke in two.

14

Henrik leaned over his desk, flanked by Mark and Lisbeth. Lotte had joined them, looking as though she had just risen from her bed. Something Henrik was doing his best not to think about.

('Here you go again,' said his wife in his head.)

'What do you think? Same girl, or someone different?' he said, pointing to the picture from the care home which he had placed on his desk next to the picture he had retrieved from Vagn Holdved's allotment.

'Could be the same girl,' said Mark. 'Looks different in that second photo, though.'

'It's the make-up. From schoolgirl to party girl. Quite the transformation,' said Lisbeth.

'I am not sure,' said Lotte, yawning. 'Besides, what if it's the same girl? Just some crazy coincidence, six degrees of separation and all that.'

'Anette Olsen, the daughter, has no idea who this is,' said Henrik, pointing to the party girl. 'Never seen the photo before.'

'So?' said Lotte. 'The old woman is mad.'

74

'Demented, not mad.'

'Same difference. Could belong to another of the residents. Somebody else's relative, she wouldn't have a clue either way.'

'Have you checked the photo from Vagn Holdved's cabin with his family?'

'Not yet,' said Lotte. 'His son's in Dubai on a business trip, his daughter lives in Berlin. I emailed it to both of them. My guess is it's the daughter when she was young. They'll get back to me tomorrow, I am sure.'

Henrik sighed, picked up the photos and handed them to Mark. 'Take these to forensics. Ask if it could be the same girl. And see if they can find out how old the photos are.'

'Sure thing, boss,' said Mark.

'And Lisbeth, ask around at the care home in Lyngby if anyone knows the girl. Lotte is right, could be someone else's relative.'

Lisbeth frowned. 'But why—'

'For fuck's sake, Lisbeth, just do it, will you?'

Lisbeth and Mark walked out of the room, leaving a bad atmosphere in their wake. Lotte stayed put, with her heeled black boots on Henrik's desk. Her eyes were closed.

'You look done in,' he said to her.

'Thanks a million. Went to bed early to catch up on sleep. All went according to plan until you called.'

'You didn't have to come.'

'You got me curious.'

'But now you think I've wasted your time.'

Lotte just about managed a smile. 'How are you doing anyway, Henrik?'

'How am I *doing*?' He knew very well what she meant. Everyone at the station wanted to hear how he was after the shooting incident in Magstræde back in January.

He didn't want sympathy.

Didn't need it.

Especially not from Lotte.

'Never been better,' he said, straightening his back and tightening his stomach muscles.

He looked at her more intently. Was she married? There was no ring on her finger, but that didn't necessarily mean anything.

'What?' she said. 'Why are you looking at me like that?'

He laughed. 'I was just wondering ... whether you've had anything to eat yet? I could go out and fetch us something. A couple of beers, seeing as we're both off duty?'

Her eyes narrowed. 'Are you chatting me up, Jungersen? Your wife kicked you out, and now you're looking for a consolation prize?'

'Who told you that?'

'Monsen mentioned something. As if I couldn't work it out for myself. When did you last shave? Or have a shower even?'

Henrik felt the unwelcome warmth of a blush spreading across his face and neck. 'Much as I like you, Lotte, I wasn't proposing dinner by candlelight. All I did was suggest we go and get something to eat, seeing as we are both at a loose end after a work meeting,' he said.

It was supposed to be a humorous remark but came out as a whine.

Christ, what was happening to him?

('You're pathetic,' said his wife.)

'See that's where you're wrong, Jungersen,' said Lotte, taking her boots off the desk and zipping up her padded black jacket as she walked off.

Henrik couldn't help glancing admiringly at her trim body. He knew she kept in shape by pounding the pavements around the office during her lunch hour. As if she knew what he was thinking, she turned in the doorway and looked at him pityingly. 'You might be at a loose end, but my boyfriend's at home warming the bed for me as we speak, so thanks, but no thanks.'

15

Henrik switched the engine off, leaned back in the driver's seat and sighed deeply. Diagonally across the dark and deserted street, behind a beech hedge was the yellow two-storey period house that he and his wife had bought together twenty years ago and filled with three kids and the detritus of family life. Though this particular district of Copenhagen, close to Frederiksberg Gardens, had been less fashionable then, it had still been way beyond the means of a high-school teacher and a policeman.

At first, he had refused the offer of a loan from her father. The last thing he needed was for the pompous git to use his money as a means of controlling the two of them. But his wife had waged a campaign, and, in the end, he had conceded.

Sooner or later, he always did where his wife was concerned.

Thankfully the loan had never again been mentioned, nor called in. Henrik had never asked his wife, but he guessed she had warned the old codger that any kind of interference in their lives wouldn't go down well with her copper husband.

Many times, over the years, Henrik had sat parked up outside the yellow house after another punishing shift, watching the comings and goings behind the brightly lit windows, before plucking up the energy to join the fray.

He and his wife had worked their fingers to the bone restoring the place, sanding the floors, replacing the old sash windows. Weekend after weekend had been spent picking out bathroom tiles and paint. Not six months ago, his wife had insisted on having a brand-new kitchen installed.

Despite this, he still struggled to believe he belonged there, in a house so different to the red-brick terrace in which he had grown up. 'Flashy', as his father had put it when he had first visited them.

Dressed in his faded windbreaker, feet at ten to two, the old man had looked awkward and lost in the high-ceilinged rooms and, ever since, get-togethers with Henrik's family, such as they were, had taken place at his father's.

Well, Henrik wasn't going to get anywhere near the fancy house now.

Not tonight.

Perhaps never again.

All he had left now were these secret nightly visits before bed to make sure the house was still standing with his family safe inside it.

He checked his phone. No messages from either Jensen or his wife.

He was still smarting after his exchange with Lotte. It had been stupid of him to think that he had a look-in there. Five years ago, maybe. ('Try ten!' his wife would say.)

Like any good detective, Lotte could smell male desperation a mile off. It wasn't even that he was into her, he told himself, more like he needed to prove that he still had it, whatever *it* was.

God.

What was more pathetic than a middle-aged man pitying himself?

Oliver, his youngest, only seven, would be fast asleep. With

Mikkel and Karla, the older two, it was anybody's guess. His wife had drawn down the blinds in the bedroom she had shared with Henrik until a few weeks ago, which meant she was getting ready to go to sleep. Rather late for her on a school night, wasn't it? He felt an icy spike in his abdomen. What if she wasn't alone in there? What if she had decided that two could play at his game?

'Don't be daft, Jungersen,' he said out loud to himself. She wouldn't bring another man to their house this soon, would she? Jensen coming anywhere near the house was unimaginable.

Wives and sweethearts.

May they never meet.

If only he could speak to his wife, actually be in the same room as her for just five minutes. He would lock eyes with her, hold her tight, so she couldn't wriggle free. 'Tell me you don't love me,' he would say. He knew exactly where to touch her, which buttons to press. She needed him, like he needed her.

('Yeah, like a hole in the head!' he heard his wife say.)

'Jesus, Jungersen, get a fucking grip,' he said out loud, rubbing his face hard. Seeing Jensen had been a bad move. He should have known that he would feel the same as he always had. When she had left the car, he had wanted to run after her, hold her, say he didn't mean it.

If only she was married, too.

Things would be easier.

However much he wanted to, he couldn't be the man she deserved. He told himself she would soon tire of the Irene Valborg case when she discovered that he had shut the door on her and would no longer supply the titbits of information that had sustained her through the Magstræde investigation.

Let's see how well you do now, he thought.

Thank God she didn't know about Ulla Olsen, or she would be getting under his feet on that case as well.

Were the photos from Vagn Holdved's cabin and Ulla Olsen's

bedside drawer really of the same girl? And if so, why were they there? If Lotte was right, and the photo in Ulla Olsen's room belonged to one of the other care home residents, was that person somehow related to Vagn Holdved?

Not improbable. Copenhagen was a small city. You could easily walk down Strøget, the main pedestrian street that ran like an artery through the city centre, on a Saturday afternoon and bump into someone you knew.

A woman with a small white dog on a lead was approaching the car on the opposite pavement. She was looking in his direction. Henrik shrank into his seat, waiting for her to pass. She lived a few doors down and would have noticed by now that he hadn't been around for a couple of months, starting to ask herself questions.

If only Irene Valborg's nosy neighbour had done the same.

A sudden thought crossed his mind. A stupid idea, perhaps, but one he had the time and the inclination to check out. At this time of night, he could be in Klampenborg in less than twenty-five minutes.

He watched as the light went out in his marital bedroom. He imagined his wife in there, her reading glasses folded on the bedside table next to her book, the air scented with the fragrance of the hand cream she always applied before bed. Was she thinking of him? Wondering where he was, and if he was OK?

Yeah sure, Jungersen, you believe that.

He turned the key in the ignition, glanced one more time at the dark house that contained his whole life and drove off from the kerb.

16

Wednesday 23:29

Jensen left her bike in *Dagbladet*'s courtyard shed. She had handed in her access card when she had left the newspaper, but the back door was locked with a key code, and no one had changed it since she was last there. She looked around before entering, an unnecessary precaution this late at night.

She had already gone to bed and had been lying under the covers in the Christianshavn flat, listening to the rain on the Velux window, when on an impulse she had got up again, got dressed and gone out. She needed to work, to distract herself.

The conversation with Gustav was playing on her mind. Since Margrethe had first forced her to take him on as an apprentice, Gustav had refused to say what had got him expelled from school. Usually, he would laugh off her prying questions, so why, this time, had he stomped off in a huff? Something was up, pulling like a lead weight at Gustav's normally buoyant mood. Was it the prospect of getting up early and doing homework that was bothering him, like it would any lazy seventeen-year-old? Or was it the specific high school Margrethe had picked, a private one in the Østerbro district? Jensen would have some sympathy for Gustav in the case of the former. Perhaps she could talk to Margrethe, make her see that her nephew just wasn't cut out for school?

As she ascended *Dagbladet's* dusty back staircase with only the torch on her mobile to light the way, she thought about the missing necklace. There had been nothing about Irene or her husband Ove online. Plenty of pieces on Regitse, but her parents had pre-dated Google. If there was anything to know, only one person in Copenhagen could tell her.

The grey-painted door to what was known as the reporters' corridor creaked on its hinges as she entered the building's top floor. She went to her old office. As she suspected, the room had not been re-occupied. The two desks were still pushed together, the notice board that had once separated her and Gustav shoved to one side. A small pile of mail had been dropped in the wire basket on top of the bookshelf. She grabbed it and stuffed it in her bag.

Her finger came away thick with dust when she wiped it on the desk. A stack of used notebooks sat in the corner, containing her illegible scribbles, the wastepaper bin was full of discarded paper coffee cups from Liron's. Jensen hadn't seen him for weeks. She wondered if he was still there with his tiny van in Sankt Peders Stræde, peddling his black gold like so much magic, or had decided to take a break from business during the wet weather.

The coffee machine pitcher was empty, most likely finished off by Henning Würtzen. *Dagbladet's* former editor-in-chief, who had left retirement to become the newspaper's obituary writer, was fond of cold coffee, preferably scavenged from other people's offices.

Jensen leaned into the dormer window where she used to sit and ponder her future. She looked out across the red-tile rooftops of Copenhagen. Rain was streaming down the windowpane, distorting the view. She missed the newspaper, the pulse of it, its readers across the country. She didn't miss the pressure on its shrinking band of reporters to feed its insatiable round-the-clock hunger for copy.

In the dark room, Jensen turned her head and listened, relieved to hear faint music coming from the direction of Henning's office. He had to be somewhere in his late eighties, perhaps even past ninety. One day, not too far into the future, she knew she would find him gone. What would she do then, without his paper library of clippings on Denmark's great and good?

'Good evening, Henning,' she said, knocking on the door frame as she entered.

Henning turned slowly from the open window through which he was smoking a cigar in circumvention of fire regulations and all manner of health and safety rules. He was wearing a long, dark green coat over his suit and a fur hat that made him look like an aged Russian spy. Was he dressed for going out, or merely to withstand the low temperature in the room? Jensen guessed the latter, having never seen Henning outside the building.

'You,' he said with a voice ravaged by decades of late nights putting *Dagbladet* to bed.

'Do you ever go home to sleep?' she asked.

Henning took a drag on his cigar and turned to face the window again, letting the smoke stand about his face in a cloud. 'You can talk,' he said.

'I wanted to ask you something.'

'You don't work here anymore.'

'No. I am trying to discover what happened to a necklace missing from the Klampenborg home of one Irene Valborg. She was found murdered a couple of days ago. I am investigating on behalf of her daughter.'

Henning turned to look at her. 'So you're a private eye now?'

'What if I am?'

83

Henning chuckled softly to himself.

'Got anything under Valborg?' Jensen said, a bit more impatiently than she intended.

'Never heard that name before,' said Henning.

'How about Regitse Lindegaard, their daughter?' she said. 'I believe her husband is CEO of a firm in Aarhus. Industrial pumps or something. He must be close to seventy now.'

Henning looked at the ceiling as he reeled off the facts from his extraordinary memory: 'Factory was founded by his father, Preben. Died in 1998, I think, or was it 1997? One of the old Danish industrialists, if a minor one. The son has continued to run the company, but less successfully. New competitors from Germany, I believe.'

Henning spent his days with stacks of Danish newspapers (diminishing stacks as titles had gone out of business), cutting out articles and marking the date with an ink pen.

'He can't be doing too badly, though, judging by his wife's appearance,' said Jensen.

Henning shook his head, puffing on his cigar and squinting into the smoke. 'For someone who is supposed to be a great journalist, you can be very naïve, young lady.'

'What do you mean by that?'

'If they're that rich, what is the woman doing hiring you as a private investigator?'

'I solved the Magstræde case. I am good at investigating.'

'Be that as it may, why care about some old necklace?'

'She says it's priceless.'

'There you go then. She needs the money,' said Henning, scratching his chin.

Jensen turned to go, then thought of something. 'Ever heard of a man called Carsten Vangede?'

'Vangede, Vangede.' Henning closed the window, stubbed out his cigar in the brass ashtray and went over to one of his filing cabinets. 'Name rings a bell.' He pulled out a file and flicked through it. 'Ah yes. Small-time restaurateur, owned a few places in Nørrebro. Went bankrupt and killed himself. What do you want to know about him for?'

'I am not sure it was suicide. I think he'd got hold of some information, something big that someone didn't want anyone to know about.'

'Oh, you do, do you? And who is paying you to investigate *that*?'

Good question, Henning.

She watched as he plonked himself heavily onto his desk chair, still wearing his coat and hat. The midnight news came on the radio. He closed his eyes and began to breathe heavily.

Jensen knew she wasn't going to get any more information out of him. If she was going to make any progress on the story, she would need access to Vangede's property and so far she hadn't heard as much as a peep out of his sister Christina.

'Goodnight,' she said to the sound of Henning's gentle snoring, feeling a wave of affection for the old editor. 'See you around, Henning.'

17

Wednesday 23:57

The officer on guard duty had been withdrawn from Irene
Valborg's property when forensics had finished up earlier that
evening, but the police tape was still up, fluttering softly in the
wind at the end of the drive alongside the no-entry sign. Henrik
parked in a side street and walked up to the villa, taking care
to stay out of the streetlight. The last thing he needed was that
nosy cow next door spotting him and kicking up a stink.

Inside, he switched on his torch and moved slowly through
the dark rooms, trying to remember the layout. He went
through the lounge first, then the dining room, eventually
making his way to the kitchen. He was trying not to think about
what had happened upstairs. He knew Irene's corpse was long
gone, but the house still gave him the creeps.

Quickly, he ran his torch over the walls, shining it inside the
kitchen cabinets. They were full of identical tins of lobscouse with
a picture of a blue-and-white chequered tablecloth, a silver cande-
labra and a plate of glistening stew. Henrik guessed this bore no
resemblance to the contents. There had to be fifty tins or more.
What had Irene Valborg been preparing for? A nuclear winter?

He left the kitchen, standing for a while in the hall at the foot of the stairs, almost having a heart attack when the gilded clock on the mantelpiece struck midnight.

He knew he still had to search the first floor.

But he didn't want to.

'Come on, Jungersen, for fuck's sake,' he said, beginning to ascend. The cone of light from his torch found the dark stain on the floor. He searched the two smaller bedrooms first. There was one with floral wallpaper which he guessed had belonged to Regitse, and another with wood panelling that looked like it had once been an office. A set of cupboard doors opened on a small wash basin with an ancient bottle of eau de cologne on a glass shelf. It bore a picture of Venice and smelled faintly of lemons.

Finally, he went through Irene's bedroom again, shining his torch along the walls, feeling behind the backs of the paintings and inside the safe.

Still nothing.

He had been right to think it was a stupid idea. Good job he hadn't told anyone about it. He went back out onto the landing and shone his torch along the low bookshelf where the bronze elephant had stood until the killer had crushed Irene's skull with it. The first shelf held a row of leather-bound books, but on the second shelf there were photographs, mostly black-and-white, some in faded colour. Pictures of Regitse as a little girl, wearing a sunhat on the beach. Wedding photos of the Valborgs grinning at the camera in a time long gone.

Then he saw it.

The frameless photo was tucked in amongst the others, curled at the edges. Regitse had been so focused on detecting missing valuables that she must have overlooked it.

The odd one out.

Henrik put on his gloves and retrieved the photo from the shelf. It couldn't be Regitse, could it? The photo looked more recent. The girl was standing on the edge of a swimming pool, wearing a costume and a cap, with a medal around her neck. She was smiling. Henrik thought he recognised her.

He turned the photo over and studied the faint slug trail of glue reflecting in the torchlight.

Two photos could be explained away, but three were not a coincidence. Henrik put the picture in an evidence bag and headed back down the stairs. The person he wanted to tell all about it was the only person he couldn't: Jensen.

18

Jensen and Gustav asked at the basement restaurant for Ernst Brøgger and were pointed to a table in the furthest corner of the back room. The restaurant was of a kind Jensen didn't think existed in Copenhagen anymore. Oak panelling and brass oil lamps suspended from a low ceiling. Green leather benches and chairs set around small tables decked in starched white tablecloths. A tiled wood-burning stove in one corner. Paintings of deer in beech woodland clearings. All that and not a single ironic hipster barman in sight.

It was at least an hour too early for lunch in Jensen's opinion, but the man hidden behind a copy of *Dagbladet* had already polished off half a slice of ryebread with marinated herring, red onion, capers and curried egg mayonnaise. On the table in front of him was a bottle of Carlsberg and a shot glass of aquavit wet with condensation.

They stood for a while, awkwardly watching the man, until Jensen cleared her throat and spoke. 'Ernst Brøgger? My name is Jensen, and this is Gustav. I emailed you?'

The man looked up with no particular urgency. Horn-rimmed

89

spectacles, a neatly trimmed beard, assuredly affluent in a white shirt, navy-blue corduroy trousers and a purple V-neck jumper.

He smiled broadly.

What the hell?

Deep Throat?

Jensen was stunned to find her anonymous informer seated in front of her, a man she had only met once, in the dark at Copenhagen's Assistens Cemetery.

'Long time, no see,' Brøgger laughed, turning to Gustav and pointing a mayonnaise-covered knife at him. 'And you, young man. I believe last time our paths crossed you were hiding in the bushes. Am I right?'

Gustav's jaw dropped. 'How did you . . .?'

Brøgger smiled enigmatically, tapping the side of his nose. 'Take a seat,' he said, indicating the two chairs in front of him.

They sat dumbly.

Brøgger finished his open sandwich before speaking again. 'Can I offer you something?' he said, wiping his mouth on a starched napkin.

A waiter hovered, wearing a white apron reaching to his knees. Jensen and Gustav shook their heads in unison, and the waiter left.

'I come every day,' said Brøgger. 'I have taken my lunch here for thirty years or more. They keep this table for me.'

Jensen held up one hand to interrupt. 'Can I just . . . *You* are Irene Valborg's solicitor? *You*?'

'I think you mean *was*. And no, I was her husband Ove's solicitor, but only as a favour to my father who went to school with the unfortunate man at Ordrup high school. So naturally I kept an eye on his affairs for his widow. Didn't meet her, if I could help it. You couldn't find a more unpleasant woman in Copenhagen. Insufferably dull too.'

He drained his beer.

A group of men and women in office dress entered the room

and were directed to a large table. Brøgger nodded and smiled at them. 'Look,' he said. 'I can tell from your faces that this isn't making much sense to you, so let me put you straight. It was me who recommended you to Regitse. She came barging into my office yesterday, going on about finding that necklace. I told her I knew just the person for the job. I thought, seeing as you weren't answering my calls, it might be the quickest way to get through to you, and here we are.'

Jensen thought of the praise Regitse had heaped upon her and was oddly disappointed. All that would have come straight from Brøgger.

'Poor Regitse has no more charm than her late mother, but you will have discovered this for yourself by now.'

Jensen was slowly regaining her composure. 'I know I should have called you back before, but the fact is I haven't got much further looking into Vangede's death. I know you wanted me to, but there is nothing to go on. That is, there's this pair of glasses that belonged to the person he thought was a benign accountant and whose name is *not* Bjarne Pedersen. I spoke to the optician.'

'And?'

'He clammed up. It was strange.'

'Strange how?'

'It was as if he was afraid to talk to me.'

'Perhaps he was advised not to.'

Jensen nodded. Someone was clearly determined to keep Bjarne Pedersen's identity a secret. Why did a mere fraudulent accountant inspire such fear in people?

Brøgger's eyes were smiling as he studied her. 'You're giving up, Miss Jensen?'

'Never,' she exclaimed, eliciting a low laugh from Brøgger. She thought of what Henning had said. 'But right now it's Regitse who's paying my bills.'

'Touché.' Brøgger laughed again, folding his paper and

gesturing at the waiter who nodded to him on his way past with a full tray of draught Carlsberg.

'So, you think the necklace was stolen?' Jensen asked.

'That's for you to find out.'

'But you must have your own theory about what happened to your client?'

Brøgger pointed at *Dagbladet*. 'Says in here that she was the victim of a violent burglary. You have information to the contrary?'

'No,' admitted Jensen. 'Apparently, Irene inherited a lot of money long ago, before Ove died.'

'Apparently so,' said Ernst.

He wasn't going to make it easy for them.

'Any idea whom she inherited from?'

'I didn't deal with that side of things. She treated it very much as hers, nothing to do with Ove.'

'But you do know she used it to buy an expensive diamond necklace?'

'Ove told me,' he said, checking his watch.

'The safe was empty.'

'So I gather.'

'Think she might have hidden it somewhere?'

'I wouldn't put it past her, the crafty old bird.'

'She bought a new alarm system just before Christmas, and a new door lock and an Alsatian. Any idea why?'

'Nope.'

'Just seems odd,' Jensen said. 'I wonder what made her do it.'

'Couldn't tell you.'

'Was there anywhere that Irene liked to go, to your knowledge? Any special places?'

'There's Gilleleje. The Valborgs had a summerhouse on the coast for many years. Still do, though I doubt anyone has been there since Ove died. It was his sanctuary. He used to go up there on his own for the weekend. I believe Irene and Regitse preferred the luxury of Copenhagen.'

'What's the address?' said Gustav, ready to punch it into Google maps.

'Oh, I doubt very much you'd find anything there,' said Brøgger, signalling to the waiter. 'For one, how would Irene have got all the way to Gilleleje?'

'By taxi?' offered Gustav.

'At her age, with a diamond necklace in her handbag? I can't see it somehow. Besides, Irene was the sort of person who complained about the price of milk. What would a taxi to Gilleleje cost? Must be a journey of what ... an hour?' said Brøgger, edging out of his seat. 'But if you insist, I'll email the address to you as soon as I get back to the office. Speaking of which, I really must go now.'

The waiter brought his camel overcoat and scarf, leather gloves and an umbrella with a wooden handle. Finally, when Brøgger was dressed for the outdoors, he shook hands with Jensen and Gustav and headed towards the exit.

'Wait, don't you have to pay?' shouted Gustav after him.

'Not since I bought the place,' said Brøgger without turning. His laughter trailed after him.

'He didn't like Irene much, did he?' said Gustav when they were back outside in the street.

'No one did,' said Jensen.

'Perhaps *he* took the necklace. Perhaps she gave it to him to keep safe, and he kept it for himself.'

'No. Regitse would have been all over him like a rash, if there was even the remotest chance of that. Besides, something tells me a diamond necklace would be a mere plaything to Deep Throat.'

Just like she and Gustav were his playthings. Deep Throat was enjoying messing with them.

19

Thursday 14:32

Minna Larsen was sobbing into her handkerchief while her burly husband glowered at Henrik and Mark as if holding them responsible. Kent Larsen was seated in the apartment's best armchair, placed at a vantage point in the corner of the living room from which he had an uninterrupted view of the television. On a table to one side of the armchair was the remote control, a stack of gossip magazines, a large glass of water and an assortment of pill jars. The chair was of the kind you saw in daytime TV adverts, with a footrest that flicked out to accommodate Larsen's slippered feet and a lever to eject him from the seat whenever nature called. He looked inordinately proud of his throne as he presided over the coffee table, on which stood the tray with the thermos, mugs and biscuits that Minna had spent ages assembling in the kitchen when they had first arrived.

Next to Kent, Minna was a slip of a thing, humming with nervous energy and jumping up at the merest hint that anyone needed something: sugar, milk, napkins. She had dropped a mug in the kitchen earlier, emitting a small yelp when it had shattered on the floor. Hendrik and Mark had pretended not to notice, both knowing the effect a conversation with the police had on people. At long last, Minna had sat down, and the mere mention of Irene Valborg's name had set off her waterworks.

'Excellent coffee,' said Mark, ever chipper, as Minna's tears tapered off into sniffles.

'Thank you,' she said, blowing her nose noisily.

'We need to ask you a few questions,' said Henrik, sensing Mark opening his notebook beside him, pencil at the ready. Henrik never took notes, preferring to concentrate on what people were saying.

And not saying.

Especially what they were not saying.

'Now we aren't accusing you of anything, Minna.'

'I bloody well hope not,' piped up Kent.

Henrik ignored him. 'But if you would just tell us, in your own words, how Irene came to let you go?'

Minna glanced at her husband, hesitating. Kent took it as his cue. 'Bloody disgrace that woman. My Minna kept house for her ladyship for forty-five years, and then it's goodbye without so much as a thank you.'

Henrik turned to him, close to losing his patience. 'I am going to have to ask you to let your wife talk, unless you prefer that we take her down to the station and interview her there?'

Kent folded his arms across his chest and glared back at Henrik but held his tongue.

Minna's red-rimmed eyes were open wide. 'I don't like to speak ill of the dead, but Kent is right. Suddenly, out of the blue, she just told me not to come back anymore.'

'How did you get the job? Must have been, what, back in the late eighties?' said Henrik.

Minna nodded, grateful to be back on safe ground. 'It was Ove, Irene's husband, who put the ad in the paper. Regitse was

95

just a little girl then, and Ove saw that she couldn't deal with her daughter and that big house. Kent and I had just married and needed the extra cash, and it was easy for me to cycle over to Klampenborg, so I took the job.'

'And how did you find it?'

'The house was a mess, took me weeks to straighten everything out. Irene was difficult, nothing was ever good enough, but Ove persuaded me to stay. He was so grateful, and he paid well, so—'

'But after he died?' Mark interrupted, shrinking a little at the look Henrik shot him.

'I thought about leaving, but I guess that, over the years, me and Irene had learnt to rub along. Not easy to find well-paid cleaning jobs.'

Henrik thought about it. There was nothing obvious connecting Minna Larsen with the murder. On the other hand, she was the only person who had had regular access to Irene's house.

They had already spoken to the gardener who, in keeping with the general lack of sympathy for Irene, had been more concerned about his imminent loss of income. He had been coming less often in the winter, he claimed, and last been to Irene's house three weeks ago. There had been nothing unusual to remark upon that occasion; Irene had stayed inside the house the entire time, as was her habit. They would need to check out if his story held up, of course, but Henrik reckoned the gardener had been telling the truth.

Minna and her husband he was less sure of.

'What's the real reason you left, Minna? Did you and Irene argue? Did she accuse you of something?' said Henrik.

Red-faced, Kent leaned forward in the armchair to protest, but Henrik held up a hand to silence him and kept his gaze on Minna.

'I don't know what you mean. There was nothing ... I didn't ...' she said, flustered.

Henrik said nothing. People liked to fill awkward silences; Minna was no exception.

'It started when I asked her about the tins.'

'The lobscouse?'

'Yes. She had them delivered, from the supermarket on Ordrupvej. It didn't make sense. I told her that if she needed any shopping done, I was happy to do it for her.'

'And?'

'She bit my head off. Accused me of spying on her.'

'Tell them what she said,' said Kent.

'She said I'd been talking to people about her.'

'What did she mean by that?'

'I don't know,' said Minna miserably. 'I think she was afraid of the house being broken into. She was jumpy, kept walking to the front door to check that it was locked.'

Henrik nodded. 'She changed the lock, put in a new alarm system. She also got a dog.'

Minna suddenly appeared to realise the implications of what he was saying. 'You don't think she did all that because she was afraid of me? I didn't ... I would never ...'

She began to cry again, sobbing, big tears dropping on her sinewy hands.

'That's enough,' said Kent. 'You've upset my wife. I want you to leave now.'

Mark's phone rang. To Henrik's intense annoyance, Mark looked at the display and got up, walking towards the front door to take the call outside. Knowing the conversation was over, if not because of Kent's command, then definitely because of Mark's insensitive interruption, Henrik got up and thanked Minna for the coffee. He looked one last time at the flat: neat, tidy, decorated with the same sort of furnishings and knick-knacks as his father's terraced house. The view from the window, a communal lawn with flower beds and bare trees, set between yellow-brick blocks, was orderly, respectable, normal.

The only thing that didn't fit the picture was Minna Larsen, crying her heart out over a woman no one liked. Unless they were tears of misery for being stuck at home with her oaf of a husband.

'What do you think?' asked Mark when Henrik had joined him in the car.

'I think don't answer your phone in the middle of a bloody interview.'

'Yes, boss. Sorry, boss,' said Mark putting his phone away. 'You think Minna had anything to do with Irene's death? Or her husband?'

'Him? He couldn't walk five yards without struggling for breath.'

'She looks quite lean and sprightly, though.'

'Smashing her employer's skull because she was angry about being sacked? Can't see it somehow,' said Henrik. 'But the two of them did protest a lot. I wonder why.' He switched on the ignition and eased out of the parking lot to join the main road back to the office.

'What was it anyway that was so important you had to take a call in the middle of questioning a key witness?'

Mark perked up. 'Oh yeah. You know Irene Valborg's dog? The one we found in the garden in Klampenborg?'

'What about it?'

'It got picked up by this animal home in Hvidovre near where I live. They read the story in the newspaper and offered to take it in.'

'OK,' said Henrik, keeping his eyes on the traffic.

'Whenever they take in a dog it gets the once-over by a vet.'

'Mark, I do hope this is going somewhere, because I swear to God . . .'

'So the vet called us and said there was no evidence that the dog went without food during the fortnight that Irene lay dead.'

Henrik swerved to avoid a cyclist pulling out into traffic.

'The vet said, and I don't know what this means, but I think we need to find out . . .'

'WHAT?'

'She said it looked as though someone had been feeding it.'

20

The dog shelter in Hvidovre was housed in a series of low-lying sheds and yellow-brick buildings. A cacophony of barking greeted Henrik and Mark as they got out of the car. Mark, half man, half Labrador, leaped ahead happily towards the entrance. He was familiar with the place, having done a week's work experience there when he was a boy. Henrik had listened inattentively on the way as Mark had rambled on about how he had formed a bond with a Golden Retriever called Monty. He had been wondering how they were going to make any headway on the case without the sort of information that usually helped them build up a picture of a murder victim: emails, social media accounts, mobile phone records. Irene's landline had offered no clues, all the calls having been accounted for, including one Kent Larsen had admitted to making on the day his wife had been sacked. Irene had hung up immediately.

Lotte Nielsen had had no more luck in the Vagn Holdved case. 'He had a mobile phone, but never used it. His digital footprint was non-existent,' she had said.

That about summed up Irene Valborg and Ulla Olsen too. Her family had given Ulla a tablet, but she had stopped using it when her dementia had become too pronounced. There was nothing of interest on it.

The vet met them by the entrance, wearing purple scrubs and a padded dark green gilet. Her dark, curly hair was gathered into a messy ponytail exposing a butterfly tattoo below one heavily pierced ear. She was younger than Henrik had expected. ('It's you who is old,' he heard his wife say.)

'Emilie,' she said, shaking Henrik's hand with surprising strength. 'It was me who called you.'

She led them through a series of covered-over walkways between cages before stopping by one of them. Henrik recognised the Alsatian he had last seen in Irene Valborg's driveway in Klampenborg by the soft golden patch between its eyes.

'This is Samson,' said Emilie, opening the latch.

The dog licked Henrik's hand. He sat down on his haunches and ruffled the fur behind its ears. 'I gather you think someone has been feeding him?' he said.

'I am not sure, but I was surprised to find no signs of under-nourishment. I read about the case. In a dog this size and age, I would expect to see the signs of starvation after a fortnight of being locked in a garden. Trust me, I've some experience of animal abuse.'

Henrik ignored her huffy tone. 'Could Samson not just have eaten some stuff lying about on the ground?' he said.

'Such as?'

'I don't know, some old fruit or a dead bird?'

Emilie smiled broadly. 'I don't know about your garden, Detective Inspector, but mine tends not to have a lot of fruit in it this time of year. And Samson here would have needed more than the odd dead bird to keep him fed.' She leaned over the dog and rubbed its flank. 'Yes, you would.'

'How did Samson end up here?' said Henrik.

'One of our volunteers must have read about him online and called the police.'

'What do you mean, volunteers?' said Henrik.

Emilie laughed cynically. 'You didn't think we have enough funding to actually pay people, did you?' She patted Samson's fur. 'Having said that, our animals do give a lot back. There are those who prefer dogs to humans.'

Henrik nodded. He knew what she meant. Dogs bestowed a calm on you, an uncomplicated love that humans couldn't.

'It takes a real knack to form a bond with the animals, to make them feel safe. Especially when they've been victims of neglect or trauma,' said the vet.

'Hang on, I thought you said Samson wasn't traumatised.'

'No, I said he wasn't starved. Being stuck outdoors in the garden for two weeks would most definitely have traumatised him.'

'But he did eat.'

'It would appear so.'

Emilie looked exasperated, like she was starting to regret having phoned them.

'So, let me get this right,' said Henrik, pushing against the resistance he was sensing from the young woman. 'While Samson's owner was lying dead on the carpet indoors, someone came every day and fed him?'

Emilie shrugged. 'I don't know. I couldn't tell you how it happened.' She spoke softly to Samson, leading him back into the cage and closing the latch, before checking her watch. 'I'm afraid I am out of time now. Stuff to do, thanks for coming. Like I said when I called, if this might help in any small way, I wanted you to know about it.'

As they drove back to the office at Teglholmen, Henrik could feel Mark's silent reproach. He knew Mark was bristling at the way he had spoken to Emilie who, after all, had only observed what she had found. 'Well, what do you think?' he said, while

Mark stared out of the passenger window as if finding the view of the motorway of great interest. 'Does it sound like a logical scenario to you? There has got to be some explanation why the dog didn't starve, we just have to find out what it was. And find out who called us.'

His phone rang, saving him from Mark's awkward silence.

Mark would be OK. He always was in the end, incapable as he was of holding a grudge for very long.

Unlike my wife, Henrik thought.

He was grateful to hear Lisbeth's voice ringing out from the in-car speakers. 'OK, so I have spoken to everyone at the care home, about that girl in the photo.'

Henrik felt Mark prick up his ears. It was just what they needed now. A break in their investigation. Something to go on.

Pretty please.

'And?'

'Absolutely no one has a clue who she is.'

21

Thursday 17:06

'We've got to walk and talk. I am late for Borgen,' said Margrethe, towering above Jensen in an unshapely navy-blue raincoat with her bag over one shoulder and a stack of papers under one arm. Her long-suffering personal assistant Yasmine thrust a coffee mug into her free hand.

Rushing down the stairs, Margrethe nodded left and right at the passing *Dagbladet* staff who stared at Jensen with open curiosity, mumbling to each other.

'Come to ask for your job back?' said Margrethe.

'No, but thank you all the same,' said Jensen, almost having to run to keep up with Margrethe's giant strides.

'What have you done with my nephew?'

'I dropped him at your flat.'

'And you are here, and I am asking myself why.'

It had finally stopped raining and bits of blue sky were showing through the leaden clouds, but the day was raw with a lingering wintry chill. They passed Copenhagen City Hall heading down Løngangsstræde towards the parliament at

Christiansborg, tourists scattering at the approaching freight train that was *Dagbladet*'s editor-in-chief.

'It's about Gustav,' said Jensen. 'I want ... I need to know what happened to him, why he was thrown out of school. I noticed he didn't like you saying he had to go back.'

'I bet he didn't,' said Margrethe, sipping coffee. 'Gustav thinks that he is the finished article.'

'Maybe he doesn't need to go.'

'Said the school dropout.'

'I got a job, didn't I?'

'And where is it now?'

'But you took me on, and I never finished high school.'

'You had already proved yourself.'

'Gustav worked with me on the Magstræde case. Our articles were praised by all and sundry.'

'One swallow doesn't make a summer.'

'So I'm just a glorified babysitter, is that it?'

Margrethe stopped suddenly on the pavement, papers flapping under her arm, long hair snaking around her face.

'What do you want, Jensen? No really, what do you want from me?'

'I want to know what happened to Gustav. If I am meant to be his keeper, will you at least tell me what I am dealing with?'

Margrethe swept hair from her eyes and mouth and pushed up her glasses. The harsh March sunlight caught the greasy fingerprints on her lenses. 'No, I won't. If you're so determined to know, you'll have to find out for yourself.'

Margrethe began to walk again, clearly tiring of their conversation. Jensen grabbed her arm. Margrethe shot her a sharp look. 'Look, for the last time, I don't care what anyone says, there isn't a bad bone in that boy's body. He takes after his mother in that way.'

Margrethe was famous all over Copenhagen for her cynicism but when it came to Gustav, she was clearly ready to believe anything.

105

'If you won't tell me what it was, how can I help him?' Jensen shouted after her.

Margrethe increased her speed without turning. 'Much as I love you Jensen, you are beginning to get on my nerves, and I have a newspaper to run, so this is where we say goodbye. Gustav may be sulking at the moment, but he'll be fine. You just leave him to me. Instead, why don't you try and find a story to write? Or have you given up already on that freelance bureau of yours?'

Jensen watched Margrethe disappear towards the dark façade of the parliament building, a woman on a mission.

Well, that made two of them.

22

'But you are sure the photos pre-date the millennium, and you can tell that from the paper they are printed on?'

Henrik's day had brightened considerably when Kenneth, one of the lab guys, had phoned him with the results of their analysis. He liked Kenneth. The two of them were life-long supporters of Brøndby football club and often chatted (or commiserated) at length when the opportunity arose. Today, however, Henrik had dispensed quickly with their small talk, detecting a note of disappointment in Kenneth's voice when he steered them onto business.

'Yes, the paper is the kind used in commercial labs. Remember when you used to take a roll of film to be developed?'

'Nah, too young,' said Henrik, eager to avoid the avenue to further chat that Kenneth was trying to lead them down. 'But you say that the school photo is different?'

'Different paper, but I would imagine that one was done by a photographer coming into school and parents ordering copies from a contact sheet.'

'And can you get a bit closer than before the millennium?'

107

'Not through technical analysis, no. But if you want my educated guess?'

'I do. God help us we have nothing else to go on.'

Kenneth laughed. 'I'd say we are looking at the mid-nineties.'

'Based on?'

'Based on the way the quality of the photos has deteriorated, and also the jeans. That whole high-waisted faded denim thing that is back in fashion now. White T-shirt rolled up at the sleeves. Big hair, big earrings.'

'I wouldn't know,' said Henrik.

'I can't be accurate about the year, of course.'

Henrik wasn't too worried about the year. As far as he was concerned, there was only one thing that counted here, and they were finally getting to it.

'Is it the same girl, in all three photos?'

'Yes. I am ninety-nine percent certain that it is, looking at the shape of the face. Anyway, the glue has the same properties, which indicates that the three photos were taken from the same album.'

'Excellent. Don't suppose you could tell me who she is as well?' said Henrik, only half joking.

'Sorry mate,' Kenneth laughed. 'If I had a crystal ball, I wouldn't be working in this dump.'

Henrik quickly made his excuses and hung up, drumming a little tune on his desk. He checked his watch. With a bit of luck, he could catch the Chief Super before he left for home. He did so every day at five o'clock unless he had something on in the evening and there wasn't time to return to his villa in Lyngby beforehand.

On the way to Monsen's office, Henrik ran into Jens Wiese, who had a deep frown on his forehead. Though he was younger than Henrik, the Superintendent wore his reading glasses permanently on the tip of his nose, peering over the edge of them whenever he wanted to make a point.

Henrik's heart sank whenever he saw Wiese. The man only brought bad news. He had no sense of humour whatsoever.

Henrik knew that he did not have it in himself to climb the greasy pole past Detective Inspector. One more promotion and the tidal wave of paperwork and bureaucracy would drown out the reason he had first joined the police: the excitement of the chase. Wiese, on the other hand, already had his sights on the big jobs, including Monsen's. The reading glasses were part of his act. He held up a hand. 'Henrik.'

'Sorry, I can't stop,' said Henrik, jogging past.

'We do have to catch up sometime,' said Wiese.

'I know,' said Henrik. 'Let's have a meeting. I'll get my people to call your people.'

'And for the last time, see that psychologist,' shouted Wiese behind him.

The psychological debrief had been mandatory after Henrik fired his gun, and his one-to-one session with the psychologist was overdue by weeks. Henrik didn't feel like he needed to speak to anyone, but he knew that Wiese would never let a thing like that go.

More was the pity.

He caught Monsen just as the big man was easing himself into his raincoat and switching off the lights. His desk was swept clean, no sign of any work having been carried out recently, if ever. In other words, everything was reassuringly normal, Monsen managing to dodge just about every task handed down by higher command. 'Ah, Jungersen. Just the man,' he said, turning to Henrik with a big smile.

'Glad I caught you. Two minutes?'

'For you, always, but you don't mind if we walk, do you?'

He grabbed his laptop bag and headed for the corridor. Wild horses couldn't stop Monsen from downing tools. Henrik knew that he had three minutes before they reached the car park where Monsen's grey Volvo would be waiting yards from the entrance.

'You know the photos we found?'

'What about them?'

'The lab guys reckon they're from the nineties and it's definitely the same girl.'

'That may be, Henrik, but as I understand it, they weren't found by forensics.'

'No. I found the ones at Irene Valborg's house and Vagn Holdved's allotment. Ulla Olsen's daughter found the one in the care home in my presence. What are you saying?'

'That the photos might not have been left by the killer.'

'Of course they were. Forensics just wouldn't have noticed them. Hiding in plain sight, sort of thing.'

'But if someone wanted to place the photo at the scene for you to find after the event, they had ample time in which to do so.'

'Monsen, listen to yourself, this is madness. Why would anyone other than the offender have placed the photos on the scene?'

Monsen had reached the two flights of stairs leading down to the reception area. He was shaking his head. 'It's too random. If the offender wanted to tell us something, they wouldn't have left it to chance.'

'OK, so someone put the photos there afterwards. Why?'

'To distract you, trip you up, watch you fall.'

'Someone on the force, you mean?'

'What, you think no one would do such a thing? Come, come, you weren't born yesterday.'

Henrik stopped in his tracks. Did Monsen have a point? There were plenty of people who didn't like him. People who had worked with him and come to regret it. People he had argued with.

Lots of people he had argued with.

But to drop photos of a girl into a crime scene. Who would do such a thing just to get at him? 'I want to join up the three investigations,' he said, a little too loudly.

110

The receptionist, a woman who carried her reading glasses on a chain around her neck looked up sharply, as he and Monsen passed. Monsen kept going. 'If you want to convince me of that, you'll need to come up with more than a few old photos. Find a connection between the victims or we carry on as planned. Good evening.'

Henrik watched Monsen disappear through the sliding doors without looking back once. 'Fuck,' he said, eliciting another sharp glance from the receptionist.

As he stood on the stairs, he envied Monsen's ability to go home, to shut the door on the world and not be a policeman.

Just for one night.

A normal person.

('Oh yeah, like that's going to happen,' he heard his wife say.)

23

'Before we start, let me just make clear that I cannot comment on individual cases,' said David Goldschmidt.

'Got it,' said Jensen.

She had asked to see the pathologist, hoping he would remember the time Henrik had brought her along to a post-mortem. 'How could I forget?' he had replied.

They were seated in David's warm cave at the Forensic Institute, with the only light coming from his anglepoise desk lamp. David had changed out of his white trousers and tunic and was wearing jeans and an open-necked check shirt that showed off his dark chest hair. He had got them both a black coffee from the machine in the corridor. It smelled bad. Liron, her coffee pusher with his tiny van in Sankt Peders Stræde, would have chucked out the brown liquid immediately, but Jensen was cold after the bicycle ride to the institute. With her hands clamped tightly around the paper cup, she was slowly regaining the sensation in her fingers.

'And you can't quote me for anything,' said David, rolling up his sleeves and smiling at her warmly.

Jensen held up her hands. 'Promise.'

'Glad we understand each other. Now, how can I help?'

'I want to know if it's possible to make murder look like suicide by hanging.'

'Very hard to pull off.'

'But not impossible?'

'I've heard of cases in other countries. Professional hitmen, that sort of thing.'

'What would be involved?'

'For starters you'd have to stop the victim from fighting back. A struggle would leave marks.'

'So you'd drug them, or get them drunk?'

'Yes, but the drugs or alcohol would show up in the blood. Too much, and we'd question someone's ability to go through with suicide. Besides, it's difficult to force someone to drink without bruising them in some way.'

'But if the victim was an alcoholic, you might not question the amount of alcohol in their system.'

'Perhaps. The alternative would be to tie them up, but there'd be ligature marks.'

'What else?'

David pointed to the side of his throat. 'You could break their neck in exactly the same place and in exactly the same way as it would through hanging, then hoist them up into the noose after death.'

'OK?'

'But there would have to be more than one of you, and you would have to know exactly what you were doing, and how to completely cover your tracks. Not easy.'

'Like you said, a professional job.'

David Goldschmidt laughed. 'Not sure if it's wise for me to give you tips about getting away with murder. Anyway, I can't remember dealing with a single case where a suicide has been faked, and I have seen a lot of suicides.'

'By hanging?'

'Sadly yes. Sometimes you see that people have worked a hand up under the ligature, as if they've had last-minute regrets. The body's will to live is amazingly strong.'

'Not much good if someone's determined to kill you, though.'

David Goldschmidt cocked his head to one side and looked at her intently. 'Do I need to remind you that if you have cause to suspect that a crime has been committed, you need to tell the police?'

'It's just a hunch.'

'Still, should you not be talking to DI Jungersen about whatever's on your mind, seeing as the two of you are friends?'

'We're not friends anymore.'

'Since when?'

'Since he broke a promise to take me to the airport.'

That and a thousand other promises.

David held up his hands in mock surrender. 'I am staying out of this.' He zipped up his jacket and put on his bike helmet. 'I said I'd be home for bathtime tonight. First evening this week, if I make it,' he said, gesturing at a photo of his husband with a smiling toddler. 'Hope I have been of some help to you, though I can't think how.'

Jensen stayed put. 'His name was Carsten Vangede. Found hanged in his home in Gentofte a few weeks ago. I had met with him shortly before. He told me that he thought some bad people were looking for an item in his possession. He had also booked a flight to Thailand mere hours before he is meant to have hanged himself. I mean, who does that?'

David closed his eyes, looking as though he had suddenly developed a headache. 'I am going to forget what you just told me. It would be unethical to discuss any individual case with you. And now I really must go.'

'Aren't you in the least bit curious?' said Jensen.

'No. Speculation is not my thing, but DI Jungersen does a roaring trade in it.'

24

Christina Vangede clacked loudly over the parquet flooring in her suede boots and wet-look black leggings. Her brother's garden flat looked like it had last been decorated sometime in the nineteen-eighties with its chrome, glass and leather furniture. On the walls were red and black posters of burlesque dancers, and at one end of the living room a bar with optics and beer mats. Yucca plants stood about on the floor in varying stages of dying.

'Cool,' exclaimed Gustav, immediately throwing himself onto one of the hydraulic barstools and running a hand noisily along the wine glasses suspended from the shelf above the counter. He had been jittery and loud all the way to Gentofte, like he didn't care, like he *wanted* a fight.

Jensen sent him an angry look, but Christina wasn't paying attention. She was walking around purposefully, yanking each set of red curtains apart and opening the windows wide. The fresh air was welcome. The rooms smelled of beer and unwashed clothes with notes of damp.

'Who found your brother?' she said.

'Postman. Got suspicious because Carsten hadn't taken in a parcel though his Beemer was parked outside. Looked through the window, saw Carsten and rang the police.'

'Where was he?' said Jensen.

'Banister,' said Christina, pointing to the stairs to the first floor with a shudder. 'With a cable.'

The three of them looked up at the landing and, for a moment, Carsten's ghost dangled between them. Christina shook her head, her features set hard with no sign of the grief that had dissolved her face at the funeral.

'You were right, by the way. Carsten was broke. I mean completely. It's all got to go. Not a krone left for me and the kids.'

'I am sorry,' Jensen said.

'Yeah, well, I should have known. I went in after they'd taken the body, got his jewellery out, some cash he'd stowed away. And good job I did.'

'What do you mean?'

'Well, someone broke in, didn't they? I knew they would. They read the papers to find empty houses they can burgle. And to think I wasted my own money on that death announcement.'

Jensen saw out of the corner of her eye that Gustav had climbed on top of Vangede's bar counter and had positioned his head under one of the optics, from which vodka flowed into his mouth. She gestured at him to get down, drawing a finger across her throat, and stepped closer to Christina. 'When was this break-in, did you say?'

'Must have been Tuesday night. Neighbour called me Wednesday when she noticed the door was open. Weird thing was they didn't take the TV or the stereo or anything.'

'So what *did* they take?'

'Dunno. Some of Carsten's papers were all over the floor in his office, but that was it.'

'Strange. When I saw Carsten in January, he thought he'd had a burglary back then, but nothing had been stolen.'

Christina didn't look interested. 'Can't say I care. There's a guy coming tomorrow to clear the flat, and the proceeds are going to the creditors. Anyway, what was it you were going to look for?'

Jensen didn't know. If the people who had defrauded Carsten were behind the two burglaries, there would be nothing important left. 'Could you show us his office?' she said.

The room faced the garden and felt dark and cold. A tree half-obscured the view and condensation had formed on the windowsill. It looked as though Carsten had once had the intention of filing stuff away properly, with ring binders diligently marked with contents and dates. At some point, however, he had abandoned the system, judging by the amount of papers scattered across the desk, along with dirty coffee mugs, paperweights and cables. The uncollected parcel that had alerted the postman was there. It was a stack of vintage car magazines bought online. Another strange thing to do for someone about to end it all, wasn't it?

'No computer?' said Gustav, peering over Jensen's shoulder. He began to rummage through the papers on the desk, coming up with a black pin plug. 'There was a laptop here.'

'I never saw a laptop,' said Christina, frowning. 'There wasn't one here the first time I came, or I would have taken it. No phone either. He used to have a mobile, I am sure of it, but I looked everywhere.'

'Could it be at Zoom bar?'

'No. I checked,' said Christina. 'Maybe he sold them if he was struggling for money?'

A few hundred kroner for some used devices would be neither here nor there against the size of Carsten's debt, thought Jensen. Someone had taken his stuff.

'So,' said Christina. 'Are you going to write an article then? I told my boys that their uncle is going to be in the paper.'

'We need to do some more research. Try to build a picture of what the last weeks of Carsten's life were like.'

'Pretty miserable by the look of things,' said Christina nodding at the overfilled ashtray and empty bottles of vodka in the wastepaper bin. Then her eyes were caught by something: a framed picture of her and her sons. She picked it up and wiped dust off the glass with a pink shirt sleeve, suddenly pensive. 'Thing is, we were his only family. Makes you sad to think that whatever Carsten was struggling with, he was all alone in the world.'

25

'How long are you going to keep this up for?' asked the psychologist.

She was pretty, though her long hair was completely grey. Henrik tried to imagine what it would look like if it were chestnut coloured and decided it would work very well with her brown eyes. He thought of what it would be like to take off her clear-framed glasses, remove the notepad from her hand and place it forcefully on the table between them.

'By my reckoning we've got another thirty-seven minutes,' he said, checking his watch.

He began to whistle to himself. The window was overlooking the road and beyond it the office car park. It had begun to rain again after a respite of a few hours. Cyclists passed every few minutes, heads bent.

'We could talk?' she tried. 'We may as well, now that you're here?'

'I'm here because my boss said that I had to see you. He didn't mention anything about talking.'

The woman smiled at him, her eyes a little sad, and guilt

flooded through him. 'I'm here to help,' she said. 'I'm on your side. You can talk to me about whatever you want.'

'Look, lady,' he said, knowing he was being patronising and insufferable, but unable to stop himself. 'I am sure you are well-meaning and good at your job and all that, but here's what happened: I fired my gun at a suspect and wounded him, saving someone's life in the process.'

Someone.

He hadn't allowed himself to think about how he would have felt if Jensen had died. It was impossible to imagine a world without her in it.

Stop it, Henrik, for fuck's sake.

He felt his legs beginning to bob up and down and forced himself to hold them still. The psychologist hadn't flinched. She was watching him intently, studying him. 'If I may, you seem ... tense, angry. It's hard sometimes for us to recognise the signs of stress when they first appear.'

'I'm not stressed,' he said, a little more aggressively than he intended.

Was he? Stressed? Angry?

If he was, he had reason to be. Sleeping night after night on the hard sofa in the office, locked out of his home, his wife never answering his calls or text messages. But actually, his anger had mellowed over the years and was now a rare occurrence. There had been just the one incident during an interview back in January when he had lost his temper and luckily Mark had intervened before it had turned into assault.

Of course, there had been times when life had got to him, but then work had always been his salvation. The steady, plodding beat of it. And now, even that had been called into question, as Monsen had dismissed his theory that the murders of Valborg and Holdved and the assault on Ulla Olsen were connected. Ulla was still in a coma, and even if she woke up, with her dementia it was doubtful they would get anything useful out of her.

'Tell me what you're thinking?' said the psychologist, whose name was Isabella.

It was the wrong name for her. She was more like a Lene, or Lone, the name of someone uncomplicated and calm who would give her husband the benefit of the doubt before showing him the door.

('I gave you eighteen years. How much longer do you want?' he heard his wife say.)

'I'm wondering whether you're single,' he said, leaning forward in his seat.

Isabella didn't react but kept looking at him without malice until he was forced to look away. Henrik gathered she must have heard it all over the years from pratts like him. After a minute's pause, she gathered her green cardigan around her and closed her notebook. 'There are no shortcuts in psychology, no magic bullets,' she said. 'For this to work, you have to want it. Why don't you reflect on what happened here today, then book another appointment with me for some time next week?'

She smiled forgivingly, and her genuine warmth, despite his appalling behaviour, made him well up.

My life is falling to pieces, he thought, as he left her office.

His phone buzzed in his pocket.

Jensen, he thought, feeling another spike of guilt.

But the text message was from his wife.

I want a divorce.

26

The jeweller's shop was in one of the narrow streets off Købmagergade in the centre of Copenhagen. It looked like it had seen better days, an anachronism amidst the global chain stores that had made the city's main shopping precinct look like most others in the world. The necklace in the window looked second-hand but would have made a striking display if someone had bothered to dust it. A large red-and-white sticker announced a closing-down sale.

'Bet that's been there for years,' said Gustav, teenage cynic.

The original Hermansen, of Hermansen & Sons, was long dead and his offspring, Jørgen Hermansen, looked past retirement with his white hair and seafarer's beard. He let them in, after opening a complicated sequence of locks. 'Burglary last year,' he explained. 'Broad daylight. Guy got off the back of a motorbike, walked straight in and pointed a sawn-off shotgun at me,' he said, shaking his head. 'I don't know this city anymore. Thank God for the insurance.'

'Did they take a lot?' said Gustav.

'Yes,' said Jørgen, and Jensen could tell that the matter of his insurance claim wasn't something he was prepared to discuss any further.

The glass display cases inside the shop were half-empty. 'I'm closing,' said Jørgen. 'Too old for this game.'

So, the sign really was true.

Jørgen sat down behind the counter on a swivel chair covered in a worn tartan blanket. He was halfway through a crossword and had recently made himself a coffee. On top of the crossword sat a piece of paper. 'I think I found what you were asking for,' he said, patting it. 'This is a copy of the invoice for the necklace Irene Valborg bought from my father on Thursday the ninth of January 1997. Twenty-four carat. Eight hundred and thirty-eight thousand kroner.'

'And today?' said Jensen.

'Something like this? Depends on the condition, but at least a couple of million I should have thought. I can tell you, after looking into it, that it was categorically the most expensive necklace my father ever sold. American, over twenty-one carats worth of Asscher-cut diamonds, another six carats of round brilliant-cut diamonds around each of the larger stones. It would have been very impressive.'

'Can you tell us why she bought it?'

'Who's to say, but the Valborgs got their engagement rings here in 1956 and wedding bands the year after. That was when the shop occupied the basement, too. Quite the place to come for jewellery in Copenhagen in those days.'

'Bit odd though. Why blow her entire inheritance on a necklace she never wore because it was too precious?'

Jørgen shrugged. 'People develop obsessions where diamonds are concerned. I've seen people return, time and time again, to look at the same piece, barely noticing my presence, almost like they are madly in love. She used her sudden windfall to buy a bit of luxury she had always wanted.'

'We were told she was really tight with money,' said Jensen. 'Nagging her husband endlessly for not earning enough.'

'There you go then. She came into a bit of cash and blew the lot on a necklace she had fallen in love with. Or . . .'

'Yes?'

'She didn't want to fritter away the money and thought diamonds might be a good investment.'

'Was she right about that?'

'No, not recently,' said Jørgen. 'Which is another reason I'm closing.'

'You deal in second-hand jewellery, so you must be getting all sorts of people trying to flog stuff to you,' Gustav piped up, ignoring Jensen's instructions to keep shtum. He was resting his skinny behind on one of the glass display cases and rolling a cigarette, to Jørgen's obvious dismay.

'Get down from there.'

Gustav jumped off the case and held up his hands. 'I am only saying that you must get people offering you stolen goods all the time. Did someone try to sell you the necklace? Did they?' He pretended to look around. 'Is it here?'

Jensen stared at him in disbelief. 'Gustav!'

Jørgen sat still for a moment while his face grew a deep shade of purple. 'Get out,' he said finally. 'Leave my shop. Come in here, accusing me of selling stolen goods. Out, the pair of you.'

The door slammed behind them, locks rattling shut one by one.

'What the hell was that?' said Jensen to Gustav when they had descended the steps to the street.

'Guy was an arrogant bastard.'

'We were trying to get him to talk to us, to help us find the necklace.'

'Stupid prick doesn't know anything.'

She grabbed his arm. 'What the fuck, Gustav?'

'Leave me alone.' He twisted free, got on his e-scooter and

zipped off down the street, his puffer jacket billowing out behind him. A woman stared at Jensen in alarm as she walked past on the opposite pavement. Jensen stared back childishly.

Nothing to see here. Walk on by.

What was it Margrethe had said? That Gustav was a good person?

She looked at her phone. Five missed calls from Regitse. At this rate, they were never going to find her mother's necklace. She thought of phoning Gustav to give him the severe telling off he deserved but decided against it. If he was anything like she had been as a teenager, it wouldn't be worth talking to him until he had calmed down. Something was going on inside his head, something to do with school. It was high time she went to Aalborg to discover the truth about his expulsion. Aalborg meant passing close to her mother's house. It would be weird to go without dropping in. She hadn't visited once since she moved back to Denmark.

Jensen dismissed the unhappy thought, pushed her bike towards Købmagergade and stood for a moment, lost as the crowd of strangers eddied around her. There was only one person in the entire city she wanted to see.

Once, it might have been Henrik.

27

To her relief, Jensen spotted the tiny coffee van as soon as she
turned into Sankt Peders Stræde. She had never understood why
Liron had swapped Jerusalem for Copenhagen. There had been
a Danish girl once, she knew, and countless others since, but
love did not seem enough to keep anyone in the freezing north.

Love was overrated.

She dropped her bike against the black fence plastered with
generations of posters and almost ran towards him.

'Fucking Jensen is that you?' he said, spreading his arms like
wings. 'Come to papa.'

She jumped into his embrace and wrapped her legs around
his waist. He held her there for ages, thankfully saying nothing.
She buried her head in his wild hair and breathed in his scent
of cardamom and aniseed. When he had set her down on the
pavement, he kept one arm around her, operating his coffee
machine one-handed. He produced a tiny paper cup of espresso,
blowing on it to cool it down before letting her take careful sips
of the smoky black liquid, like she was a patient he was nursing
back to health.

Not a million miles from the truth.

Liron's coffee was the best in Copenhagen and draining her tiny cup, she realised how much she had missed it.

'I thought you had gone and fucking left me,' Liron said, softly. 'Where have you been hiding?'

'Long story. Let's just say that I needed some time to put myself back together.'

Liron looked her up and down as if checking that her limbs and eyes and ears and nose were in the right places.

'Liron?' she said, when she had choked back the tears triggered by his genuine concern for her.

'Tell me.'

'If you had stolen a really expensive diamond necklace, where would you sell it?'

'Did you steal a necklace, little girl?' he said, keeping his face serious.

'Of course I bloody didn't,' she laughed. 'It's a story I am working on.'

'OK, Sherlock. In that case. Have you tried online sites, *Den Blå Avis*, for example, or Facebook?'

She shook her head miserably. It felt foolish that she hadn't. Still, she reckoned the odds of finding the necklace offered for sale were about one in a million. Her and Gustav playing private investigators seemed like a bad joke now. When she got home, she would call Regitse, tell her it had all been a big mistake, return the money. Back to square one.

'You're crying because of a stupid necklace?'

'No!' Jensen pushed his shoulder affectionately. 'It's really Gustav I'm worried about if you must know.'

'That little boy who came to get coffee from Liron?'

'He wouldn't like you calling him that, but yes.'

'What's he done to you?' said Liron.

'He hasn't done anything, except drive me mad. All sweetness and light one minute, temperamental teenage monster the next.'

127

'It's hormones, Jensen.'

'No, it's not that. There is something bothering him, something serious.'

'Ask him,' said Liron, taking her empty cup from her.

'I tried but he won't talk to me.'

'Want Liron to have a word?'

'No,' said Jensen, wiping her nose. 'I am going to have to find out for myself.'

'That's my girl.'

He pulled her towards him, her head fitting neatly in the armpit of his leather jacket. He kissed her hair. Standing there, looking about her at the town where she was born – the town she had left and returned to – Jensen felt that she had more in common with Liron than her fellow Danes milling around them to get out of the rain.

28

'OK,' said Henrik, closing the door to his office and facing Lisbeth and Mark. 'We've got to find a connection between our three victims. Irene Valborg, Vagn Holdved and Ulla Olsen.'

'*If* one exists,' said Lisbeth.

'Well, we know there's at least one link,' said Henrik, ignoring her weary tone.

It had been difficult to persuade the two of them to slip away from the rest of the team. Lisbeth was sceptical and had managed to infect Mark with her doubt. She kept looking at the door.

Several different lines of enquiry were now being pursued. With her necklace and husband's gold watch missing, burglary still seemed the most likely motive for the killing of Irene Valborg. In the case of Ulla Olsen, they were taking a close interest in the other residents at the care home. And Lotte Nielsen now believed that Vagn Holdved had been attacked by a neighbour on the allotments with whom he had been seen arguing the day before his murder. Apparently, the same neighbour had called in the crime in an agitated state.

'Of course he was bloody agitated,' Henrik had argued. 'He'd just found the old bloke next door with his head near as chopped off.'

But Lotte wouldn't listen.

No one would.

Henrik had to admit, it was far easier to spot the differences between the three cases than the similarities. Irene Valborg had taken steps to protect herself, which suggested she had an inkling someone was coming for her. Vagn Holdved had done no such thing, and Ulla Olsen had been in no fit state to. And whereas Irene and Vagn had both been killed pretty decisively, Ulla was still alive. Just.

'We have the photos of the girl,' said Mark.

'Yep,' said Henrik, looking at the small display he had arranged on the whiteboard, with the pictures of the three victims matched to the respective photo of the girl that had been found next to them: schoolgirl, party girl, swimming girl.

Mark had been through hundreds of photos and pretty much ruled out that she was a missing person.

'But leaving aside the girl, what other connection might there have been between them? Did they go to the same school, maybe, or work for the same employer, or belong to the same religious sect? I want you to look through absolutely anything you can find on them and do so discreetly.'

'Whilst we carry out our day jobs, you mean?' said Lisbeth.

She looked tired, and Henrik sensed she was losing faith in him. He could tell that had already happened to a few of the other investigators on his team. Inconsequential people. But Mark and Lisbeth? His best boy and girl? After everything the three of them had been through together? Without them in his corner, not even Monsen would be able to save him from self-destruction. 'I promise to lighten your load,' he said. 'Meanwhile, I'm going to make the photos public. There has to be someone out there who knows who this girl is.'

'Wiese will never agree to it,' said Lisbeth.

That much was true. Superintendent Jens Wiese (and Henrik himself, if he was being completely honest) feared ridicule and humiliation if it turned out that there was a perfectly logical explanation for the presence of the photo at the three crime scenes. Some reason no one could think of right now, but that would keep them laughing for years to come.

Henrik's thoughts turned to Jensen. Maybe she could get the picture into *Dagbladet* somehow? She would demand to know why, though, and generally be a pain in the arse. And if his wife found out they had been in touch, there would be no mercy.

I want a divorce.

Well, they would see about that. He had phoned and texted her multiple times, demanding a meeting, but as usual she wasn't picking up. You couldn't actually divorce someone without talking to them, could you?

'Boss, are you OK?'

Henrik stared into Mark's upturned face, surprised to see genuine concern there. 'Why wouldn't I be?'

'Sure,' said Mark. 'Of course.'

'No, tell me, what makes you think I'm not OK?'

'I . . . I,' Mark's face had turned a dark red.

Lisbeth came to his defence. 'Come on, Henrik, you're not OK. You're wired, distracted. We're not the only ones who have noticed.'

'Oh yes? Everyone's talking about me, is that it?'

'Wiese says—' Lisbeth began.

'Since when have you cared what that dusty bean counter thinks?' said Henrik.

He knew the answer to his own question. The smarmy git had begun to seek Lisbeth out, invite her to meetings, give her little tasks of his own, as though she were a poodle he was teaching

131

to walk on her hind legs. After his unsuccessful appointment with the psychologist, Wiese had given him 'the talk', suggesting that he had come back to work too soon after the shooting incident, that he was exhibiting classic signs of stress. Henrik wouldn't be surprised if Wiese had asked Lisbeth and Mark to spy on him. 'Look', he said, his fists slowly unclenching. 'I am not going to do anything stupid. But, for whatever reason, a photo of the same girl has turned up at three different crime scenes. If it's a red herring, then I apologise for having wasted your time,' he said, staring intently at them both. 'Let's keep this between us. Deal?'

Mark and Lisbeth both nodded, more or less reluctantly. He reckoned he had at least bought himself some time.

'But the photos,' said Mark. 'How will you—'

'Leave that to me,' said Henrik.

If he couldn't ask Jensen for help, that left one obvious option. The more Henrik thought about it, it might just work.

29

Jensen had just emerged from a hot shower when her doorbell went. She had felt like clearing her head after spending hours online searching in vain for the diamond necklace on all the resale sites she could think of. The doorbell rang again, twice in quick succession. Only Gustav knew where she lived. 'Come to apologise?' she said into the entry phone, buzzing him in and leaving the door on the latch while she climbed the spiral stairs to the mezzanine and quickly threw on a T-shirt and a pair of joggers.

'What the hell got into you today?' she shouted over the banister when she heard footsteps on the landing. She was rubbing her hair with a towel.

Her visitor opened the door.

It wasn't Gustav.

On the floor below stood a tall, broad man who looked like he might once have carried a few kilos too many. A man who liked to live, but had reined himself in. Dark hair and stubble. Anywhere between late thirties and mid-forties. Jeans, boots, shirt, jacket, coat, a killer gaze as he smiled up at her. 'I came as soon as I could,' he said.

'What?'

He laughed at her confused face. 'I'm Kristoffer.'

'OK.'

'Your landlord?' he said. 'I understand the washing machine isn't working. Which is very odd because it's brand new.'

'Right,' said Jensen. 'Oh God, yes, sorry.'

She wrapped her hair in the towel, ran down the steps and pointed to the machine, next to the sink, as if he didn't know where it was. 'Sorry, it's just—'

'You were expecting some hunky repair guy? Like the porn films?' he laughed again. 'I studied engineering. I like fixing things. Besides, this flat was my first in Copenhagen, so I've a certain emotional attachment to it.'

'What, you mean you like remembering that you were once a poor nobody like me?' she said, smiling.

'Ouch,' he said. 'But I suppose I should have expected that from a journalist of your calibre.'

'You know me?'

'I looked you up.'

He moved in close, dwarfing her as he offered his hand. 'Kristoffer,' he said.

'Jensen.'

His hand was warm, lingering in hers. 'No first name?'

'It's . . . I never use it. Everyone just calls me Jensen,' she said, pulling back her hand. 'I hear you run your own business?'

Kristoffer held her gaze, something sharp flashing quickly across his blue eyes. 'It's just . . . and this is going to sound big-headed but it's rare these days that I meet someone who doesn't know who I am. It's refreshing.'

'I've been living abroad for a long time.'

'London, wasn't it?'

Her phone rang, saving her from having to explain. She pointed at the washing machine. 'I'll leave you to it.'

Gustav.

Boy of the impeccable timing.

'Where are you?'

'Home,' she said.

Next to her, Kristoffer had taken his coat and jacket off and was rolling up his sleeves, before starting to ease the machine out from under the kitchen counter. She turned away from him, lowered her voice. 'What was that all about earlier, Gustav? We're working together and suddenly you blow your top and disappear?'

'I . . . I'm sorry, OK? I don't want to talk about it.'

Kristoffer had managed to pull the washing machine all the way out from the wall.

'That's OK, Gustav,' she said. 'But we can't work together, if you keep flying off the handle like that.'

'I know, and I won't. But listen . . .'

'A-ha,' exclaimed Kristoffer triumphantly. 'Of course.'

'Who's that?' said Gustav.

'It's just . . . the washing machine repair guy.'

Kristoffer grinned up at her.

'Wait, just listen for one second,' said Gustav. 'I rang all the taxi companies. Told them Irene was my grandmother, that she was confused and thought she had left her purse in a taxi . . .'

Nice work Gustav.

'And?' she said.

'She *did* go to Gilleleje. On the twenty-second of December last year. She told the driver to wait outside. Came out after about ten minutes.'

Jensen thought about what Brøgger had said about Irene being a crafty old bird.

'Are you still there?' said Gustav.

'Yes. Got to go,' said Jensen, ending the call.

'You won't believe it, the water intake was switched off,' said Kristoffer. He pushed the machine back into place and started a washing programme. Water began pouring into the drum. 'You can thank me now,' Kristoffer said.

'Thank you,' Jensen said, but her thoughts were far away and moving at speed. She got out her phone and began searching for the nearest e-car, barely noticing as Kristoffer Bro let himself out. 'See you some other time, I hope.'

30

Henrik felt his mood improve as he followed the road around
the national hospital to the Forensic Institute. He was conscious that looking forward to visiting the morgue would be
absurd to most people, but he liked David Goldschmidt and
his warm, unassuming intelligence. Sometimes, he was almost
envious of the pathologist and his calm oasis under the streets of
Copenhagen. Above ground, life was chaos, violent and unpredictable, a tangled mess of human interactions, but in David's
subterranean world all was ordered and quiet. He had thought
of stopping by the hospital to check on Ulla Olsen but decided
it was easier to phone Mark, who had informed him that Ulla
was still in a coma and that the doctors couldn't tell them how
much longer it was going to be.

He found a free parking bay and jogged across to the low concrete building. He had already received the email with David's
post-mortem report on Irene Valborg. Henrik could have read
the details in the comfort of his office, but he liked chatting to
David in person and wanted to run his thoughts on the case past
him. The two of them weren't friends exactly. Henrik couldn't

imagine inviting David out for a beer. Though their relationship was about more than work for him, he suspected that, without the investigations to glue them together, they would struggle to find common ground. He didn't have David down for a football fan. The subject had never come up as it did all the time with other men of his acquaintance, though he wouldn't exactly call any of *them* friends either. He couldn't talk to them about anything that mattered, such as the state of his marriage. No one knew about that, except, ironically, Jensen whose very existence had caused the problem in the first place.

Or had she?

Had the problem not been there all along, buried deep inside him? This desire to prove himself with women as if he couldn't believe that someone as beautiful and smart as his wife had chosen him for a husband? Isabella Grå, the psychologist whose time he had wasted along with his own, would have had a field day with such thoughts, he reckoned as he flashed his badge to be let into the institute.

He found David finishing a phone call, signalling for him to wait. David's office was warm and Henrik felt himself relax as he took a tour of the bookshelves. The titles were mainly medical textbooks, in among journals and folders, but dotted here and there were personal ornaments, wooden figurines and postcards. Henrik picked up a framed photo of David, his husband and the baby they had had together last year by a surrogate mother overseas. He wondered idly if it was David who was the child's father, or his husband who was Nordic-looking and pale. They looked happy, the two of them leaning into the shot, with the baby strapped to David's chest.

'That was taken when Max was just three months. He is walking already, can you believe it?' said David behind him, having ended his call.

'Congratulations,' said Henrik, setting the photo back down. 'They're lovely when they're little.'

'Now there's a world-weary man if ever I heard one,' said David, laughing. 'Was that meant to warn me to stop at one?'

'Not if you're cool with abandoning sleep for the next twenty years of your life. Not to mention the slow loss of any control you might once have had.'

David smiled, studying him more closely. 'Are you sure you're OK, Henrik? Something on your mind?'

'Me? Never better.'

For a minute he felt like coming out with it. That he had been a fool with Jensen, that he had been kicked out of his home and lost access to his kids, that he didn't know what to do with himself. But the words wouldn't come. He realised that to make David understand what he was really feeling, he would need to be a completely different person from the sarcastic, hardboiled cop that the other man thought he knew.

'Irene Valborg,' he said, instead. 'Need you to talk me through.'

'Of course,' said David. 'That's why you're here, right?' he said, the question mark hanging for the briefest moment between them, before Henrik shut it down with a nod.

It was easy to talk to David about work. Their roles were pre-assigned: Henrik was the ignorant speculator and David the tolerant expert who refused to get drawn into anything unsubstantiated by facts. The truth, as Henrik knew only too well, was to be found somewhere in the murky world between them.

David led them through to the post-mortem room where Irene's body had been laid out on a stainless-steel table. He turned on a bright overhead light and Henrik recoiled at the sight of the small, purple corpse. He was glad of the surgical mask that covered most of his face, so David couldn't see the sweat that was beginning to prickle his top lip.

'The stage of decay means we can say with some confidence that she would have been killed fourteen to sixteen days before her body was discovered,' began the pathologist.

'Let me guess. Last meal was some kind of meat in gravy?'

'Why do you ask?'

'Found loads of tins in her kitchen cupboard. Lobscouse. Apparently, she had stopped shopping for fresh food altogether.'

'I see. No, she hadn't eaten anything for at least twelve hours by the time she died. As you can see, she was quite severely undernourished.'

This was an understatement. Irene had been what could only be described as skin and bones, the bowl of her pelvis jutting up from the table. Henrik looked away. 'Any evidence of medication?'

'Not according to the bloods. But there was something. She was suffering from advanced breast cancer. There are tumours in both breasts and signs of metastases in her brain.'

'Undiagnosed?'

'No mention in her medical records.'

They looked at each other for a while without saying anything.

'Could she have been unaware that she was ill?' said Henrik.

'It's possible. She would have had little appetite, though, most certainly some pain.'

'Maybe she had an inkling but didn't want to go and see a doctor about it,' said Henrik, thinking about how reluctant Irene had been to leave her house for the last few months of her life.

'There might have been cognitive changes.'

'Something that made her act irrationally?'

'It's possible.'

Henrik had to look away again as David pointed to the damage to the back of Irene's skull. 'She would have died within minutes of sustaining this injury. It is consistent with the bronze elephant found by the body.'

'Could it have been an accident? Someone trying to stop her, but catching her at the wrong angle?'

140

'No, I don't think so. Whoever picked up that statue and connected it with Irene's head would have had a reasonable assumption that it would cause her death. She was struck just the one time, splintering the bone.'

'Man or woman?'

'Could be either. But a considerable amount of force was used, I can tell you that much. So someone strong, or angry.'

'Hm,' said Henrik. 'You know it's odd . . .'

'What is?'

'There are these photos of an unidentified schoolgirl. I found one at this woman's house, and another out at Amager on the allotment where Vagn Holdved was murdered.'

'Ah, he wasn't one of mine. Let me look him up for you,' said David, heading across to a laptop sitting on a counter that ran the length of the far wall. 'You're saying that the two are related?'

'We don't know yet.'

David typed in Vagn Holdved's name and studied the report flashing up on his screen. 'Multiple blows to the head with a spade. Quite a sustained attack.'

'Could it have been the same killer?'

'That's not for me to say. But there is no reason why not, despite the difference in the number of blows. Both victims were struck from behind, which suggests they were running from their killer.' David stopped and looked at Henrik. 'You look pensive.'

'It's just . . . a photo of the same girl also turned up at another crime scene. The victim, Ulla Olsen, is still alive, just . . . if it's the same offender, why did he spare her? It happened in a care home for dementia patients, so there is always the possibility that he was interrupted.'

David looked lost. 'These photos . . . are you sure they are related to the crimes? Could there not be some innocent explanation?' he said.

'That's what everyone thinks. Perhaps they are right,' said Henrik.

He felt his heart sink. If there was a link between the victims to explain the photos, it wasn't David who would supply the evidence.

'Oh, I almost forgot,' said David. 'That friend of yours was here yesterday, the journalist?'

'Jensen was here?'

David nodded. 'Asked me loads of questions about how a killer might go about making something look like suicide.'

Jensen.

What is she up to now?

Henrik felt love stir deep inside him, then remembered the misery of his predicament.

As if he had read his thoughts, David lowered a sheet over Irene's body and switched off the bright light over the trolley. Then he walked over to Henrik and put a warm hand on his shoulder. 'Did something happen between you and Jensen?' David said, and Henrik thought that if he answered the question he would begin to weep and never be able to stop himself again. 'What is it, Henrik?'

'Nothing,' he said, taking off his mask and heading for the exit, so David couldn't see his face. 'Just one too many late nights.'

31

Friday 22:16

Jensen had almost turned around half a dozen times on the way
to Gilleleje. There had been no e-cars available nearby, so she
had cycled to the Central Station where she had managed to
catch a train to Hillerød and, from there, the local train service
to the coast. Each time the train doors had opened it had seemed
like a prompt for her to step out and return to Copenhagen,
sleep on it, come back with Gustav by daylight.

But she had to know.

She had pedalled as fast as she could from Gilleleje station to
the summer cabin, breathing hard in the raw night air. On the
entire journey, she had seen just one car.

She hid her bicycle in the bushes to one side of the summerhouse, then stood for a moment in the dark, trying to calm
herself. She could hear the gentle lap of waves against the nearby
beach. It was just an old wooden cabin, there was no one else
around. Everything was going to be fine.

Using her torch, she picked her way through the wet vegeta-
tion, crying out once when her trouser leg got caught on brambles
and it felt like someone was tugging at her, holding her back.

Fuck's sake, Jensen, will you get it together?

She switched off the torch for the last stretch of the drive, her eyes slowly getting used to the dark. It felt better like this, less conspicuous, as if she was not really there. As long as no one could see her, she would be safe.

She pushed gently against the front door. The smell of pine-wood and mildew hit her instantly as the door yielded in its rotten frame.

There was a large mouldy stain on the once beige carpet in the lounge, stretching its fingers into all corners of the room. Mouse excrement peppered the floor. At least Jensen hoped it was mice.

She went to the teak bookshelf next to the wicker sofa arrangement and picked up an old paperback. *The Godfather*, by Mario Puzo. Its pages were stained and curled with damp. The bar cabinet was still stocked with whisky (Johnnie Walker black label) and in the hallway was an assortment of fishing rods next to a pair of green wellington boots. It was easy to imagine Ove Valborg here: content, gently tipsy, at peace from his nagging wife.

She searched the three bedrooms, opened all the kitchen cupboards one by one.

Nothing.

Irene wouldn't have been able to move anything heavy, which ruled out the back of the fridge or oven or wardrobes. She searched the lounge. There was nothing under the book-shelves, or behind the paintings or under the sofa and chairs. Jensen shivered in the damp. There were electric radiators in all the rooms, but no power. She wondered whether Ove would have left a fire ready the last time he had been to the house, not realising that he would never be back. Perhaps if she could find some matches, she could light a fire and dispel the cold and damp. There was an open brick fireplace in one corner of the room.

Jensen frowned. Could it be that easy?

She bent down and looked up into the chimney. Nothing to see. She felt with one hand in the narrow space which was greasy and cold with soot and damp.

It was just where the flue bent backwards, a small paper parcel with something hard inside, taped to the wall. She pulled it out.

'Yes!'

There was something written on it by hand, joined-up in blue ink. 'This belongs to Irene Valborg.' Jensen ripped the parcel open and the diamonds spilled out, luminous in the dark. She smiled.

And froze.

Bluish torchlight was flashing through the dirty windows of the cabin and painting stripes on the ceiling.

'What the hell?'

32

Friday 23:00

After a good amount of pointless but satisfying cursing, Henrik finally managed to find a parking space two streets away from Margrethe's Østerbro flat. He had done his homework and knew that Margrethe was out of town at a conference in Jutland and wouldn't be returning to Copenhagen until tomorrow. At first, there was no answer when he pressed the doorbell, but stepping back, he saw that the lights were on in the windows on the fourth floor. He pressed the bell again, this time leaving his finger on it, until the intercom scratched with an insolent, adolescent voice. 'What?'

'Detective Inspector Henrik Jungersen, Copenhagen Police,' he said in the scariest voice he could muster

The boy didn't miss a beat. 'Your girlfriend doesn't live here anymore.'

'No idea who you're talking about,' said Henrik. 'It's you I need to speak to.'

'Me? At eleven o'clock at night?'

'Police work is twenty-four seven.'

Gustav buzzed him in.

Henrik arrived on the fourth floor, panting heavily with exertion. It was days since he had last been to the gym and, what with the dirty takeaways that passed for meals these days, he was getting unfit. He lifted his chin, looking down at Gustav, who was waiting for him in the open doorway. He was taller than the boy, just, and considerably broader.

'What do you want?' said Gustav. He seemed wary. A pair of headphones dangled from his neck and greasy hair cascaded over his spotty forehead.

The face of things to come, thought Henrik, whose eldest boy was just a year off being a teenager. 'Let me in and I will tell you,' he said.

The state of the flat hinted at why Gustav had been so reluctant to let Henrik in. There were pizza cartons and glasses everywhere, items of clothing, phone chargers and crisp bags trailing across the floor.

'When the cat's away,' Henrik said, tutting.

Gustav shrugged and plonked himself back on the settee where he had been lying comfortably, judging by the shape of the cushions. He was staring at his phone as if he had forgotten that Henrik was there.

The flat was huge with double doors opening through successive rooms and would once have been elegant, though the decor now looked tired and outdated. The walls in the living room were dark green and almost entirely covered with portraits painted in oils. The art wasn't to Henrik's liking. The people's faces were distorted, their bodies angular and contradicting every law of nature, their mouths stretched out of shape. Everywhere there were books, crammed into shelves, stacked on the floor, lying open across the oriental carpets. His wife would have torn the heavy curtains down, walked across the floor with black bin liners and scooped up everything in her wake, then rolled the walls with white paint. She abhorred any kind of mess and nagged him daily

147

about leaving his keys and mobile phone on her precious kitchen island.

Or used to nag him, rather.

How was it possible to miss being nagged at?

He supposed the editor-in-chief of one of Denmark's oldest broadsheet newspapers had better things to do than worry about how her digs looked.

'If you've come to warn us off the case again, go and speak to the boss,' said Gustav without taking his eyes off the screen. 'As you can see for yourself, she's really not here.'

'I told you already, it's not Jensen I am after. What the two of you get up to on your own time is up to you, as long as you don't interfere with my investigation.'

'You've changed your tune.'

'I've had time to reflect.'

Gustav looked at him apprehensively. Henrik knew that look. It was one his very presence as a police officer often produced in people who had something to hide.

'I've done nothing wrong,' Gustav said, as if reading his mind.

His face told Henrik otherwise, but he wasn't here to probe the boy's guilty conscience. He suspected it was to do with weed. You could smell the stuff everywhere in Copenhagen these days. 'No one says you have. I am here because I need a favour.' He reached for his phone and found the photo of the unknown girl. He passed it to Gustav.

'Who's she?'

'That's what I want you to find out.'

'How?'

'Post it on social media. Say you're writing a story. Say whatever you want, as long as you get someone, if not the girl herself, to respond with her name. The photo is likely to be from the nineties, so she will be in her forties now and looking quite different.'

Gustav was feigning reluctance, but Henrik could tell he was interested. Either that or he was just relieved that Henrik wasn't there on other business. He was sitting bolt upright now. His phone pinged on the coffee table as he sent himself the photo. 'What's this to do with?' he said.

'I can't tell you.'

'Don't you have people in the police who can find out about this sort of thing?'

'It would seem not.'

'Why don't you put it on social media yourself?'

The boy was smart. Either this was genetic, or his time working with Jensen had rubbed off on him. It was exactly what she would have asked. 'Sometimes we have to do things without people knowing it is us who are doing them.'

Gustav put the photo down. 'OK,' he said. 'I'll try. But if I find out who it is, I want in on the story.'

Henrik laughed. 'We'll see about that.'

'Or I could just tell Jensen instead, if you'd rather I did that?'

Gustav had some spark. He was trying to look tough. Henrik felt a rush of tenderness for the lad, recalling the first time he had seen him, lying in a hospital bed at Riget, his face beaten to a pulp. Not quite an adult yet, he was trying to make his own way in the world. He could do worse than being Jensen's assistant.

'No, don't tell her,' said Henrik. 'This has to stay between us. If you help me on this one, maybe there is something I can do for you in return?'

Gustav made a face as if to say that he really couldn't imagine what this would be.

'When did you leave school?' said Henrik.

A sudden blush. 'I . . . last year. I . . . didn't get on with it.'

'Me neither,' said Henrik.

'Really?'

'Left at sixteen. Worked for a bit, then joined the police. And you? What happened?'

149

They didn't get any further because at that moment Gustav's phone pinged on the table again. His eyes widened as he read.

'Has something happened?' said Henrik, instantly on his guard.

Gustav didn't reply. He held the screen up to Henrik's face. Jensen.

At Irene's summer house in Gilleleje. There's someone else here. Call the police!

33

Jensen dropped to the floor and crawled on all fours into the hallway. There was nowhere to hide that wasn't obvious. In the end she crawled into the bathroom and hid in the tub, yanking across the mouldy shower curtain.

Could it be Irene's killer? Someone who had been frustrated at not finding the diamonds in her safe where they thought they would be? Someone who had managed to find out about Irene's little trip to Gilleleje? After all, Gustav had done so easily by calling a few local taxi firms.

Someone was entering the house now. There was nothing tentative about the footsteps.

Fuck.

She shrank further into the tub, trying not to think about the nature of the moisture that was seeping through her jeans and connecting with her skin. The bathroom stank of decay. She could hear the intruder moving through the kitchen, opening and shutting cupboards and sweeping stuff onto the floor.

Come on Gustav.

How long would it take for a patrol car to reach the house?

151

Thirty minutes? If they would even come out for something like this.

The intruder was moving through the living room, knocking stuff over. Jensen stared at the shower curtain. It had little white sailing boats with red sails, faded and streaked with dirt. She couldn't risk making a run for it. She could only wait and hope to God that the intruder wouldn't think to look in the bathroom, or that the police would get there first.

Neither prayer was answered. She heard the intruder approaching methodically, through each room in turn. Finally, the door to the bathroom was flung open so hard it slammed into the wall, the shower curtain yanked back in a single move. For a few seconds Jensen screamed at the top of her voice, blinded by torchlight.

'Jensen?'

She stopped screaming.

'Regitse?' she said, shielding her eyes against the bright light. 'Is that you?'

'You found it, didn't you?' said Regitse.

Jensen struggled to her feet in the bathtub. 'Shit, Regitse, what are you—'

'You haven't answered my question.'

'Yes, I found it,' said Jensen, feeling for the diamond necklace in her pocket. 'Look, can you put that torch down, I can't see anything.'

Regitse wasn't yielding.

'I thought you didn't believe your mother could possibly have hidden the necklace here,' Jensen said.

'I recalled something she said to me a few months back, about the plot being overgrown and it made me think how she could possibly have known that, unless she had been here recently.'

'And so you thought, you'd drive all the way over from Aarhus and get the necklace for yourself to avoid paying me?'

'It's my house now. I can do what I want. Hand it over,'
she said.

'When you've paid me,' said Jensen.

'Show it to me first,' said Regitse.

Reluctantly, Jensen fished the envelope with the necklace out
of her jacket pocket.

There was a loud curse as someone stumbled into the hall.

'Police. Stay where you are!'

Two officers crowded the small bathroom, shining their
torches from one face to the other, then at the diamonds in
Jensen's hand, unable it seemed to make sense of what they
were looking at. In the confusion, Regitse turned to Jensen in
disbelief. 'You called the police? You stupid, stupid girl.'

Then there was a shuffle of bodies as another man entered
the room. A bald man in black jeans, white shirt, leather jacket
and a pair of wet Timberland boots.

Face like thunder.

'What in the name of the almighty God is going on here?'

34

Saturday 01:34

Henrik had spent ages persuading the two uniforms that no crime had been committed. This had been followed by a stand-off with Regitse over the necklace, one the woman was always destined to lose, given the mood he was in. The necklace was evidence in a murder investigation, as far as he was concerned. She would just have to wait for him to feel inclined to release it. 'For fuck's sake, Jensen, what am I going to do with you?' he said to her as they watched Regitse pick her way down the driveway, cursing.

To his great surprise, Jensen began to cry. He could count on one hand the times he had witnessed this. Mostly it had been his doing. He told himself that she was all right, and that the tears were no more than a release of tension. After all, she had been hiding helplessly behind a shower curtain, fearing that a killer was coming for her. He had seen people cry in similar circumstances more times than he cared to remember, but still he felt himself weaken. It was the hold she had over him, this ability to transform his feelings in an instant, not matter how cross he was, or how determined to steer clear of her.

He reached out and pulled her close, feeling her stiffen in his arms, then relax, her shoulders heaving with quiet sobs. They stood like this in the dank, dripping jungle that had once been a front lawn proudly mowed by Ove Valborg, and he thought 'I love this woman.'

Of course, the moment didn't last.

Slowly, Jensen recovered her composure and wriggled free. 'I'm fine,' she said, wiping away tears on her coat sleeve. 'Really. You don't need to ... God, I don't know what I am crying for.'

'Is now a good time to ask what the *hell* you were thinking coming here on your own in the middle of night? Have you learned nothing?' he said.

'I didn't ask you to rescue me. What are *you* doing here anyway?'

'Your juvenile assistant told me you were in trouble.'

'Gustav?'

Henrik decided not to tell her that he had actually been with Gustav in Margrethe's flat at the time. No need for her to know that. He only hoped that Gustav was going to heed his warnings and keep his mouth shut. 'He was worried sick about you and quite right too. How are you going to get back from here?'

'I've got my bike.'

'Oh that's all right then, and you're going to cycle back to Copenhagen? No trains this time of night.'

She hadn't considered this. 'I'll be fine waiting at the station for the first one in the morning.'

'Don't be daft, Jensen. Come on, I am taking you home.'

He put her bicycle in the back of his car, shoving aside sports bags, cardboard boxes of Coke Zero cans and a gym towel with a streak of dirt on it.

When they reached the motorway, he took her hand and squeezed it hard. 'How did you work it out?' he said.

'I had this hunch that Irene had hidden the necklace. All that extra security, the dog, the new lock, she wouldn't get

155

that only to leave her most prized possession in the house. So when Gustav found out she took a taxi to Gilleleje just before Christmas, I thought it was worth taking a look.'

'You should have waited till the morning.'

'Good job I didn't or Regitse would have got there before me, and we would have been none the wiser,' she said.

'Or called us in.'

'And miss out on my fee? No chance.'

Henrik let it go. He was hardly in a position to lecture Jensen on patience after his own midnight foray to Irene's house. Not for the first time, he thought of how alike the two of them were: impulsive, taking stupid risks, acting alone.

The discovery of the necklace was important, but not conclusive. A burglar could have broken into Irene's house to steal it, found the safe empty and killed Irene out of frustration. Or more likely, given that Irene was struck from behind on her way to her bedroom, she had been killed to get her out of the way before she had time to pull the security grille across. But burglars weren't killers, or at least not very often. And David had talked of someone striking Irene with great force. What had Irene done to deserve that? He felt Jensen's eyes on him. 'What do you think happened to Irene?' she said.

'I don't know.' Suddenly, he felt mortally tired. 'Jensen, I'm in trouble.'

'I know,' she said.

'I mean, I'm really losing it. I need to get back to what I was. I need to get back into that house, with my kids, put back together what I have broken.'

How many times had he and Jensen sat like this, together in his car, with Denmark zooming past the windows in a blur, like a parallel universe on wheels? He had always felt safe with Jensen in the car, as though no one could see them. It had never *felt* like betraying his wife, not as long as they were on the move and shut away from other people. Now he knew this was a lie.

His betrayal was not what he did with Jensen, but what he felt for her. To know her was to cheat.

'Jensen, we can't do this anymore. I wasn't here tonight, this didn't happen.'

'It's OK,' she said. 'I am out of your hair now. Regitse's got what she wanted, and I'll get my money, and that will be me done investigating.'

'That's not what I heard from David Goldschmidt.'

'Ah, he told you.'

'Yes.'

'Completely different story, though. It's this guy, Carsten Vangede who is supposed to have hanged himself, but—'

'Never heard of him.'

'I don't think he did hang himself. I think—'

'Jensen, please don't . . . I can't, I just can't. You and me, we can't *be*.'

'I understand,' she said, the brightness in her voice crushing him. 'You can trust me completely. Isn't that what you once told me, Henrik?'

He was ashamed to think of it. He had been testing her, trying to impress upon her that they needed to keep their affair secret. 'The problem with you, Jensen, is that you remember everything.'

She turned away from him and leaned her head against the window, watching the dark countryside of North Zealand rush by. 'And the problem with you, Henrik, is that you remember nothing.'

35

Jensen stood in the dark and listened to the rain tapping against her kitchen window. Someone nearby was having a party. The deep thump of the music was giving her a headache. Her hair and clothes were damp, and she was exhausted, but couldn't bring herself to go upstairs and get into bed. Not yet. She had told Henrik that she was done with the Irene Valborg case, but it didn't feel like the end. Too many unanswered questions.

Carsten Vangede was another conundrum altogether. Only Christina, Gustav, Deep Throat and herself seemed to care that he had gone, yet many of the circumstances surrounding his death still disturbed Jensen profoundly. His laptop and phone, gone when his sister first entered the flat after his alleged suicide. The subsequent burglary where nothing had been taken. The terror in the voice of the Randers optician when he had finally called her back.

She reached into her bag, relieved to find the spectacle case still there with the glasses rattling inside. Her hands brushed across the mail she had picked up on her late-night visit to

Dagbladet. She laid it on the dining table and turned on the light, shrugging off her coat.

It was time she went away from Copenhagen for a while, a research trip to gather her thoughts away from the noise of the city. She made tea and sat down and looked at her letters. An invitation to a reception at the British Embassy, old payslips and a slim jiffy bag that weighed nothing. No return address. She shook the envelope and a USB memory stick with a Carlsberg logo dropped onto the table. She opened her laptop and inserted the stick, but the drive wouldn't open. Then she felt inside the envelope again.

A folded sheet.

In case something happens to me.
  Be careful.
  Carsten Vangede

36

Saturday 08:56

Henrik tried to concentrate on what the man opposite him was saying, none of which seemed to have any bearing on his investigation. He and Lisbeth were in an office on an industrial estate in Rødovre, seated around a Formica table with the general manager of the alarm firm that had kitted out Irene Valborg's house. The manager, bald like Henrik himself and looking like he might have put a career in crime behind him, was seated next to a younger man who was busy chewing his nails down to the quick. The two of them were wearing identical dark blue fleeces with the company logo, an eye inside a keyhole. The office was sparse and unkempt, a couple of sick plants expiring quietly on the windowsill. On the wall, a calendar from last year with pictures of different dog breeds. Henrik's eyes kept going back to it. They had stopped turning the leaves last October (a Boxer).

Beside him, Lisbeth radiated reproach. She had found him out cold on the sofa in his office earlier. He hadn't got back from Gilleleje until almost 3 a.m. and had struggled to fall asleep for thinking of Jensen. The first thing he knew was Lisbeth

160

shaking him awake with a worried frown on her forehead. He had mumbled something about crashing after working late. She hadn't responded, but her eyes had taken in his sleeping bag and clothes on the floor. Stupidly, he had left his washbag and shaver on the windowsill.

Her disapproving looks had put him in a bad mood on the way to Rødovre. He was thinking of Jensen's determined face when he had dropped her off outside her flat in Christianshavn in the early hours. She didn't need him. Like his wife didn't need him. In all areas of his life, he seemed surplus to requirements, and now Lisbeth was giving him the cold shoulder. He would have to make her swear not to tell Wiese that he had been staying nights in the office.

'Excuse me,' he said, cutting off the manager mid-flow. 'But can you just answer our question? When and how did Irene Valborg contact you?'

The manager put on his reading glasses and consulted his tablet, an elaborate gesture to gain some thinking time, if ever Henrik saw one. Surely the man had looked up the date before they got here?

'Eighth of December last year.'

'How did she find you?'

'She'd seen our flyer.'

'Show me this flyer, please.'

The manager sighed, walked across to his desk and handed Henrik a neon-yellow sheet of A5 with the logo of the keyhole with an eye inside. *Burglaries are on the rise in this area. Don't be a victim!* it said in bold black letters.

'Long way from Rødovre to Klampenborg. Just the size of your catchment area, or more of a bespoke approach to frighten little old ladies living on their own?'

The manager turned bright red. 'You just told us this was a murder investigation. Seems to me we weren't wrong to highlight the risk.'

'Shame it didn't do her any good, though. The alarm system was off when she opened the door to her killer, and she didn't have time to close the security grille behind her before she had her skull crushed.'

The younger man shifted uncomfortably in his seat. 'I told her to get a panic button, by the front door, but she said it cost too much.' The manager laid a hand on his arm. 'I don't see how this has anything to do with me or Tommy. We've done nothing wrong.'

Lisbeth glanced sideways at Henrik, and he gave her a slight nod, permitting her to take over the questioning. He was glad they were still a team, despite their differences. When they got back to the office, he would tell her that.

'Detective Inspector Jungersen and I aren't accusing you of anything. We just want to know if Irene hinted at what she was afraid of?'

'No. She just said she wanted to discuss her security. Tommy, tell them what she told you when you called.'

Tommy fiddled with his earring. He had a tattoo on his finger, a cross of some sort. Henrik wondered if he had been inside, too, and decided the answer was yes.

'Nothing. She just said what she wanted and I gave her the price and we arranged a time for the fitting.'

'Really?' said Henrik, folding his arms across his chest. 'You said you tried to sell her a panic button, so which is it?'

'I tried to. I told her that many of our clients want a panic button in case they feel threatened after opening the front door to someone.'

'And?'

'She bit my head off, saying that if people were stupid enough to open their front door to a stranger, even someone posing as a meter reader or a policeman, then they deserved to have their house burgled. She made me push my business card through the letterbox, asked me all sorts of questions before letting me in. She wasn't some gullible old bird, if that's what you're thinking.'

If that was true, then Irene probably knew her killer, or at the very least, it was someone she expected. And she hadn't been killed in her entrance hall, so some sort of conversation must have taken place before she had tried in vain to get herself to safety upstairs.

'And you're sure she didn't mention why she wanted the extra security?' Henrik said.

'Positive, and I didn't ask. We've rigged up hundreds of houses like hers. It wasn't anything unusual except it's normally the kids who call us.'

'The kids?' said Lisbeth.

'A son or daughter fearing for their elderly parents' safety,' explained the manager.

No chance in hell that Regitse would have harboured such worries, thought Henrik. He glanced up at the dog calendar, a sudden idea crossing his mind. 'Irene got herself an Alsatian not long after your visit. We're wondering where she got that idea from. Any thoughts on that, Tommy?'

'What the—' the manager began but Henrik held up a hand to silence him.

'Tommy?'

The boy squirmed. 'I didn't do anything. It was her, she wanted it. She asked me if I knew someone.'

The manager looked astonished. So he didn't know.

'Nice little side-line?' said Henrik. 'Guard dogs for people too old to walk them? Do you know that Samson spent over two weeks locked in Irene Valborg's back garden? You stupid fuck.'

He felt something shift inside him as he scrambled to his feet, and the boy recoiled into his seat, sensing that Henrik was about to lash out.

'Stop!' Lisbeth shouted, loud enough to make him freeze mid-punch.

163

'And you?' she said, jabbing a finger at Tommy in a way that made Henrik feel proud of her. 'Don't say another word. We'll deal with you later.'

'Thanks,' said Henrik, when they were back in the car. 'I owe you one.'

He could tell that, despite his outburst, he had regained some credibility with Lisbeth for rumbling Tommy. He'd bet his pension that the boy wasn't a registered puppy trader. Not that it made any difference to their investigation whatsoever.

'Henrik—' Lisbeth began, but he stopped her.

'I know what you're going to say. I was unprofessional in there. Put it down to tiredness. I didn't get much sleep last night.'

'You need help,' she said, avoiding his eyes. 'Why don't you take some leave, see someone?'

This was how he knew that Lisbeth was going to go far in the police. Mark would not have dared venture onto such personal ground.

'You've been talking to Wiese.'

'I am worried about you. Mark and I both are.'

'Come on, Lisbeth. We're in the middle of an investigation. There's stress, sleep deprivation, all the usual crap.'

'I think it's more than that,' said Lisbeth quietly.

'Thank you, and I appreciate your concern, but please cut me some slack. Don't go running off to Wiese about what happened today, please. We'll keep it between us, yes?'

She didn't reply but started the ignition and began to back the car out of the space next to the white transit van with the logo of the eye in the keyhole.

'Come on, Lisbeth. How long have you and I been working together?'

'That's not fair.'

Not fair, no. HR would have a field day with him. Leaning

on a junior detective to cover for his unacceptable behaviour. But team players were meant to have each other's backs, weren't they? At least, those were the old ways of the police force he had joined two decades ago. He feared things were changing for the worse, presided over by the likes of Jens Wiese. 'I'm not perfect, I make mistakes.'

('No shit,' said his wife in his head.)

'But when have I ever not got the job done?'

True, his anger had been bubbling back up of late, but if he could only move back home to his family, then things would be under control again. He would put Jensen out of his mind for good, and never stray again as long as he lived.

'It's not like that anymore,' said Lisbeth, avoiding his gaze. 'Whatever you are going through, you don't have to just grin and bear it.'

37

Saturday 10:43

Jensen's mood was lifting with each mile separating her from Copenhagen. She had slept badly, thinking about Carsten Vangede's letter. In the end, she had got up early, packed and gone to Margrethe's flat to drop off the USB stick with Gustav, so he could take a look while she was away.

'Of all people, why did you call Henrik last night?' she had asked him.

'You said to call the police,' Gustav had replied, standing in Margrethe's doorway in his underpants, scratching his midriff.

'And there was no one else you could find in the entire police force?'

'OK, so he was here at the flat already,' said Gustav.

'What?'

'Wanted me to do him a favour.'

'What kind of favour?'

'Can't tell you, I'm afraid,' Gustav had said, yawning so hard it brought tears to his eyes.

By the time the tall concrete gateways of the Storebælt suspension bridge had towered above Jensen, with the sea grey and choppy to either side, she was starting to look forward to her break, despite the rain lashing against the windscreen of the hire car.

She had told Gustav that she was going away for a few days, and he hadn't asked any questions. Not that she was going to tell him what she was up to. Two could play at secrets.

She felt a twinge of jealousy that Henrik had asked Gustav for help and not her.

'I need to wipe you from my mind for good,' he had said when he had dropped her at her flat in Christianshavn in the small hours of the morning.

She knew Gustav was sore about the way she had rebuffed him when he had suggested that the two of them should advertise as private detectives. 'Why not?' he had said, desperate to feed his aunt a decent excuse for not wanting to return to school.

'Because I expect we'd be spending most of our time staking out lovers or spying on people claiming sick pay while playing golf. This is Copenhagen, Gustav, not LA,' she had told him. 'Just take a look at what's on Vangede's USB and text me when you've got something. And don't show it to anyone.'

Be careful.

Careful about what?

Regitse hadn't wanted to talk when Jensen had rung her earlier. Grudgingly, she had agreed to transfer the remainder of Jensen's fee via Mobile Pay.

'Just one more question,' Jensen had said when her phone had pinged to confirm that the money was in.

'You said to me when we first met that you had no idea who your mother might have inherited from.'

'So?'

'I find that odd. You must at least have a guess?'

'Nope and can't say I care two hoots.'

'Do you have any relatives who might be able to tell me?'

'Why?'

'Call it professional curiosity. No extra charge,' Jensen had said.

'There's a cousin in Svendborg who's into family history. Dreadful bore.'

And so Jensen had ended up driving across the island of Funen instead of taking the ferry to Aarhus and going north to her mother's house. It was only a small detour, a pitstop. She was going to tie up this one loose end, then leave the Irene Valborg case to Henrik. She had heard on the radio news that police were appealing for anyone with information on the murder to come forward.

Jensen parked outside the yellow house on the outskirts of Svendborg and sat for a while listening to the rain and the crackling of the engine as it cooled down after the long drive. The house shone warmly in the gloom, surrounded by a neatly kept lawn and white picket fence. It looked cosy and inviting after her journey.

The front door opened and Bo Koppel, Regitse's cousin, lifted his hand to greet her.

Her phone buzzed.

Kristoffer Bro.

Again.

> I have been racking my brain for something in the flat that needs fixing, so I can see you again. Put me out of my misery, would you Jensen, please?

Why was she always the woman men cheated with? She thought of the man's actress girlfriend and resolutely deleted the message. Then, tossing the phone into her bag, she opened the car door and waved smilingly at Bo.

38

'This is your final warning,' said Jens Wiese, looking at Henrik over the rim of his reading glasses.

Henrik wanted to rip the glasses off the man's face and push him up against his neatly organised bookshelf with its legal lexica and framed photographs of Wiese shaking the hands of assorted dignitaries.

Keep it together, Jungersen.

Losing his patience now would mean certain suspension, and he didn't want to give Wiese the satisfaction.

I want a divorce.

His wife had refused to answer his angry questions.

'If that illegal dog trader scum has made a complaint, I hope we both agree where he can stick it,' he said, feeling his face grow hot.

'No one has made a complaint, yet, but if you carry on like you are, it can only be a matter of time.'

Henrik sat back, folding his arms across his chest, sensing that Wiese had more up his sleeve. 'I understand from your team that you have been lashing out lately, and am I correct that you slept in the office last night?'

Thanks very much, Lisbeth.

'It was a one-off. I worked late, crashed on the couch.'

'You sure about that?'

Henrik stared back in silence. He didn't know what Wiese had picked up from Monsen and, if he had learned anything from his career on the force, it was never to volunteer information.

'Henrik,' Wiese began.

Henrik pushed his hands under his thighs to prevent himself from reacting. He could guess what was coming next. It was a repeat of a conversation Wiese had had with him a few times now. 'Just two months ago you experienced a trauma during which you fired your weapon and injured a man.'

'To stop said man from killing again.'

Wiese took off his glasses, rubbed his eyes and put his glasses back on as if exercising a great deal of patience. 'I am well aware of that. No one has accused you of acting inappropriately, Henrik, but I think it's obvious to everyone that what happened has taken a considerable toll on you. You were encouraged to take leave at the time.'

'I did.'

'Two days.'

Henrik remembered it well. He had planned to take a week off, but his wife's decision to kick him out had forced him to check into a hotel and he had very quickly got stir crazy. 'I felt fine.'

'How are things at home?' Wiese said.

So he *had* spoken to Monsen.

'Fine,' said Henrik, staring Wiese out.

Wiese squirmed in his chair, not willing to challenge him on information he only had second-hand. 'I understand you saw Isabella Grå. How was that?'

'Fine.'

Wiese sighed.

'I can't help you if you won't help yourself, Henrik. The

psychology sessions are voluntary. But if I hear of another angry outburst from you, you'll be on sick leave with immediate effect. And just so we're clear, from now on I will be watching your every move.'

Henrik got up to leave. 'Fine.'

Wiese looked at him, perplexed. 'That's all you've got to say, "fine"?'

But Henrik had already opened the door and was halfway into the corridor. He walked straight to the investigations room and signalled to Lisbeth and Mark to follow him into his office. He could tell from their dragging footsteps that they were wary, sensing he was about to blow.

'How many times have I told you to speak to me first if you have a problem?' he said when they were inside, and he had slammed the door after them. 'We're meant to be a team.'

Mark was staring down at his shoes but Lisbeth, at least, had enough gumption to look him in the eye. 'We did speak to you,' she said. 'A few times now, but you never listen.'

'So you thought you'd go running off to Wiese?' he said.

Lisbeth shrugged. Mark shuffled his feet. 'You seem stressed,' he mumbled.

'Of course I am bloody stressed.'

Lisbeth's phone dinged. Mark and Henrik exchanged glances while she checked the screen.

'It's Ulla Olsen,' she said. 'She is awake.'

39

'Regitse?' said Bo Koppel, rolling his eyes. 'No one likes Regitse.'

Jensen was starting to seriously warm to the man. In half an hour, during which Bo and his wife Annemette had served her coffee and home-baked cinnamon buns at their dining table overlooking Svendborgsund strait, she had learned more about Irene Valborg, née Koppel, than she ever had from Regitse.

'The apple doesn't fall far from the tree, if you know what we mean,' said Annemette, who supplemented her husband's recollection with sentences that wove themselves seamlessly in and out of his. Both spoke with the sing-song lilt of Funen natives. It was an accent in which it was impossible to convey menace.

'Irene was a piece of work all right,' said Bo.

He had told her that Irene and Ove had not believed they were able to have children, before Regitse had turned up when Irene was the grand old age of thirty-five, which back then had made her an 'older mother'.

'It wasn't a success,' said Bo.

'Motherhood didn't suit her,' added his wife.

172

'Not at all,' said Bo. He was the son of Irene's older brother Svend, and according to him, there had been no love lost between the siblings. 'But my father liked Ove,' said Bo.

'Everyone liked Ove,' said Annemette.

Bo continued. 'I think my father felt sorry for him being stuck with Irene.'

'Did you ever visit them in Klampenborg?' said Jensen, helping herself to a second bun from the dish offered to her by Annemette.

'A few times, with my brother and sister. We thought the house was enormous, almost like a castle with so many dark rooms and that huge garden. I remember my parents talking about it in the car on the way back to Svendborg, what on earth Irene and Ove wanted a big place like that for, on his salary. My father said Irene was a snob. It was the first time I'd heard that word, so I asked what it meant, and he explained it to me. He was straightforward like that.'

'She didn't like having you kids in the house,' said Annemette.

'She told us off for being noisy. We weren't allowed to touch anything. And then, when Regitse came along, my father and Irene fell out and we never saw them after that.'

He looked down at the dining table and Annemette laid her hand on top of his. They had the same wedding rings: wide silver bands. Jensen nodded, moved by the sight of the two of them.

'Show her,' said Annemette.

Bo reached for the spiralbound A4 book with a plastic cover which had been laid out next to the ceramic coffee mugs and matching plates.

The Descendants of Hansigne and Aloysius Koppel

Hansigne and Aloysius stared out sternly from the black-and-white photographs. Inside, were pages of family history with photos from the past. 'Took me three years to put together,' said Bo.

Bo pointed to the page showing Svend and Irene's

great-grandparents. Against each descendant Bo had printed the name of the spouse and any children, occupations and addresses neatly recorded. Bo and Annemette were retired teachers, Jensen noted. Regitse's occupation was noted as 'housewife'. She wouldn't have been pleased with that, thought Jensen.

'Tell me,' she said. 'According to Regitse, Irene inherited in 1996. She spent the money on an expensive diamond necklace. Can you think who she might have inherited from?'

Bo shook his head. 'My father would have told us kids if he'd inherited. Shared everything with us, he did.'

'Someone could have bequeathed to Irene only. Was there someone in the family, perhaps, with whom she had a special relationship?' said Jensen.

Bo stared back at her incredulously. 'We *are* talking about the same Irene here?' he said. 'I don't believe my aunt had a loving relationship with anyone. Didn't attend the funerals of her own parents, let alone anyone else's.'

'She had no interest in her family and Regitse is just like her,' said Annemette.

'Come to think of it, I don't think anyone passed away in 1996.'

'Or 1995?'

'No', said Bo. 'And if anyone had, it is extremely unlikely they would have made Irene the beneficiary. We were never a rich family. I think that's why Irene's delusions of grandeur rankled so with my father.'

'So if she didn't inherit the money, where did she get it from?'

Bo and Annemette shrugged in unison.

'And can you think why anyone would have wanted to kill her?'

'Don't get me wrong,' said Bo. 'Irene wouldn't have won any popularity contests, but bashing an eighty-six-year-old over the head? I just don't understand how anyone could bring themselves to do that.'

174

'The newspapers say it was a burglary gone wrong,' said Annemette.

'Yes,' said Jensen, draining her mug. 'That still seems most likely.'

40

Saturday 13:53

'I will have to warn you,' said Anette Olsen, intercepting Henrik and Mark outside the hospital room. 'Mum is extremely confused and what happened has only made matters worse.'

'I understand,' said Henrik. The last few times he had visited his father, they had been forced to talk outside in the garden, because his stepmother had been upset at repeatedly finding what she thought was a stranger in the house.

'Just as long as you manage your expectations,' said Anette. 'And I am going to have to ask you to be quick.'

'We'll be out of there before you know it,' said Henrik.

The room smelled of disinfectant and decay. Ulla Olsen had a bandage around her head and an oxygen tube under her nose. Her face was swollen, one eye closed and puffed up like a blue egg.

'Mum,' said Anette. 'There are some men here to see you. They need to ask you a few questions.'

Ulla Olsen moaned quietly, her one good eye staying closed.

'Ulla,' Henrik began. 'Someone came into your room and hurt you. Do you remember? We need you to try and describe the person to us.'

There was no reply. In the silence, Henrik could hear the rhythmical whirring of the drip next to Ulla's bed, and the low hiss of the oxygen flowing into her nose.

'Mum,' said Anette. 'Try to look at us.'

Finally, Ulla Olsen blinked. She squinted at Anette. 'Åse?' she said.

Anette glanced at Henrik. 'Åse was her little sister. I think I must look like her.'

'Åse,' said Ulla, beginning to cry.

'No, it's me, Anette. Who attacked you, Mum? Try to remember.'

Ulla looked at her daughter. 'I want Åse,' she said.

The conversation was going nowhere, but there was one more question Henrik needed to ask and quickly. Ulla was getting agitated. She was jerking her hands back and forth, pulling at the drip. 'Åse . . .' she repeated.

Anette tried to calm her down. 'Mum . . . it's OK. Nothing is going to happen to you.'

It was now or never.

Henrik pulled the picture of the girl in the swimming costume from the inside pocket of his leather jacket and held it in front of Ulla's face, ignoring the questioning look Mark sent in his direction. 'Ulla, Ulla, look at me.'

Finally, she turned to him, with a look of terror.

'We found this picture in your bedside drawer. Do you know who it is?'

Ulla Olsen began to scream.

41

The Lindegaards' modern mansion in suburban Aarhus was lit up like a Christmas tree in the gloom. Jensen shuddered in the cold wind as she looked up at the house between the sand dunes. It hadn't been designed for privacy. Dwarfing its neighbours, the house was made of glass, giving any passing dog walker a full view of the couple's sparsely furnished rooms. Regitse was sitting alone by the dining table, no sign of Preben.

From the back, the house was all concrete and rusty metal, uninviting and impersonal. Jensen rang the intercom and looked at the camera.

It was a long while before Regitse replied. 'What do *you* want?' she said, her voice slurred.

'Can I come in?'

'Suit yourself.' The gate buzzed open on a bare courtyard. A couple of olive trees were dying in their pots. Grass had appeared in the cracks between the grey flagstones.

Regitse was in her bare feet, her stiletto boots lying discarded in the hall next to her wheelie suitcase. Her silk shirt was untucked from her leather trousers. She staggered into the house, off her face. Jensen saw that the rooms weren't just sparsely furnished, but almost empty bar a few cardboard boxes and paintings covered with bubble wrap and gaffer tape.

'You're moving out?' said Jensen.

'What does it look like?' snapped Regitse, tipping the last of a bottle of red wine into her glass and knocking it back. 'Preben's left me, his business has gone tits up, this place has to go.'

'I'm sorry to hear that.'

'The fuck you are,' said Regitse.

'At least you have the diamond necklace, and the house in Klampenborg.'

'Ha,' said Regitse. 'The creditors will take it all.'

'Oh.'

'Yes, oh.' Regitse squinted into her empty glass. 'Why are you here? Come to gloat?' she said.

'I saw your cousin in Svendborg.'

'Surprised you got away without getting bored to death.'

'The money your mother used for the necklace?'

'What about it?'

'She didn't inherit it.'

Regitse looked at her with one eye closed. 'So?'

'So where did she get it from?'

'How should I know? It's not enough anyway.' She began to cry: child-like, self-pitying sobs.

Perhaps Regitse was only a victim of her mother. Perhaps, deep down she was a decent human being. Deserted, penniless, she would have to start again, but at least she was free from the burden of being Irene's daughter. 'I am sorry,' Jensen said. 'About everything that's happened to you. I hope something good comes of it, even if it doesn't feel like that now.'

'Leave me alone,' said Regitse, but her voice had lost its sharpness.

Jensen saw herself out. Before she got into her car for the journey to north Jutland, she texted Gustav.

There was no inheritance, so ask your new best friend how Irene paid for the necklace.

42

Henrik stuck his head round Lotte Nielsen's door. 'Is it safe to come in or will you bite my head off again?'

Lotte looked up from her screen, frowning absentmindedly. Her blonde hair was scraped back from her face more tightly than usual, giving her a stern look. 'From what I hear, you're the one with the temper issue,' she said.

'I see. Word's got around.'

'When did it ever not in this place?' said Lotte, gesturing for him to sit.

Her office was identical in size to his, but considerably tidier. There was a black blazer on a hanger on the back of the door, a framed art poster from the Louisiana museum of modern art on the wall, a row of trainers neatly lined up on the floor. 'You look knackered, Henrik.'

'Thanks very much.'

'No, I mean it. Why don't you just take leave, chill out for a bit.'

'Chill out? In the middle of a murder investigation?'

'You're not the only one around here who can handle an investigation.'

'I have the best record on the force.'

'So you keep saying. You're only as good as your last case, though,' she said. 'Screw this one up and that's all anyone will remember.'

Henrik picked up the bitterness in Lotte's voice. She was a competent and thorough investigator, but a couple of years ago she had been suspended for messing up the evidence in a murder case that saw the chief suspect go free.

There but for the grace of God, he thought.

'Why are you here? I've got work to do,' said Lotte.

'It's about Vagn Holdved.'

Lotte moaned. 'Oh God, tell me you're not still looking for a connection.'

'Just hear me out.'

Lotte leaned back in her chair and folded her arms across her chest. The text message from Gustav had made Henrik think. Jensen had found out that Irene hadn't inherited, so she must have got the money some other way. Mark and Lisbeth were still looking into her bank records, but they had been told it could take days, if not weeks.

'Was Vagn Holdved wealthy?' he said.

'Why?'

'Do you think it's possible that he came into a large sum of money in 1996?'

'If he did, there is no sign of it. He rented his apartment in Emdrup. His car was a wreck, he didn't even own a television.'

'But he was a former bank manager.'

'Doesn't necessarily make you wealthy.'

'But you'd expect him to have a bit of money set aside, wouldn't you?'

'Not a man with his gambling habit.'

'Oh?'

'Bankrupted himself and his family. Hence no love lost between him and his children.'

182

'Did he have a pension?'

Lotte shook her head. 'He lived off his state pension, which means extremely frugally.'

Henrik knew from his father what that meant. 'But you can't rule out that he came into a lot of money about twenty-five years ago?'

'Henrik, where are you going with all this?'

'I want you to check it out. Surely you can do that for me? Go through his bank records, ask around, let me know what you find?'

Lotte stared at him. 'Have you not heard?'

'Heard what?'

'We've arrested Vagn's neighbour. Guy with previous for GBH. Found his prints on the spade.'

43

Jensen felt the years peel away as the white walls and thatched roof of her mother's cottage slid into view among the leaning, weather-beaten trees. It was as if, with every mile, she had travelled back to her youth.

She had been fifteen when her mother had uprooted the two of them from Copenhagen and bought the cottage in the North Jutland dune plantation, miles from anywhere. 'I like the light, and the peace and quiet,' her mother had said, though Jensen knew it had more to do with the latest man who had made the mistake of falling for her.

It wasn't that her mother didn't love the man back. It was that she loved everyone. Jensen no longer remembered the man's face, only his desperate voice as he begged to be let in to their flat in Nørrebro.

For one whole year, Jensen had struggled through the tenth grade at the local North Jutland school, cycling to and from the cottage in gale-force winds when she wasn't able to persuade her mother to drive her or – more likely – their car had broken down again. She had the wrong accent, the wrong clothes and the wrong face for the local kids and didn't play handball which they all seemed to be into.

That summer she had landed a job with a local newspaper and informed her mother that she wasn't going to high school in Aalborg after all but would be moving into a rented room in the city, saving her from travelling back and forth every day. 'Sure,' her mother had said, as though Jensen had told her that she wouldn't be home for supper.

She got out of the car and breathed in deeply. The air smelled of pine trees and wet sand. You couldn't see the ocean, but you could hear it, like a prolonged exhalation in the dark.

'Isn't it lovely? All this space,' her mother had said on the hot summer's day when they had first arrived ahead of the removals van with their furniture from Copenhagen.

At first, exchanging a cramped and dark inner-city flat for an idyllic cottage on its own plot of land had seemed like a dream. They would cycle to the beach every day to swim, get fish off the boats in the local village, or buy ice creams and eat them sitting with their legs dangling from a bench overlooking the sea. But the reality of living five hours' drive away from her friends had dawned on Jensen all too soon. The house had been a wreck, still was, despite the conveyor belt of men, and some women, who had loved her mother over the years, throwing themselves (enthusiastically, at first) into fixing it. Jensen had never understood where her mother met all those people: the bearded, bespectacled poets and artists and musicians who were always there whenever she visited during the holidays. Cooking complicated vegetarian meals, playing the guitar outside in the lyme grass and making earnest, but ultimately doomed, attempts at mending the loo which kept blocking. She had given up a long time ago on getting to know her mother's passing lovers. They had all left eventually, tired of the broken house, or of her mother, or both, and through it all her mother had been oblivious, spending most days painting in her studio, huge canvases of the ever-changing North Jutland skies. People attached themselves to her, but she attached herself to no one, perhaps conscious that it would only be temporary anyway.

Occasionally, she would sell a painting and for a while there would be more money but, to her cost, she didn't care about seeing her art on the walls of people's homes or, God forbid, an art gallery. It was the process of creating something out of nothing that mattered to her.

Jensen approached the old front door, which had been painted dark green by a famous Danish author one hot summer. The house looked cosy from the outside, with golden light in the low-slung leaded windows, but Jensen knew this was an illusion. She let herself in; the door was never locked. 'No need around here,' her mother always said. Nothing to steal, Jensen supposed, setting down her overnight bag. The only thing of any value in the house was her mother's art, the paintings stacked six-deep in her studio.

'Hello?' she shouted. The low-ceilinged rooms were cold. The fire hadn't been lit. 'Marion?'

Her mother didn't like to be called 'Mother' or 'Mum' or 'Mummy', as she had made clear to Jensen when she had grown old enough to understand.

During her fifteen years in London, Marion hadn't visited once, though Jensen had offered to pay for her ticket and put her up in a hotel. She rarely left the cottage, let alone North Jutland.

Jensen could smell the turpentine from the studio. She walked through to the back of the house where an ardent lover from Norway had once knocked through the wall and erected a ramshackle conservatory, which during the day was flooded with light. Her mother greeted her from behind the easel which was rigged up with a huge canvas. 'Is that you darling?'

Jensen went up to her mother and smiled, knowing better than to attempt bodily contact.

'Good to see you,' Marion said. She kept painting, a bright splash of orange across a grey landscape. Sometimes she would

186

take her canvases down to the sea and paint there. 'What do I call you these days?'

Jensen laughed. 'We've been through this. Everyone just calls me Jensen now.'

'I don't understand. When you have such a beautiful name.'

'It's a ridiculous name, as you would have known if you'd sat through school with it.'

'I can't call you Jensen.'

'Then call me nothing. Call me *you*.'

'All right *you*,' said her mother smiling.

Jensen had waited impatiently through her teenage years to be allowed to change her name by deed poll at eighteen, but when she had got to it, she was already writing under the by-line of Jensen and no first name had seemed quite right.

'Have you eaten? Not sure I've got much in,' said Marion.

'I'll cook us something,' said Jensen.

Marion never had anything in and could go for days without food. Knowing this, Jensen had foraged for dinner on her way from Aarhus.

'How long are you staying for?' said Marion.

'There's this guy I am seeing tomorrow afternoon, on the air base at Aalborg. Might head straight back afterwards.'

Marion nodded, keeping her eyes on the canvas. Her lovers were fewer and further between these days, but she never appeared lonely, never nagged Jensen to visit or stay longer. Never invited her, but never turned her away. In her early sixties, she was still a beautiful woman, taller than Jensen, slender, with long white hair and a year-round tan. Her eyes were dark blue and intense, like Jensen's own. Her denim dungarees were splattered with paint as was the scarf she had used to tie back her hair. She never seemed to sense the draught that crept into every corner of the house. 'Just need to fix this,' she said, and Jensen reflected as she always did on her mother's total lack of curiosity in her life.

Her bedroom was to one side of the house. It felt cold and damp. She plugged in the electric heater she had once brought with her to the house, adamant she wasn't going to spend another night frozen half to death. She sat on the bed in her coat as the room slowly warmed and checked her phone. There was no broadband, and no mobile reception except for a small hill 500 metres from the house, but she saw that she had received two text messages on the journey.

The first was from Gustav. *When are you coming back?*

The next message was from Kristoffer. *You're avoiding me.*

44

Henrik left his car by the emergency vehicles and ran through
Dyrehaven, nodding at a couple of uniforms he recognised. It
was pissing down as usual, and his boots, which he had cleaned
painstakingly that morning in the loos at work, were soon
covered in mud up to the ankles again. Jonas Møller, another
detective inspector, was already on the scene. Henrik knew he
shouldn't be there; he had no business meddling in another DI's
case, but he had to ask. Just one question. Was that too much?

He had been to the deer park north of Copenhagen a few
times with his family, walking as far as the Hermitage hunting
castle on the plain, looking all the way down to the narrow blue
strip of Øresund. Sometimes, they had been to Bakken, the old
amusement park in the woods.

Today, however, the park with its tall red entry gates felt dark
and sinister as he ran further in between the trees. Ulla Olsen's
terrified scream was still ringing in his ears. Had the unknown
girl in the photo attacked her? Or was he going mad? He had
spent all night and most of the morning brooding. Was he
wrong and everyone else right?

189

Mark and Lisbeth, despite turning every stone, had found nothing yet to link Irene Valborg, Vagn Holdved and Ulla Olsen, except for their advanced ages.

There was one glimmer of hope. Forensics had been unable to account for a few blonde hairs found at Irene's house. Her gardener, Troels, had been interviewed and discounted as a suspect, and the hair wasn't Minna's or Regitse's. But if there was no DNA match on the database, they would be none the wiser. As always, they were in the uncomfortable position of having to wait for something, anything, to turn up.

The runner, a woman in her fifties, had been found by a dog-walker on one of the deer park's lesser-trodden paths. Albeit considerably younger than the others, she was the fourth mysterious attack in a few weeks, which was enough to make Henrik interested.

The area between the trees had been cordoned off. He was stopped by a uniformed officer. He flashed his badge and insisted he needed to speak to Jonas urgently. Eventually, the officer lifted the tape and let him through.

Henrik couldn't see Jonas anywhere but jogged over to one of the younger detectives, a tall redhead who greeted him with a frown. 'Jungersen, what are you doing here?'

'What happened?' he said, sensing her reluctance to answer. 'Come on, you know who I am. This is in connection with another case.'

The redhead sighed deeply before she spoke. 'Sexual assault, attempted strangulation, still alive. Look, I've got to go. I don't know any more. Talk to the boss,' she said.

Henrik spotted the tall, thin figure of Jonas in among the trees. He was wearing a red cagoule and holding an umbrella, talking to one of the scene-of-crime officers.

'Hey Jonas,' he shouted, running towards the two of them.

It annoyed him that Jonas was already looking at him warily. He suspected everyone on the force was talking about him.

No matter. He had to know. 'Did you find a photograph?' He pulled the school picture of the girl out of his pocket and shoved it under Jonas's nose. 'Of this girl?'

'What are you talking about?' said Jonas.

'Just answer the fucking question,' said Henrik. 'Have you or have you not found a photo?'

The officer in the white moon suit began to walk off. 'What about you?' Henrik shouted after him. 'Someone must be able to tell me.'

'Henrik,' said Jonas. 'For fuck's sake. This is a crime scene. We're right in the middle of it.'

People around them had stopped what they were doing and were staring at the two of them. Henrik felt something inside himself go. Perhaps it was his lack of sleep. Or his wife's refusal to answer his messages. Or just feeling utterly lost. He grabbed Jonas by his cagoule and pushed him up against the trunk of an oak tree, shouting at him: 'Did you or did you not find a photograph?'

'No,' shouted Jonas, 'We did not. Now leave, or I will have you arrested.' He pushed Henrik away with a surprising amount of force. Henrik slipped and landed on his backside in the mud.

One of the uniformed officers laughed. Jonas shook his head at Henrik and backed away with a pitying expression on his face. 'You fucking loser.'

45

Though he wasn't wearing military garb, which for some reason she had expected, Jensen immediately recognised Claes Skov when he walked into the Aalborg coffee shop. Not just because of his above-average height and penetrating gaze, both traits he shared with his sister, but because of the way he carried himself as if he had a broom handle stuck down the back of his trousers. In his early fifties, Gustav's father had short-cropped grey hair and was dressed as if about to go for a long walk, in jeans, walking boots and a waterproof jacket. Except for his chin, which hinted at a familial stubbornness, there was no likeness at all to Gustav and Jensen decided that the boy must take after his mother.

'Claes,' he said, almost crushing her hand.

'Jensen.' She had chosen the café because she remembered it from her time as a reporter. A little bit of Paris in North Jutland, with tables and chairs outside on the pavement. The interior was decorated with chandeliers and a wooden bar sparkling with glasses and bottles lined up against a mirror wall. Claes looked uncomfortable among the students scattered about the round bar tables, their faces flushed with candlelight and beer.

'Margrethe told me to talk to you. She says you want to help Gustav.'

'I do,' said Jensen. 'I like him.'

'I should really be thanking you,' Claes continued. 'For taking him under your wing.'

'He'd make a great reporter.'

Claes frowned, glugging sparkling water straight from the bottle. 'You do realise it's temporary, right? I've already spoken to Margrethe. Gustav's going back to high school. He'll have to start in year one again, but that's the price he'll have to pay.'

The price for what?

Jensen studied Claes's face. No real trace of warmth, or tenderness for his son. She could see why Gustav didn't get along with him. 'I didn't go to high school,' she said. 'Not everyone has to.'

'I'm not going to watch Gustav throw his life away because of what happened to his mother.'

'What do you mean because of what happened to his mother? I know she died, but—'

'Margrethe hasn't told you? That's when it all started. When my wife's cancer came back, Gustav was distraught. Frankly, he became impossible to deal with. I was in Iraq with the NATO mission at the time. Came home straightaway when I heard she was dying, but he refused to speak to me.'

Jensen remembered Gustav telling her how his mother had first been diagnosed with breast cancer when he was nine, only for it to return aggressively and take her life when he was sixteen. He had been blasé about it, stopping dead any attempt at conversation.

'Me and Gustav's mother were separated then, had been for a couple of years. I thought that was it at first, that he had to get used to me, and my way of doing things.'

'Which is . . .'

'I like things straight. Gustav was messy. He'd been allowed

193

to get away with it for too long. I tried to impose a bit of structure on his life.'

Jensen could well imagine that Gustav wouldn't have been
too keen on that.

'Anyway, he was leaving his senior school the summer after
his mother died, and I thought it would be a fresh start for the
two of us, in Aalborg. I got stationed at the air base, got Gustav
a place at a local high school, nice house, plenty of space, big
garden.'

Something in his voice told Jensen this hadn't been the happy
new beginning he had hoped for.

'Gustav began school last August. He didn't say much. I was
at work a lot of the time, but things appeared to be going OK.'

'What happened?'

'That's just it. Nothing did. Everything was normal, well as
normal as it can be with a grumpy sixteen-year-old boy.'

Surely, you were sixteen once yourself, thought Jensen.

'It was a couple of weeks before Christmas. Totally out of
the blue. The psychologist said grief can manifest itself in many
ways, including acts of violence. It's a kind of PTSD they said.
I should know. I've seen that sort of thing often enough in the
military.'

Jensen remembered Gustav telling her that listening to music
in his headphones helped keep him calm.

'There was a party at the high school. Some sort of play or
performance at the start of the evening.'

'What did Gustav do?'

'Margrethe really hasn't told you? He drugged two boys,
second-years, spiked their drinks, then ...' Claes lowered his
voice. 'He used a permanent marker to draw swastikas on their
faces, stripped them naked and left them seated on the stage.
When the curtain was pulled back, there they were, unconscious
and humiliated in front of the whole crowd. People thought it
was part of the play at first. They laughed and clapped. Some

194

people filmed it, posted it on social media . . . until one of the boys woke up and vomited all over himself. Gustav is very lucky they didn't press charges. The police were called, of course, but amazingly he ended up getting away with a caution thanks to his diagnosis of severe stress. The school threw him out though.'

Jensen thought of the thin, grubby, mouthy teenager she knew. How he had zipped ahead of her on his e-scooter in the rain. His cheeky grin and annoying habit of turning up where he wasn't invited. Could this be the same boy who had pulled a stunt so indescribably awful? Surely, there must have been some mistake.

'Why did he do it?'

'Same as any other bully. Push others down to stay above water yourself. Substitute your own powerlessness for the power you can wield over others. It was all in the psychologist's report.'

'But there must have been some point he was trying to make.'

'Search me.'

'You never asked?'

'Of course I did, but Gustav still refuses to talk me, and, to be honest, I'm not sure I want to know the sordid reasons. I am ashamed. Gustav is my son, my only child. I had such high hopes for him.'

Jensen was struggling to make sense of what she was hearing. It couldn't be right.

Not this.

Not Gustav.

Claes smiled bitterly. 'And you're sure you still want to help him?'

46

Henrik hadn't bothered going back to the office after his confrontation with Jonas Møller at the deer park. No point. His twelve missed calls from Jens Wiese told him all he needed to know.

Game over, Jungersen.

For a while, he had driven aimlessly around Copenhagen, stopping at one point at a car park near Øresund to try and sleep, but sleep had not come.

Towards the evening, he had found himself on the motorway heading south out of the city as if drawn there by a powerful magnet. He had known all day that he wouldn't be able to resist. Halfway up the slip road to the Brøndby exit he had pulled his car over in the emergency lane and got out.

He had walked further into the undergrowth, ignoring the wet that crept up and soaked his trouser legs. The path was still there, leading to the bald patch under the trees where they had found Trine Andresen's torso.

Nothing to see here now. Nothing but the withered stem of the rose he had tied to a tree when he had last visited the site.

He always went on the anniversary of her killing, more often if he could manage it.

Wojciech Kaminski, a Polish plumber, had been on his way from one job to the next when the litre of Diet Coke he had consumed in his van had made its presence felt. Having staggered into the bushes where Henrik was now standing, and unzipped his jeans to take a leak, he had looked down to find himself urinating on human remains.

It had taken Henrik and his team almost four weeks, digging in mud up to their shins, to locate the rest of the bones, and eventually the remains of the head, which was thought to have been carried away by a fox. The fingers and toes were gone, ingested by animals.

Henrik had always thought of those weeks, almost twenty years ago, as a metaphor for police work: thankless, painstaking and invariably unpleasant attempts at reconstructing the past from a million fragments, made by unsung heroes in the kind of dogged and unglamorous pursuit of the truth that no one wrote about in the newspapers. 'It's public service, lad. If you want reward, go join a bank,' he recalled one of the instructors at police school telling him an eternity ago.

Trine Andresen, a student hairdresser, had been identified from her dental records and her boyfriend, who had been out on parole at the time for beating up a man with a baseball bat, had been convicted of her murder.

Though far from a failure, as investigations went, it had felt like it to Henrik when he had brought her parents the news. The boyfriend had been known to the system. Three times when she was fifteen, Trine had reported him for beating and threatening her, each time ending up withdrawing her statement. When, finally, he had been locked away, she had decided to go to college. It had been a fresh start and, according to her friends, she had loved every minute. Only to get cornered and stabbed by the man she thought herself protected from.

197

A man who had gone on to dump her by the side of the road like garbage.

The boyfriend was still in prison, but for Trine, Irene Valborg and the countless other bodies Henrik had recovered in his time with the police, it was too late for justice. Sometimes, all he could see when he drove around Copenhagen was dead people. The woods, houses and waterways from which they had been carried away in body bags could never again be just places, they were graves.

He doubted anyone would have been here to remember Trine since it happened. Her parents had both died. It was as though she had never existed. As the cars droned past on the motorway, oblivious, Henrik sank to his knees, buried his head in his hands and wept.

47

Sunday 19:39

Marion asked no questions when Jensen walked back into her studio in the dunes, weary and exhausted after seeing Gustav's father. She merely glanced up from her easel and smiled distractedly as if Jensen were still sixteen and living upstairs in her teenage bedroom with the dreamcatcher dangling from a nail in the ceiling. There were times when this lack of curiosity was just what you needed, thought Jensen. Mostly, though, it was hopelessly impractical. More than anyone Jensen knew, Marion lived for the moment, uninterested in what had come before or was going to happen next. Recently, she had sold her car to buy canvases and paint, which meant she now had to cycle miles across the flat countryside for food. From the way her clothes were hanging off her, Jensen reckoned she only did so when she was starving.

In past years, things would have worked themselves out somehow. Friends with wheels would have come to stay for a while. Someone would have paid above the odds for a painting. Once Marion had decided that she could live without money altogether. She had gathered firewood in the woods around the house, picked mushrooms and berries, persuaded the fishermen to give her the fish they couldn't sell. It had gone well until winter had set in and Marion had gone down with pneumonia. A Swedish admirer, a nurse not much older than Jensen, had moved in for a few months, coaxing Marion back to strength with her love and savings.

Where were they now, all these people who had travelled past the white cottage with the thatched roof? Whose clothes had dried in the wind on the rack beside the house? Who had left books and photos and strange spices and ingredients crowding the shelves in the kitchen?

'Hello *you*,' said Marion.

Jensen held up the shopping bags from the Coop in Fjerritslev where she had stopped off on the way back. 'Spaghetti OK?'

'Lovely,' said Marion.

She was still working on the sunset, though she had now tempered the bright orange with red.

'Maybe tomorrow we can go for a walk,' said Jensen. 'I changed my mind, I'm going to be staying for a while.'

'Mm . . .'

Jensen made a fire in the woodburning stove, blowing on the flames until they caught on the wood. As the room grew warm, she cleared away the detritus that littered the surfaces: ceramic cups with dried-up tea bags, unopened bills, cans of tuna with their attendant forks, glasses with sticky finger marks, a Jesus sandal, old letters, notebooks, broken necklaces, tubes of hand cream, keys to doors in forgotten houses.

That was the thing with Marion. You wanted to take care of her, put her to rights. Besides, Jensen hadn't felt like driving back to Copenhagen after the conversation with Claes Skov. Had Margrethe known all along what Gustav had done, and still defended him? Or had she not asked because she was afraid of the truth? Both seemed implausible.

Jensen would have to go and talk to the head of the high

school in Aalborg, do some more digging. There was nothing about the incident online. The school must have wanted it to go away as fast as possible.

Claes and Margrethe had decided between them that Gustav's next school would be in Copenhagen where he would feel more at home. A great plan, except now Gustav didn't want to, because he had seen a way out, working with Jensen and becoming a journalist. 'If you care about him, you tell him to give up on that stupid idea and come to his senses,' Claes had said.

I do care, she told herself.

Gustav was lazy as hell and knew almost nothing (the latter not unrelated to the former) but there was a canniness about him, an eye for the story that had impressed her on more than one occasion. He had texted her to say that Carsten's USB contained nothing but 'invoices and spreadsheets that make no sense'.

Keep looking, she had texted back.

It took her over an hour to get Marion's kitchen tidy and clean enough to be able to put the food away. Then she tackled the dining table, shoving aside papers, and stacking dirty plates in the sink to soak off lentils and streaks of jam made from wild roses picked along the gravel track that led to the cottage.

There were a couple of final reminders, still in their envelopes. A letter dated two months ago reprimanded Marion for not attending a mammogram appointment at the hospital in Thisted. 'Fuck's sake,' said Jensen under her breath. 'What am I going to do with you?'

But she knew deep down that it was herself she was staying behind for, and not her mother, who was oblivious to any kind of sacrifice made for her benefit and would not be thanking her when the visit was over. She dropped the letter from the hospital on the pile with the others and opened the door to what had once been a garden but was now overrun with brambles and gorse bushes.

It was dark and dank and windy outside. She couldn't see the path through the undergrowth, but her feet soon found it, walking as if by their own accord through the lyme-grass-covered sand dunes towards the pebbly beach and the roaring North Sea beyond it. These days it was as close as she was ever going to get to home.

48

Sunday 20:12

Henrik's black jeans were still damp and stained with mud when he parked outside the big yellow house in Frederiksberg from which he had been banned by his own incomprehensible stupidity. Without work, without his home, what would become of him?

All the windows were lit. His wife and three children would be in there now having supper cooked by his wife. Or perhaps they had already eaten and were watching something on TV together.

He lowered the driver's seat and lay down in his leather jacket. His boots were filthy. The car was strewn with takeaway litter. There was a stack of Baresso paper cups in one cupholder, an empty can of Coke Zero in the other.

Was there such a thing as being too tired to sleep? Could you get over the other side of tiredness, to the point where you no longer knew how to close your eyes and drift off? His body felt wired, jittery, tense. There was a deep ache in his thighbones, rock-hard knots in his shoulders. He hadn't been to the gym for God knew how long. Couldn't find the energy for it.

Of course, he had made a complete arse of himself in Dyrehaven. The victim, a schoolteacher, had been interviewed and a pupil at the high school where she taught had been arrested.

Nothing to do with Irene or Vagn or Ulla.

Whatsoever.

Oh God.

The face of the unidentified teenage girl in her swimming costume was staring up at him from multiple fragments scattered in the passenger footwell. He had torn the photo to pieces in a fit of anger. What had he been thinking? There was no link between the three cases. None whatsoever. Vagn had been killed by his neighbour. Irene had paid with her miserable little life when a burglar who had turned up to steal her diamond necklace to order had found her safe empty. And Ulla Olsen had been attacked by a fellow resident at her care home.

End of.

Stop, Jungersen, stop.

Someone else would be closing the cases now. Let them.

A white estate car Henrik didn't recognise turned into the street, the driver slowing in front of the big yellow house with his wife's black Audi parked in the car port. Henrik sat up. Who was this?

A man got out of the car and jogged up the steps to the front door. There was a flowerpot there where his wife would put out Danish flags whenever it was someone's birthday. The man had a bottle of red wine in one hand.

Henrik froze.

It was Bo Petersen, a teacher from the high school where his wife was head mistress. Once, after a couple of remarks by his wife, Henrik had suspected that something was going on between the two of them. He had waited outside the school, staring meaningfully at the man as he emerged at the end of the day. That had been the end of Bo Petersen.

Or so he had always thought.

He ducked as his wife opened the door, watching in disbelief as she leaned up on her toes and kissed the man on his cheek in the light spilling from the hallway.

The way she used to lean up and kiss *him*.

The way she had kissed *him* the first time, with his back against the wooden gymnastics rack in their old school sports hall. She had been the prettiest girl in the year with her big brown eyes and long dark hair. Several inches shorter than him in her trainers. And she had chosen him when she could have had anyone.

The front door closed, leaving the steps in darkness. Henrik felt the inside of the car begin to spin, volcanic heat building up in him, dangerous and unstoppable. Out of the corner of his eye, he saw the neighbour walking her little white dog, but he didn't care as he tore open the car door and leaped across the street. Then he was standing in front of the house, all at once with his hand on the doorbell, his fingers opening the letterbox, his knuckles rapping the door.

Someone was shouting.

It was him. 'Open up. I know you're in there. OPEN UP, FOR FUCK'S SAKE!'

His wife in the doorway.

Frightened.

'Henrik, what are you ...'

He pushed past her, into the house, still shouting, words that didn't make any sense. Up, up, up the stairs to the kitchen.

Bo's voice.

Women's voices.

He looked around the kitchen island at them all. Their pale oval faces turned towards him. All the teachers from his wife's school, sipping wine, eating from paper plates. The annual supper party. He had been there many times, usually excusing himself politely after a few minutes to watch TV in the other room.

205

'Oh,' he said. 'I thought . . .'

'Henrik,' said his wife, who had appeared wide-eyed behind him. Her voice was small, gentle, like someone talking to an idiot. 'Henrik, you have to leave now.'

He turned to go, confused, mumbling to himself. At that moment he saw a sight that he knew at once was going to stay with him for ever. His youngest son, slight, vulnerable and blond, stood in the doorway. The spitting image of him, the apple of his eye, his one, simple, true, unconditional love.

And the look in the boy's eye was not fear, or anger or even amusement. It was loathing.

April

49

Saturday 08:47

Jensen pulled the duvet over her head to block out the sound of the doorbell. If this was Kristoffer Bro, it was bordering on harassment. He had been texting her regularly while she had been away. Was it so difficult to understand that she wasn't interested?

Her unwanted visitor kept hitting the doorbell, a pause of five seconds between each furious burst. 'Go away,' she shouted.

Finally, she pushed her duvet aside and got up, sweeping hair out of her eyes and squinting. To her surprise, the sky in the Velux rectangle was a deep dark blue, the floorboards bright and warm with sunlight. She could hear children laughing in the courtyard.

'Coming for Christ's sake,' she shouted, stubbing her toe on her open suitcase. She hadn't unpacked yet after the long drive back from North Jutland, having finally run out of patience with Marion. She had taken her to the hospital for her mammogram (all clear). She had scrubbed the cottage clean, fixed a leaking tap, filled the cupboards with tins and the woodshed with enough firewood for an arctic winter, realising by the end of it that her visit had served its purpose as a break from her own life in Copenhagen. Marion had remained her usual indifferent

209

self. Jensen reckoned that, when her time came, they would find her skeleton slumped over the easel, a paintbrush welded to the bones of her right hand.

'What?' she shouted into the entry phone.

Gustav's voice. 'Jesus, I thought you were dead.'

'Then why did you keep buzzing?'

'Let me in. I've got something you'll want to see.'

Jensen doubted that, but her curiosity got the better of her. Like Kristoffer, Gustav had texted and phoned her dozens of times, as he reminded her as soon as she opened her front door. 'You just vanished off the face of the earth.'

It was true that she had been avoiding him. She didn't know what to say to him, how to broach the issue of what had happened in Aalborg. Everything else they might talk about seemed less important.

'Told you I was going away.'

'For a few days. It's been three weeks. What were you doing anyway?'

'Visiting my mother,' she said.

And discovering your little secret.

She still couldn't believe that a skinny rake like Gustav with his soft, boy's hands was capable of inflicting hurt on others, but his former headmaster in Aalborg had as good as confirmed it. At first, he had refused to see her, until she had mentioned that she was working on a big article on bullying and intended to make a case study out of his school. 'I already know from Gustav's father *what* happened,' she had told him. 'Now I want to know *why*.'

In person, Ole Loft, a bald man in his fifties with worn features, had seemed genuinely regretful about what had occurred on his watch. 'You will find such ... incidents at any high school, but I can assure you that we operate with absolute zero tolerance, which is also why the pupil concerned was expelled immediately.'

210

'You mean Gustav Skov?'

Loft looked at her as if she had said a dirty word. 'I can't sit here and discuss individual pupils with journalists.'

'OK, tell me about the victims then, the two boys.'

'That's confidential also. Safeguarding reasons. Come on, you know this . . . err . . .' He studied her business card intently, looking for a first name that wasn't there.

'Jensen,' she said. 'I'll just have to ask around among your pupils then.'

'Please don't,' said Loft, forming a steeple with his hands and touching his lips. 'The matter's been dealt with. It won't serve any purpose to drag it all up again in the press.'

'Dealt with by sweeping it under the carpet, you mean?'

'What I *can* tell you is that what happened came completely out of the blue. There had been no indication whatsoever that something like that—'

'Nice couple of boys, are they?'

'I can't—'

'Discuss it? Safeguarding, I know,' Jensen said. 'All the same, it must have been tough for Gustav, coming from Copenhagen, coping with the loss of his mother while trying to fit in with a new crowd?'

Loft glared silently at Jensen with a look that said: 'Nice try, lady.' He was hiding deftly behind his rules and regulations, but Jensen could tell that the matter pained him.

On the way out of the building, she had managed to hand out her business card to a few of the kids before Loft had intervened and asked her to leave.

'Gustav, what do you want?' she said now.

'You know that favour your boyfriend asked for?' Gustav said, bright-eyed and far too awake for a teenage boy this early in the day. He even looked as if he had showered and washed his hair.

'For the hundredth time, he is not my boyfriend, and you said it was a secret.'

211

'He told me it was, but now he's nowhere to be found. I did exactly as he asked, but he's not answering his mobile. I phoned his office, but they said he is off.'

'What do you mean "off"?'

Aside from his summer holidays, which he spent in the same resort in Italy every year, like something tiresome that had to be got through, Henrik was never off work. He didn't like breaks in his routine. He was the only man Jensen knew who liked Mondays.

'Dunno. That's all his office would tell me.'

Gustav used her hesitation to step over the threshold and sit down on the sofa. He pulled his laptop out of his rucksack and flicked it open. 'There is something else too,' he said, plugging in a USB drive. Jensen recognised the memory stick with the Carlsberg logo that Carsten Vangede had sent her.

'I managed to open Vangede's secret folder,' he said.

'What secret folder?'

'The one I texted you about?'

'You said the drive was full of spreadsheets and invoices.'

'That's true but not only that. There was a folder. I missed it at first but then I noticed it had some extra encryption on it, which I thought was strange, so I went to see our friend Fie. Remember her?'

Jensen did. The schoolgirl hacker from Roskilde had helped her and Gustav crack the Magstræde case. If Fie couldn't open an encrypted file, no one could.

'And?'

'It's very odd. Come and see.'

Jensen gave in, taking a seat on the sofa next to Gustav. They both looked at the screen. A blank page. Except for an address north of Copenhagen.

'What's that supposed to mean?' said Jensen.

'I thought you might know.'

'Well, did you look it up?'

Gustav typed quickly into his browser and brought up a street-view image of a tall laurel hedge. He scrolled and the two of them were looking at a black gate. There was also an aerial view of the plot, showing a white mansion with shiny black roof tiles, a swimming pool, outbuildings and a park-sized lawn sloping down to Øresund, with a small motorboat moored at a private jetty.

'Why encrypt *that*?' said Gustav.

Jensen thought of Vangede's letter.

In case something happens to me.

'He must have been interested in whoever owns the property.'

'Speaking of which,' said Gustav, 'I haven't been able to find out who that is. What do you think it means?'

'I don't know,' she said. 'But until we find out, I'd better put that USB stick somewhere safe.'

She held out her hand. Gustav removed the stick from his laptop and placed it in her palm. Despite the sun falling through the kitchen window and painting warm squares on the floorboards, Jensen felt cold. As she climbed the spiral staircase to hide the stick in her underwear drawer, she thought of what Gustav had done. Her mind kept flashing up an image of a naked schoolboy, vomiting on stage at the high-school show, naked, with swastikas inked on his cheeks.

Why swastikas? Why naked?

None of the high-school kids in Aalborg had called her back. The headmaster must have confiscated her business cards moments after she had left. She would have to go back, spend some time hanging around outside the school, but there was a reluctance in her. What if Gustav wasn't who she thought he was? 'What was it Henrik wanted you to help him with?' she said, descending to the lounge.

'I suppose I might as well tell you, seeing as he has gone AWOL,' he said, pulling up a picture on his phone and handing it to her. The picture was faded and looked like it had been taken a good few years ago. It was a school photo of a young girl, smiling at the camera against a toned blue background. Were school photographs still a thing?

'Who is it?' said Jensen.

'That's what Henrik wanted to know, so I put it on Instagram,' said Gustav.

'Why couldn't Henrik do that himself?'

'He wouldn't say, except for some cryptic tripe about the police needing to do things without anyone knowing it's them.'

'And?'

'I heard nothing for ages. No one knew who she was, but then this woman messaged me. Said she showed the picture to her mother who used to be a high-school teacher, and that her mother recognised the girl. What should I do now?'

Jensen shrugged. She looked at the photograph again. The girl was wearing a blue shirt open at the neck. A silver heart nestled in the hollow between her pronounced collar bones. How old would she be now? 'Did you get her name?'

'Karoline Kokkedal. Nothing about her online.'

'Did you go and see the teacher yet?'

'Not sure what I would ask her.'

Could it be something to do with the Irene Valborg murder? Jensen couldn't see what connection there could possibly be between the old woman and the schoolgirl. 'Perhaps she is a witness he needs to speak to urgently about some case.'

'Ah, that might be difficult,' said Gustav.

'Oh, why is that?'

Gustav pointed to the photograph. 'Because this girl is dead.'

50

Henrik woke up when a blade of sunlight found his eyes through the gap in the faded orange curtains in his boyhood room. He turned onto his back in the narrow single bed and opened his eyes slowly, finding the knot in the pine ceiling that had always looked to him like a giant eye watching him reproachfully from above. This was where he had first had sex, aged fifteen, with Betina, the girl next door who had been a year older and a good deal more experienced. It had been an utter disaster, over in seconds, and there had been no repeat performance, though other girls had soon come along.

His eyes felt shrivelled and dry in their sockets. Was it possible that you could cry yourself empty? There was a calm in him, a sense that, from this point on, things could only get better. Downstairs he could hear his father shuffling about, washing the dishes, feeding the cat, coughing. By now, he would have started the coffee machine for the second time, his TV magazine crossword half-finished on the dining table. Soon Henrik would get up and shower on his knees in the mint-green bathtub with the shower attachment fixed to the tap. Then he would join his

215

father and the two of them would drink a cup of coffee together. To his guilty relief, his stepmother, whose Alzheimer's had reached a critical stage, had been taken into respite care for a few days. It was easier when it was just him and his father, though he could tell that the old man felt the absence of a woman in the house.

Henrik had been eighteen when his mother had died suddenly of a brain haemorrhage. His older brother had already left home, and Henrik had been just about to. Almost immediately, his father had met Birthe and proposed to her. He couldn't bear the solitude, didn't know what was up or down without being one half of a couple. Henrik understood now how his father felt. He had been just sixteen when he had got together with his own wife. As far back as he could remember, she had been there: his conscience, his interpreter to the world outside policing, his crutch. She had been surprisingly gentle after he had burst into their home, embarrassing himself in front of her colleagues.

Oh God.

He would do anything to go back and erase that awful moment. If she had refused to have anything to do with him again, he couldn't have blamed her, but the few times they had talked on the phone since, she had been understanding, kind even. If he really meant that he was sorry, and went back to therapy, she would agree to meet face to face.

Henrik had immediately made an appointment with Isabella Grå, the psychologist, whom he had refused to talk to.

Oh God.

His predominant feeling these days was shame. For the way he had come on to Lotte, or shoved Jonas Møller against the tree in Dyrehaven. The fact that his son had witnessed him making an utter tit of himself. He sat up in bed, unable to bear the thought. The sun warmed his back as he looked around the room. His old Brøndby FC posters were still there. The silverware from his brief years as a half-decent football player was gathering dust on the shelf, next to the photo of him wearing his first police uniform, grinning in blissful ignorance of the trials to come. There were no books. Henrik hadn't been into them. 'Some people have it in their heads, some in their legs,' one of his teachers had told him. Only later in life had he understood that not all intelligence could be measured in exam grades.

His mobile buzzed on the bedside table. He felt a jolt of excitement, thinking that it might be his wife or maybe even Oliver. He had work to do to build himself back up in his son's estimation.

He stopped smiling.

It was Jensen.

Need to talk to you urgently. Today.

In the fifteen years they had known each other, there had been an unspoken pact between them. Whenever one needed the other, *really* needed, they would always respond. No matter what. Henrik knew seeing Jensen, even talking to her, would be madness, especially now, but couldn't help feeling a stirring of anxiety on seeing her message. What had she got herself into now? He would stop for five minutes on his way to the gym, hear her out and be on his way, he decided, tapping the briefest of replies.

Address?

51

Henrik was already waiting in his black car when Jensen stepped out of her apartment block. She almost didn't recognise him. He had grown a stubbly beard and lost weight, and what was he wearing? She gestured at him to roll down the car window. 'Are those . . . tracksuit bottoms?' she said.

He avoided her eyes. 'What do you want, Jensen?'

'Not like this, not in the car.'

'The car is what's on offer.'

'It's important. For me?'

He sighed, cursed under his breath and got out with exaggerated slowness, donning his mafia shades. 'You've got fifteen minutes,' he said.

They walked in silence on the cobbles alongside Christianshavn Canal with its wooden boats on their moorings, past the old apartment buildings in shades of red, yellow and blue. The air was clear and sharp, the water a deep, sparkling sapphire.

Henrik was shifty and kept looking around. Years ago, in the heady first days of their affair, he had told her: 'I want to be found

218

out.' The feeling had rapidly reversed, however, and he had spent the subsequent years terrified of them being spotted by anyone even remotely acquainted with him or his wife. Now that there was nothing going on between them, this seemed insulting.

They reached Christianshavn's old ramparts, a grassy elevated path overlooking the water and partly obscured by trees. Jensen pointed to a bench. 'What happened to you?' she said, taking a seat. 'Gustav has been trying to reach you for ages.'

'I'm off sick,' said Henrik, resting his behind on the very edge of the bench, as far from her as possible, hands in the pocket of his hoodie.

'Sick how?'

'Sick and tired.'

'Of?'

'Life. Look, can we fast forward to the reason I am here?'

'OK,' she said. 'You asked Gustav to do you a favour.'

'Oh that.'

'Yes that. He found out who the girl is. Karoline Kokkedal. She is dead. Her Danish teacher from high school recognised her.'

'OK,' said Henrik, shielding his face with one hand as a woman with a long, blonde ponytail ran past pushing a twin buggy.

'OK? That's it, you're not interested?'

'Told you, I am off work. It was just a stupid theory I had. I found the photo of the girl at Irene Valborg's house. She looked very similar to a girl in some photos I had picked up on a couple of other crime scenes, including another murder.'

'Which ones?'

'I can't tell you that, but it's not important anyway. They couldn't have been left there by the killer, not obvious enough. It's either a coincidence or a prank to make me look like an idiot, in which case I'd say it's been almost one hundred percent successful.'

219

'Not funny, is it?'

'Depends who you ask.'

'Still, don't you at least want to know who the girl is?'

'Not particularly, no,' Henrik said, pushing his sunglasses up on his bald head and rubbing his face with both hands as though washing it under a cold tap. It was like the fire inside him had gone out.

For a moment, Jensen toyed with the idea of asking him about Carsten Vangede and the mystery address in Vedbæk but before she could form the words Henrik got up from the bench. 'Your time's up.'

'Wait, when will you be back at work?'

'Maybe never,' he said. 'I feel better out of it, to be honest. There's this psychologist I've been seeing.'

'Really?' said Jensen. 'Please tell me what you've done with the real Henrik.'

He looked at her deadpan until she stopped laughing. 'Good to see you, Jensen. Take care of yourself,' he said, walking away. His usual wide-boy gait was so slow it almost looked hesitant. She decided she didn't like this Henrik.

Not at all.

'Fine,' she shouted after him. 'If you won't talk to the teacher, then Gustav and I will.'

52

'I would like to apologise,' Henrik said to Isabella Grå.

They were sitting in opposing armchairs in the private consulting room she kept in her townhouse in one of the picturesque, treelined streets by the Lakes that were known in Copenhagen as the Potato Rows. Kids were playing outside on their bikes, laughing. He wondered if they were Isabella's. Her partner, if she had one, was probably some sort of artist and utterly devoted to her. He couldn't imagine that either of them would be unfaithful or even raise their voices to one another. The sun-dappled walls of the room were petrol blue, the decor a mixture of teak furniture and modern art. Isabella had scrunched her long grey hair into a bun. Her brown eyes bored searchingly into his. 'For what?' she said, her face betraying no emotions.

'For wasting your time when I saw you that first time. At the office. Being a prick and refusing to talk to you.'

'Not at all. You must have had your reasons.'

'I must have.'

'And what were they, do you think, Henrik?'

221

'Couldn't see the point.'

'But now you can?'

Could he? Really?

Last time he had seen Isabella, it had been on the orders of his boss after he had fired his gun on active duty. This time it was on the orders of his wife.

('You need professional help, Henrik.')

She was right, of course. He was hypocritical, selfish, impulsive, blunt and stubborn as hell, but some of those traits had served him well in his career with the police. The women were another matter: his flirtatious behaviour and occasional steps too far. None of it serious, of course.

Except for Jensen.

His Achilles' heel.

His downfall.

If there was anything he ought to speak to Isabella about, it was Jensen. How she had burrowed into his heart. How he was thinking about her even now, with her infuriating inability to let go once she caught the scent of a story. Was there something about those photos? Yes. Had they been left by the killer or had someone set him up? He didn't know. Was it his problem? No.

The inconvenient fact was that he loved Jensen. Not that he would ever be able to tell anyone that. 'I'd like to give it another try,' he said. 'Properly this time.'

'You've been on sick leave for a few weeks,' said Isabella, consulting her notes. 'I understand there was an incident with a colleague.'

'I was under pressure and lost it. I am not living at home at the moment. My wife and I ... well, we've been having some problems.'

Mild understatement there, Jungersen.

'And how are things now?'

'Better. We are talking again.'

'That's good,' said Isabella. 'Talking is good.' She looked at him for a long time in silence as if expecting more, but he didn't know what else to say. 'And what are your thoughts now, about returning to work?' she said.

'I am not sure I want to. When I think about it . . . it's how my life's gone to hell.'

Unbelievably, he felt the sting of tears again.

Don't start. You know you won't be able to stop.

'What do you mean by "gone to hell"?'

Where to begin? His anger, his cynicism, the impenetrable wall between him and normal people: his father, his wife, even his own children. Where had that come from, if not from policing? 'I don't think it's done my marriage any favours, for a start,' he said.

'Talk to me about that.'

'I haven't been around as much as I should have been.'

('If only you'd been around less!' he heard his wife say.)

'That's interesting. Let's look more closely at why that might be,' said Isabella leaning forward in her chair.

'Come on,' said Henrik. 'The long hours, the unpredictable work patterns. You know the drill.'

'Or you might say the adrenaline, the absorption into something that doesn't require you to confront difficult feelings? Routine can be very seductive in that way.'

Henrik shrugged. 'I suppose.'

Isabella smiled at him and cocked her head to one side. Outside in the street the kids had launched into a song from children's TV that he had heard Oliver listen to from time to time. 'What was growing up like for you?' she said.

'Normal. Mopeds. Football. Girls.'

'And what do you think the child Henrik would think about your life and how it's turned out?'

It was a brilliant question. He could see why Isabella was such a sought-after psychologist. 'He'd love my car,' he said. In fact, his younger self would have been seriously impressed knowing that one day he would be a police detective and live in a big house with a beautiful and clever wife and three kids.

Isabella smiled again. 'What do you think he'd say to you?'

Henrik laughed. 'What the fuck's wrong with you, old man? Stop making things so complicated.'

'He sounds like a happy boy.'

Happy? Henrik supposed he had been. Where he had grown up, it wasn't the sort of question you asked yourself.

'So, when did things get complicated?'

'I don't know exactly.'

Try fifteen years ago when you met Jensen.

Isabella looked at her watch. 'I'd like you to hold that thought,' she said. 'Next time you come and see me, perhaps we can start there?'

Next time? Henrik hadn't considered this. 'How long do you think it will take?'

'How long do I think what will take? What is it you want to happen, Henrik?'

He didn't have to think about it for more than a second. 'I want to go home.'

53

'Thank you for seeing us at such short notice,' said Jensen.

'Mum insisted. I am still not entirely clear what this is about, though,' replied the younger and warier of the two women seated opposite her and Gustav.

That makes two of us, thought Jensen.

'We're trying to learn as much as we can about Karoline,' she said, pointing to the photo on Gustav's mobile phone.

'Why?'

'We don't actually know, only her photo has turned up in connection with a story we've been working on. Call it a loose end.'

'But—'

Agnete Bech-Andersen rested an arthritic hand on her daughter's arm. 'It's OK, Marianne,' she said. 'What harm can it do?'

The retired Danish teacher had warm eyes that seemed to be perpetually smiling. Her flat was very small, but cosy, lined with books, cushions and house plants. No TV, but an upright piano on top of which stood family photos, including one of Marianne with two teenage boys.

'We won't quote you or anything,' said Gustav. 'Don't worry.'

We? You're getting above your station, thought Jensen.

But he was right. Marianne was just anxious to protect her mother and needed to be reassured.

Agnete looked at Gustav with a friendly smile. 'You look a bit young to be a trainee journalist?'

'I—' Gustav began, but Jensen cut him off. 'Oh, he is not an apprentice in that sense. More like work experience. Gustav is still at high school.'

'I could tell,' said Agnete, keeping her gaze on Gustav. 'What are you, seventeen?'

Gustav nodded. 'You're good!' he said, beaming at her.

'I ought to be. I spent my whole career teaching kids your age. Even taught Marianne here once.'

'Oh,' said Jensen, looking at the younger woman. 'Does that mean you were at school with Karoline?'

Marianne shook her head. 'She would have been a few years after my time.'

The atmosphere in the room had lightened after Agnete's little exchange with Gustav. 'I thought no one was going to recognise her,' he said. 'That photo did the rounds on Instagram for ages until Marianne got in touch.'

'Oh, I knew straightaway when Marianne showed me,' said Agnete. 'I remember all of my old pupils. Every single one.'

'Didn't seem to have stopped others from forgetting,' said Gustav. 'What about her family?'

'It was tragic. Six months after Karoline died the father drove his car into the woods in North Zealand and attached a vacuum cleaner hose to his exhaust pipe. The mother, Pia, went abroad. India, I think. The house was sold.'

'Any sisters or brothers?'

'A twin sister. What was it . . .? Ah yes, Rikke. A bit of a tearaway.'

'Were you her teacher too?' said Gustav.

'No, Rikke wasn't high-school material. Pia couldn't cope with her after her husband took his own life, so she ended up in foster care. You know . . .'

'Yes?'

'I often thought that Karoline's suicide was like a hand grenade that split the whole family apart. Like it wasn't one person who died that night, but four. Nothing was ever the same again. For any of them.'

'Still, you'd think someone would remember Karoline,' said Jensen.

Agnete smiled. 'She wasn't what you might call a flamboyant pupil. She was clever enough, but quiet, not many friends. And it's so many years ago now. People forget.'

'Not everyone has as good a memory as my mother,' said Marianne.

'How did Karoline die?' said Jensen.

Agnete's eyes lost their focus. Marianne spoke gently: 'Mum, if this is too much . . .'

'No,' said Agnete, swallowing hard. 'I want to. Karoline took her own life in 1996, in her second year of high school. She threw herself in front of a train. Probably not long after that photograph was taken.'

'Oh no, that's . . .' said Jensen, searching for in vain for the right word. 'What happened?'

'She was out with two of her classmates.'

'Who were they?'

'Susanne Brande and Morten Rastrup.'

'*The* Susanne Brande?' said Gustav.

'Who?' said Jensen.

Marianne looked at her as if she was slow. 'I'd say she is probably one of Denmark's richest women. Her father invented some kind of revolutionary hearing aid,' she said.

'Everyone knows Susanne Brande,' said Gustav.

'And Morten Rastrup?' said Jensen.

227

'He and Susanne were always together,' said Agnete. 'His father was the Danish ambassador in Moscow if I remember correctly. He never attended parents' evening. The mother wasn't around. Morten had his own flat near the school. Anyway, the two of them said that Karoline had been upset because of some boy.'

'Who was the boy?' said Jensen.

'I don't think anybody ever found out who it was,' said Agnete. 'I feel so sorry for Karoline, just when she was supposed to have been out enjoying herself for once.'

'What do you mean?' said Jensen.

'Susanne and Morten had invited her to a party in Copenhagen. It wasn't the sort of thing that usually happened to Karoline. Susanne and Morten were known for bullying people, including Karoline, I believe, so I must say it was a surprise to me that they would have taken her along.'

'A surprise how?'

Gustav laughed cynically. 'Yeah right, the power couple of the school want the quiet girl to come along to a party?'

'Precisely,' said Agnete. 'Still, she'd been excited about it. Her mother told me they'd been shopping for a new shirt the week before. It was the one she was wearing, when . . . when . . .' She stopped, swallowed again. Jensen could see her eyes welling up.

Marianne had noticed too. 'I think that's enough for today,' she said.

'Can I just . . .?' said Jensen. 'Do you know where we might be able to find Pia or Rikke?'

Agnete shook her head. 'I don't know if Pia ever returned to Denmark, and I heard Rikke went to prison, though she could be out now. Anyway, it's all long in the past now and perhaps best left there,' she said, blowing her nose on a tissue handed to her by Marianne.

'Does the name Irene Valborg mean anything to you?' said Jensen.

228

'No,' said Agnete. 'Should it?'

'I don't know. But try to think. Did Karoline ever mention that name? Did you ever hear it at the high school?'

'No, I—'

'I *said* that's enough,' said Marianne in a voice that suggested she wasn't going to argue about it.

'Look at me,' said Agnete. 'It happened a quarter of a century ago and here I am getting all emotional.'

She looked at Gustav, smiling as she wiped away tears. 'You're just a bit older than Karoline was when it happened. What do you think?'

Jensen could tell she had been excellent at her job. It wasn't often that anyone wanted to hear Gustav's opinion.

'I think I wish you'd been *my* teacher,' said Gustav, smiling. Jensen was astonished at the tenderness in his voice. 'And I feel sorry for Karoline, doing something like that, just because of some arsehole boy.'

'Yes, it doesn't seem fair, does it? I wish I had known what she was going through. Then perhaps we wouldn't be sitting here now.'

As they got up, ushered towards the door by Marianne, Jensen stopped in her tracks for a moment. 'The suicide,' she said to Agnete. 'Where did it happen again?'

'Oh, did I not say? It wasn't far from here, at Ordrup S-train station.'

54

Henrik put his mobile phone in his pocket, then changed his mind and put it in the glove compartment. He couldn't risk a message from Jensen flashing up on the screen while he was talking to his wife.

He got out of the car and walked towards the big yellow house. Should he have brought something? Flowers, maybe? No, he decided. To his shame, he couldn't remember when he had last given his wife flowers. If he did so now, she would be suspicious that he was atoning for more than she thought.

She had taken the kids to her parents so the two of them could speak without being disturbed. He supposed he should be grateful for that. Moving back home was all that mattered now. He would be seeing the kids soon enough.

'You're fooling yourself. I know you want to get back on the case,' Jensen had shouted after him that morning, accosting him outside the gym.

'Stop stalking me,' he had barked at her.

'What do you expect when you won't answer my calls?'

Did he want to get back to work? Jensen had discovered

230

that the girl in the photo was a sixteen-year-old who'd thrown herself in front of a train at Ordrup station. She had virtually begged him to dig out the old files on the suicide. Why had Karoline Kokkedal killed herself? And why, three decades later, had her photos turned up on three crime scenes with nothing else to link them?

'You're curious, I can see it on your face,' Jensen had said.

He had pushed past her and attacked his exercise bike with unprecedented vigour. The conversation with Isabella Grå had made everything clear in his mind. If he had to give up policing, so be it. He was going to turn his life around, get fit again, be a normal person. Nothing would be any good, if he wasn't at home where he belonged, with his family.

It felt odd to ring the doorbell at his own house. His wife made him wait. He saw her languid shape through the frosted glass panel, moving without urgency. When she opened the door, her beautiful eyes, the eyes of his children, looked at him piercingly. He tried to kiss her, but she moved her head sideways, and he felt like he had the first time all those years ago: like a clumsy oaf, unworthy of her love. 'I am so sorry,' he said.

'Don't,' she said as they walked through to the kitchen. 'Let's not have one of those conversations where you tell me how sorry you are and promise never to do it again.'

She made coffee, operating the espresso machine, and setting out the cups and the milk with movements that told him that her anger was fading, that she was tired. 'Let me get one thing straight,' she said as they sat on the bar stools by the stone-topped kitchen island whose precise shade of grey she had spent weeks agonising over. '*I* don't need you for anything.'

'I don't think that's true, strictly speaking,' said Henrik, stroking her arm.

She withdrew it instantly, rubbed it, as though she'd been

burned. 'The reason you're here has nothing to do with me. It's Oliver, he's been asking after you.'

'Really?' Henrik felt a wave of relief wash over him. His little boy, his one chance of redemption. Almost immediately, however, the feeling was replaced by disappointment. So this was it, her little rehearsed speech. What had he been expecting? That they would tumble into bed together, swearing undying love?

'I'd do anything to—'

'Save it,' she said, squinting into the blinding spring sunlight flooding through the garden window.

He wondered what was on her mind. Was she thinking about him, Bo Petersen, the teacher from her school whom he had seen at their front door when he had lost his rag completely? He thought of the way she had reached up on her toes for his kiss and something twisted in his stomach. 'I know what you'll say, it's none of my bloody business, and you're right, but are you seeing *him*?'

'Who?' she said.

'You know who I mean. Can I at least ask if there is something going on between you?'

She looked at him as if he had lost his mind. 'No, you can't.' Her headmistress energy was back, the crackle and spark of electricity in her eyes. He pitied the children who fell foul of her temper at the high school.

'I suppose I deserved that,' said Henrik. 'But I'd still like to know.'

'No,' she said, slamming down her coffee cup. 'I am not seeing him. Nor have I ever. It's typical of you to suggest that. A thief assumes everyone steals.'

The words hung between them. She had never asked him directly about Jensen. Perhaps she knew that if she did, she was going to hear something she didn't like, but there were always plenty of hints. She knew Jensen was back in Copenhagen, knew Henrik better than he even knew himself.

'I'm giving up policing,' he said, changing the subject.

She had moaned about his job early in their marriage: the unsociable hours, his irritability when he was working on a case, the way he could never relax, seeing danger at every turn. 'You are what?'

'I am handing in my resignation. Policing has fucked up my life, our marriage, everything,' he said, feeling himself well up again.

He had been wrong. Tears did not come from some reservoir in the body that could be emptied, but from a bottomless well.

'Don't be so bloody stupid,' his wife said.

Henrik looked up, astonished to see that she was angry. 'But I thought you wanted me to?'

'When did I ever say that?'

'Maybe not in so many words, but I think you made it pretty clear.'

'It might have taken me some time to get used to your job, but seriously, Henrik, what do you have in mind? Becoming a house husband? Because I can tell you right now, if you do that, then I *will* divorce you.'

'Plenty of roles in security where my skills would come in useful.'

'What, you'd sit in some office at two in the morning staring at CCTV screens? Come off it, you'd be bored senseless. You're fooling yourself, Henrik.'

His wife and Jensen telling him the same thing.

'I messed up badly. I lashed out at people at work.'

'Then say you're sorry. Do us all a favour and move on, for goodness' sake.'

She got up, snatched their coffees from the counter, though Henrik hadn't touched his, and poured them down the drain, ramming the mugs in the dishwasher. Then she looked at her watch. 'I've got to collect the kids now. You can get your stuff, come back. But it's the spare room for you. Don't go thinking I've gone soft on you, Henrik Jungersen.'

He almost cried out in gratitude.

The room lit up with her smile, so briefly he might have missed it. 'And bloody well get back to work!'

55

Sunday 11:27

Jensen turned her face up into the sunshine as she cycled north-
wards out of the city alongside the flat blue plane of Øresund,
wearing sunglasses for the first time since September. After
the long month of rain, the dry, warm weather was a novelty.
People were walking along the seafront without coats on, pushing prams, playing with dogs, pale-skinned and blinking into
the light. It felt good to be out, losing herself in the crowd. Just
another Copenhagen cyclist no one was paying attention to.

She had woken late after ruminating on the Karoline
Kokkedal story for most of the night and getting nowhere with
it. If Henrik was right and the photos of Karoline had been
planted, then what was the message they had been supposed to
send him? Karoline had jumped in front of the train long before
Henrik had joined the police, so it couldn't be related to any of
his old cases, could it? She had to talk to him, properly, before she
would get anywhere. He must have seen *something* in the photos,
or he wouldn't have asked Gustav to find out who Karoline was.

She had already been to Ordrup. Sunday morning and she
had had the S-train station to herself. From old images she had

found online, she knew that the white station building wouldn't have looked much different on the September evening in 1996 when Karoline had arrived there.

Friday the thirteenth.

Had it felt ominous?

Jensen had walked up and down both sides of the platform and sat for a while on the long wooden bench in the waiting hall with its yellow walls and white globe lampshades suspended from the ceiling.

She had tried to imagine it: the three inebriated teenagers barging through noisily, their voices echoing under the ceiling. At what point had Karoline known what she was going to do? Had her feet been dragging heavily as she walked up the steps to the station, or had she acted on impulse when she saw the train coming?

After a fruitless half-hour of speculation, Jensen had cycled through the leafy neighbourhood with the big villas where Irene Valborg had met her end until she had hit Strandvejen, the coastal road. But instead of going south, back to Copenhagen, she had cycled north. The mysterious address Gustav had found on Carsten Vangede's memory stick was in Vedbæk, just a little further up the coast. It kept playing on her mind.

She passed the granite statue of polar explorer Knud Rasmussen, looking towards Sweden with one hand over his eyes, as if he too was struggling to see in the sharp April sunlight. She remembered going there on a school trip before she and her mother had left Copenhagen. Everyone had eaten their packed lunches sitting on the sandy Bellevue Beach a little further along the road. Except Jensen, who had to make do with an apple donated by one of her teachers as there had been nothing in the fridge at home that morning.

Or any morning.

Jensen increased her speed.

*

When she arrived at the Vedbæk address, she was thirsty and sweaty, promising herself to take the train back to town.

She almost missed the property altogether. Nothing there but the tall, dark-green hedge and black metal gate that she and Gustav had looked at online. There was an intercom to one side of the gate and above it a small sign with the name of the property, Amaliekilde. She walked the length of the hedge, looking for gaps, but found that the greenery concealed a solid metal fence.

Walk on by. Nothing to see here.

What did this address have to do with Vangede?

She returned to the gate and stood for a minute with her bicycle, and looked at the intercom before pressing the button. There was no reply. Behind her, the cars were zooming past on Vedbæk Strandvej, oblivious.

The house had been up for sale a few years ago, though it had been called something different then. According to *Dagbladet* it had been one of Denmark's most expensive properties at the time. The pictures from the estate agent's website showed a palatial lounge with French doors opening onto a lawn that sloped down to the water.

When she had googled Amaliekilde, she had found that it was a natural spring on Bornholm, the Baltic Sea island. Nothing on Amaliekilde in the company register.

As she stood there, waiting for an answer that never came, she began to feel shivery, the sweat running down her back suddenly ice cold. There was a nervousness in her body that she couldn't account for, a feeling that something was happening.

What was it?

She looked up and saw the cameras mounted high up on the fence posts, zooming in, like guns pointed at her head.

56

Sunday 12:26

The suicide at Ordrup station was too far in the past for the files to be accessible digitally, but Bent Sørensen, the on-duty officer at the local police station, had agreed to see Henrik at short notice and with some enthusiasm. 'I must admit to being curious. We don't often have requests for the old paper files. In fact, I can't remember the last time it happened,' said Bent, as he unlocked the door to the basement.

He was a cheerful man of sixty-something years who had told Henrik that he was due to retire in May. Unfortunately, he had not been around in 1996 when Karoline Kokkedal killed herself. 'I was stationed in Helsingør back then. Then about eighteen years ago, I got divorced, wanted to leave town, put it all behind me. You know what it's like,' he said.

No. Henrik didn't know what it was like, nor did he want to find out. Now that he was back in his wife's good books, he swore to himself that he would never come so close again to his world falling apart.

Not for Jensen.

Not for anyone.

After collecting his things at his father's and dropping them off at home, he had phoned Jens Wiese. 'I'd like to make a formal apology to Jonas Møller for the incident in Dyrehaven. It won't happen again,' he had said. 'I'll be returning to work in the morning.'

'Wait a minute now,' Wiese had said. 'Not three weeks ago you had what I think you and I would both call a nervous breakdown.'

'Spot of trouble at home, that's all. I am not a machine.'

'No one is saying that, but—'

'Isabella Grå reckons I am ready to come back,' said Henrik, knowing that if he asked her politely, and behaved himself, she would vouch for his sanity.

'Strictly deskwork,' said Wiese, relenting on the mention of the psychologist, whom he held in high esteem. 'We'll see about you returning to active duty.'

Afterwards, Henrik had then phoned Mark to get the low-down on the three cases. To his immense satisfaction, nothing much had moved in his absence.

'Karoline Kokkedal, eh?' said Bent Sørensen, turning on the strip lighting as he went. The basement corridor under the police station smelled of wet concrete and mildew. 'And what would this be in connection with?' he added when no reply came.

The last thing Henrik needed was some busybody sticking his oar in. 'Just something we need to eliminate from our enquiries. You know what it's like,' he said.

After a few heavy hints, Bent Sørensen finally left Henrik alone with the files, which fitted into a single cardboard box. There was a small table in one corner of the room where he could go through the papers. 'I'll be up in a minute,' he said. 'I'm sure there'll be nothing here, but worth being on the safe side.'

The room was warm. Henrik removed his leather jacket,

folded up the sleeves of his white shirt and switched on the reading lamp. The police report from the incident was brief and to the point. Shortly before 7pm on Friday 13 September 1996, the S-train had been slowing as it prepared to stop at Ordrup. The driver, who was noted to be suffering from severe shock, reported seeing Karoline Kokkedal suddenly detach from a group of people on the platform and land on the tracks in front of his train. He said he had locked eyes with her for a fraction of a second before she disappeared under the train.

Henrik didn't need any further description. He had seen what was left behind on the tracks after a suicide, had been out there himself in the rain, putting a thousand unrecognisable pieces of human flesh and bone into a bag.

Karoline's mother had told the police that Karoline had left home that evening to go to a party with friends from school. She had been happy and excited, nothing to suggest what she was about to do.

The officers who had visited Karoline's parents to deliver the bad news had noted in their report that Karoline's twin sister Rikke had become so distressed that she had required restraint and sedation.

Henrik thought about it. It was a tragic story, no doubt about it, but what did it have to do with Irene Valborg, or Ulla Olsen or Vagn Holdved, for that matter? It made no sense. Except for one thing that niggled away at the back of his mind.

What was it?

Something.

Like his softening body and failing eyesight, his memory was another casualty of his ageing.

He would have to read every single one of the files in the cardboard box. If nothing else, then to rule out any connection to the three cases. He turned off the reading lamp and carried the box upstairs to Bent. 'I need copies of these files.'

'Oh,' said Bent, rubbing his hands together. 'Does that mean you found something?'

'No,' said Henrik. 'It means I didn't, but I won't be able to finish going through everything today.'

'Tell you what,' said Bent. 'If you sign for them, you can take the box away on loan. No one's wanted it for the past thirty years. I dare say no one's going to notice it's gone.'

Like Karoline, thought Henrik.

Though, clearly, someone out there still remembered her.

His phone buzzed.

Jensen.

She was about to be very disappointed.

57

Sunday 13:31

'Don't say "I told you so", but I'm going back to work in the morning.'

'I told you so,' said Jensen, trying to recover from the shock of Henrik answering his phone for once.

She was dying to discuss Karoline with him, find out what he knew. He sounded like his old self: gruff, matter of fact.

She felt the sting of tears, shook her head vigorously to rid herself of the unwelcome sentiment. After Vedbæk, she had taken the train back to town and cycled to Liron's coffee van in Sankt Peders Stræde, still trembling from the feeling of having been watched.

Liron had handed her a cold-brew coffee in a large paper cup, hot with a single teaspoon of sugar. 'Fuck, you look like there's someone after you,' he had said, before a sudden rush of customers had distracted him, and Jensen had slipped away, gratefully sipping her sweet, smooth drink.

Maybe there is, she thought.

She was sitting in a café with her laptop, a few hundred yards from her flat, trying in vain to discover more about the property in Vedbæk. She didn't feel like going home, not yet, though she was on her third pot of tea, and had no appetite for the rye-bread sandwich with chicken going stale on the plate by her side.

Stop being so tense, she thought. *Nothing happened. Nothing will.*

Henrik sounded like he was out walking somewhere. She could hear traffic in the background, a busy road. She had been phoning him repeatedly since she and Gustav had met up with Karoline's teacher, even turned up at his gym, only to be given the brush-off in person. But now something had changed. Henrik sounded bouncy, resolved.

'I have moved back home,' he announced. 'But listen, about Karoline Kokkedal. I retrieved the files, and it's all fairly standard. She jumped in front of a train. The driver didn't stand a chance. There won't have been much for her mother to look at.'

'How can you call that fairly standard? A sixteen-year-old girl dressed up for a party kills herself in front of two classmates?'

'I know,' said Henrik. 'I saw the pictures of the aftermath. Let's just say I don't think it was the fashionable look she had in mind.'

'You're joking about it?' said Jensen.

'Not joking. Trying to get the images out of my mind by way of ironic distancing. It's a police thing, you wouldn't understand.'

Jensen was quiet for a moment. She could hear Henrik getting into his car. 'You know there was a boy, don't you?' she said.

'If you say so.'

'You haven't read the files yet, have you?'

'Enough to know that the coroner delivered a clear verdict of suicide. Cut and dried.' There was a pause before Henrik spoke again. 'I guess we will never know why it happened.'

We will never know.

Those four words. To Jensen they had always been like a red rag to a bull. Karoline's Danish teacher had said that perhaps her death was best left in the past. Jensen disagreed.

243

'Agnete Bech-Andersen, the teacher, told us that Karoline had been bullied. You should speak to her.'

'Right.'

'And did you track down the twin sister yet? Rikke? Agnete said Rikke was in prison, last thing she heard. Would have thought that means even you should be able to find her.'

'Let me do my job, Jensen.'

'There has to be something else to this, you just haven't looked hard enough. A girl commits suicide, and years later, her photo just happens to turn up at three crime scenes?'

'That's the bit I don't understand yet. Like I said, it's possible that someone set me up. Plant a red-herring clue, sit back and watch me fail. None of the photos were discovered straightway. They weren't placed on top of the victims or anything like that. All three were found by me or in my presence.'

'Who'd hate you enough to do something like that, for God's sake?'

'Given how I have behaved over the years, I'd say you've a pretty large pool of people to choose from.'

Jensen wasn't going to argue with that. 'Just do me a favour,' she said, looking out at the canal outside the café window where a man was sailing past in a blue-painted boat, a small brown dog wagging its tail in the stern. 'Read the files. See what else you can find. If nothing else, then just to rule stuff out.'

'Maybe I will,' said Henrik, haughtily. 'But I'll be fairly busy the next few days, so I am not making any promises.'

58

Sunday 21:53

Jensen's front door was ajar, a sliver of her dark flat visible through the gap. 'Hello? Anyone there?'

The door moaned faintly on its hinges as she pushed it. She took a step back onto the landing and looked up and down the centre of the stairwell but couldn't see anyone. The lights went out. A TV in one of the flats was blaring out an evening news programme. There was a smell of fried onions in the air.

After speaking to Henrik, she had headed to *Dagbladet*, slipping up the back stairs and into her old office, taking care not to be seen. Keeping her coat on, she had climbed onto the dormer windowsill where she used to spend hours looking out at the city's red rooftops and promptly fallen asleep.

Now, slowly, cautiously, she entered her flat, flicking on the lights as she went. She climbed the spiral steps to the mezzanine, pulling back the duvet on her unmade bed and looking behind the clothes rail. Had someone broken in? Her laptop and phone were in her bag. There was nothing else of any value to steal.

She went back down to the lounge and stood for a while and looked across the yard to the double-bass player's flat. He

245

was sitting on the sofa, kissing a girl with long hair. Behind them stood his instrument, tall and brooding, like a voyeur in the dark.

There was only one place left in the flat for anyone to hide: the bathroom. Thinking of the uncomfortable minutes she had spent in the dirty bathtub in Gilleleje, Jensen yanked the shower curtain to one side, but the cubicle was empty.

Footsteps outside the bathroom door.

Someone *was* there.

In her flat.

Heart in her throat, she held up her mobile phone and barged out. 'Who are you and what do you want!' she shouted, filming the intruder.

Kristoffer Bro.

With his hands up.

'Don't shoot, please.'

'Shit. You scared me. What are you doing here?' said Jensen.

'Er . . . I own the place?'

'You can't just walk in whenever you want.'

'The door was open. I thought . . . what the hell happened here, Jensen? You look frightened out of your wits.'

'I think someone's been here.'

'How do you mean?'

'I just got home and found my door open.'

'Are you OK?'

'I think so.'

'Was anything taken?'

She shook her head.

Unless.

Oh no.

She ran upstairs quickly. Opening her underwear drawer, she was relieved to see Carsten Vangede's memory stick.

'What is it?' shouted Kristoffer from downstairs.

'Nothing. It's still here.'

'What is?'

'Never mind,' said Jensen.

'You know it's very odd,' said Kristoffer. 'The lock hasn't been forced. Are you sure you didn't just leave it open by mistake when you went out this morning?'

Jensen looked at him through the mezzanine railings. 'No! I mean, when did you last walk out and leave *your* front door open?'

Kristoffer held up his hands. 'You're right. You wouldn't do that. Maybe the burglar was surprised before they could steal that thing you said is still here ... whatever it is.'

'Maybe,' said Jensen.

'Right,' said Kristoffer, taking his phone from the inside chest pocket of his blazer. 'I'm calling the police.'

Jensen descended the stairs. 'No, don't do that.'

'Why not?'

'Because there's nothing they can do.'

They wouldn't even be sending a patrol car around. No immediate threat, no hurry, nothing taken. And God forbid Henrik should find out. The last thing she needed was him overreacting. 'There are only a few people in my life I would die for, and you're one of them,' he had once told her.

She wondered if that was still true.

Could it have been the people from the villa in Vedbæk? Had they seen her on the security cameras, found out who she was and gone to her flat?

Don't be stupid, Jensen. You're not that important.

'OK,' said Kristoffer. 'Here's what we'll do. Tomorrow, I am sending someone to fix new locks and install an intruder alarm and a webcam.'

'A webcam?'

'Connected to your phone, an alert if anyone tries to enter, live pictures from the flat anytime you want.'

She smiled. 'Slight overkill, wouldn't you say?'

'Not at all. I have the same set-up at my place.'

'Yeah, a luxury penthouse apartment, no doubt with all the latest Bang & Olufsen gear, not a garret with nothing to steal.'

'Nothing? That's not the impression you gave me just now.'

Touché, Kristoffer.

She looked at him, narrowing her eyes. 'You didn't say why you're here.'

'Oh that..I need to inspect your washing machine urgently, see if it's still working. I've called a few times. Must say it's a relief to finally find you home, Miss Jensen. I was starting to think you'd been abducted by aliens.'

Jensen went and stood by the front door, holding it open for him. 'The washing machine is fine, thanks all the same. Now if you don't mind, I'd like you to leave.'

'Come on, Jensen. What does a man have to do?'

'Uhm, how about take a hint?'

'I'm afraid I'm a bit deaf in that department, which is more than can be said for your neighbours, I'm sure. Mind if I come in, so we can do this in private?'

'If you must,' she said and sat on the sofa clutching a cushion, legs curled up under her.

He closed the door, folded his hands in front of him as if in prayer. 'I apologise for stalking you,' he said. 'I'm not some crazy axe murderer, I promise. It's just that ... well, I guess I'm not used to taking no for an answer.'

'No shit,' said Jensen.

Kristoffer smelled of expensive aftershave. He was wearing a collarless pale blue linen shirt, untucked, and black denims with a navy blazer. His killer gaze sparkled as he looked at her. 'I like you,' he said.

'Did you tell your girlfriend that?' said Jensen.

'I don't have a girlfriend.'

'The pretty actress from TV. I believe you live together?'

'Not anymore.' Kristoffer beamed. She imagined it was the

smile he used when closing a deal. 'Is that what this is about? Because let me tell you, I am strictly a one-woman-at-a-time man.'

A rare breed.

'Sure,' said Jensen.

'I can't stop thinking about you. You excite me. You're ... different.'

'Am I meant to be flattered?' said Jensen.

Kristoffer laughed. 'I can see you're not going to make it easy for me, and I wouldn't want it any other way, but let me at least introduce myself properly? There's this little restaurant I know just down the road. Might help you take your mind off things?'

'What, now? It's ten o'clock at night, on a Sunday.'

'Ah but this is a special place. They will keep it open for me, and besides they're Italians, so this isn't late for them at all.'

Jensen was hungry. It was hours since she had eaten the few bites of her chicken sandwich, and wine might help her sleep. 'Do I need to dress up?' she said.

'Absolutely not. As I look at you now in that fetching leisure ensemble, I cannot remember having seen a more beautiful woman in all my life.'

59

By the time Henrik arrived in the office canteen, clutching a takeaway coffee and a tub of anaemic-looking fruit salad, Mark was waiting for him at their usual table in the corner. It was the one nearest the wall-mounted TV screen on which the two of them sometimes watched the football. Mark was eating a Danish pastry with custard. The sweet smell of it made Henrik salivate, but he had promised himself to stay off junk food. Things were going to be different from now on.

'Good to have you back, Henrik,' said Mark. 'You look great.'

'Thanks,' said Henrik, spearing a piece of hard melon with his wooden fork. 'You're a terrible liar. Where is Lisbeth?'

'On her way,' said Mark. 'She worked late last night. I suppose she is keen to prove herself now.'

'What do you mean, prove herself?'

Mark dropped the half-eaten pastry on his plate as if he had suddenly lost his appetite. 'You don't know?'

'Aside from Wiese yesterday and you this morning, I haven't spoken to anyone in this place since early March. What's going on?'

'It's Wiese. He has offered Lisbeth a job. It would mean a transfer, into organised crime.'

Henrik felt a spike of irritation that she hadn't discussed it with him. Then he remembered that she had texted him a few times, messages that he had deleted immediately along with anything else remotely related to work. 'You think she'll take it?' he said.

'I think she's thinking about it seriously.'

Lisbeth would go far, Wiese had spotted this long ago, and who could blame him? He was doing what any good manager would do. Looking at it less favourably, though, Wiese was undermining Henrik by pinching his best people.

As the man well knew.

The total bastard.

'I am sorry you had to find out in this way.'

Henrik shrugged. It took all his willpower not to reach across for Mark's discarded pastry and wolf it down. 'Lisbeth can do what she wants. Good luck to her.'

He would need to talk to her, find out what really lay behind it. She had been terse with him even before he had gone off sick.

'Wiese said you'll be on desk duty for a while,' said Mark.

'We'll see about that,' said Henrik.

'Yes, boss,' said Mark. 'Boss?'

'Yes, what is it?'

'We're OK, you and me, aren't we? I haven't done anything to offend you?'

Henrik looked closely at Mark's earnest face, trying to read him. Mark wasn't someone you worried about. The disagreements they had had over the years, the times when Henrik had lost his temper and been an arsehole, none of those had appeared to stick in Mark's mind, unlike Lisbeth who seemed to be running a score.

Henrik knew Mark had his own career ambitions. They had talked about it a few times, Henrik trying to manage Mark's expectations. Was it the talk of Lisbeth's manoeuvring that had made Mark feel insecure? Henrik duffed him affectionately on the shoulder. 'Of course not, mate, don't be daft. Why do you say that?'

'I just . . . don't worry about it,' said Mark.

'Things all right at home?' said Henrik, feeling like the world's greatest fraud for asking.

'Yeah, well,' said Mark, shrugging. 'You know what it's like when you've got small kids.'

Henrik nodded, though of course he didn't know. He had left his wife on her own with everything for far too long, excusing himself with work. He was glad that Mark wasn't about to make the same mistake. 'Now,' he said. 'I want the full lowdown on our two murders.'

Mark waved his phone at him. 'Three, boss. Ulla Olsen died of her injuries last night.'

'Shit.' Henrik thought about her daughter Anette and how she had painted the floor red with her mother's blood.

Ulla Olsen. Something about that name was stirring in Henrik's memory. 'Anything new turned up in that case?'

Mark shook his head. 'It's gone to Laurits Tønder. The lead theory is still that one of the other residents at the care home did it, an eighty-four-year-old. About ten days ago, he struck one of his carers, so he has previous for violence.'

Lashing out at a carer was bad, but hardly the same as evading detection to sneak into the room of a fellow resident and battering them over the head, before making off without as much of a drop of incriminating evidence. An octogenarian dementia sufferer wasn't up to that kind of cunning, was he?

He knew Laurits Tønder well. Nice guy, but as weak as they came. Recently promoted to detective inspector. Over-promoted in Henrik's book.

'Sounds unlikely to me,' he said. 'What about Irene Valborg?'

'Also with Laurits. He hauled the daughter in yesterday. He has another twenty-four hours to interview her. Nothing so far.'

'What's he got on her?' said Henrik. Regitse Lindegaard was a first-class bitch, and there had been no love lost between her and her mother, but a murderer?

'Her life's fallen to pieces. She was picked up in a bar in Aarhus, semi-conscious with drink. The big house has gone, all the money, husband's left the country. Laurits believes she killed her mother to get her hands on her property and diamond necklace.'

'How?'

'She travels to Copenhagen to try and get money out of her mother. Irene lets her in, of course, not suspecting her own daughter wishes her harm. Regitse forces her mother to open the safe and loses her rag when she finds it empty. Irene flees, Regitse grabs the bronze elephant and, boom, hits Irene over the head.'

Henrik shook his head. 'She was lying on the carpet, facing her bedroom where the safe was, not running away from it.'

'It might still have been Regitse,' said Mark.

'You're forgetting about all the security Irene installed before she died. I refuse to believe that was all because she was afraid of her daughter.'

'There might be an innocent explanation. Rising crime rates and what have you.'

'Dismisses her cleaner. Removes her most precious object to her summer cabin. Fills her cupboards with tinned food. Stops going out. That's not rising crime rates. Irene Valborg had been threatened by someone. Someone who had scared the living daylights out of her. Next?'

'Vagn Holdved's neighbour has been charged. Seems there's pretty watertight evidence against him.'

'His fingerprints on Vagn's spade, you mean?'

'Yes,' said Mark. 'And a gardening glove with Vagn's blood on it.'

'Nothing else? The man's clothing would have been covered.'

'The theory is he got rid of the clothes.'

'But not the glove.'

'Left it out by mistake.'

'And how does he explain the blood on the glove?'

'Says he heard a commotion on Vagn's plot and went to investigate. He saw Vagn lying on the ground and tried to shake him awake, which is when he got the blood on the glove. He says he ran back to his house and phoned the police straight away. He says he was worried about being a suspect because he and Vagn had been seen arguing in public, so he panicked and buried the glove in his compost heap.'

'Not the kind of story you'd make up, is it?'

'Well, Lotte Nielsen thinks he is lying, and the prosecutor agrees.'

The morning rush in the canteen was over, and the staff were heading back to their desks, clattering crockery onto the trays stacked on trolleys by the kitchen. A few of them glanced at Henrik with a look of surprise. He grinned at them, tipping his imaginary cap.

Down but not out.

It was when he and Mark were getting up from their table that it suddenly came to Henrik. 'Ulla Olsen,' he said out loud.

'What about her?' said Mark.

'She used to go walkabout. Her daughter said that when Ulla was still living in her flat in Bispebjerg, she'd go to random places and forget why she was there and how to get herself home. But it wasn't random, was it? It was where that young girl threw herself in front of a train.'

'Who.'

'The girl in the photo.'

'I don't follow you, boss. Where do you mean?' said Mark.

Henrik got up, his dining chair falling away with a loud noise. 'Ordrup station.'

60

'Why do you think she jumped?' said Gustav. He was lying on Jensen's sofa, his long legs dangling over one armrest, his head propped against the other.

Jensen was face down on the rug next to the coffee table. She was trying to decide whether she had the energy for a conversation with Gustav. Her head was still aching with rare determination after her night with Kristoffer, despite the handful of painkillers she had taken. She was longing for one of Liron's special hangover coffees but couldn't face cycling all the way to his van in Sankt Peders Stræde.

The restaurant Kristoffer had brought her to was in a pretty, red Christianshavn townhouse with potted laurel trees and flickering storm lamps on the front steps.

The Italians had ushered her and Kristoffer into a private room and fed them one rich delicacy after the other and plenty of wine. By the third course, Jensen had been unable to see straight, while Kristoffer had spoken to her of his love of Italy, his business, his parents (both dead) and how he wasn't driven by money.

Yeah right.

Easy to say when you were rich enough to keep a restaurant open after hours and handpick the most expensive bottles from the wine cellar. 'Then what *are* you driven by?' she had asked him, barely able to speak.

'The deal. Closing. Winning.'

'That killer instinct,' she had said with a cynical little laugh, finishing what must have been her eighth glass of wine.

Kristoffer had looked at her intensely, his eyes flashing. She had squinted, trying to bring her eyes into producing just one image of him. 'You may not be driven by money, but money changes everything,' she had said, shaking her empty glass at him.

'I'm aware what it can buy, if that's what you mean. I like my luxuries as much as the next person, but I'm still very much me.'

How was it possible that he could be so sober after the amount of alcohol they had consumed? Not willing to let him off the hook so easily, Jensen had continued the third degree. 'These waiters, hovering around us, you think they'd be remotely interested in you if you were skint?'

'Actually yes. I used to wash dishes here. When I made my first serious money, I bought a share in the restaurant.' He nodded at a thick-set bald man who was supervising the others. 'That's Andrea, the manager. His son works for me. I am god-parent to his first grandchild Giulia. And that's Giorgia over there, from San Remo. She lost her sister to breast cancer two years ago. Everyone here is like family to me.'

The thought of it made her cringe now. When they had got back to her flat, she had asked if Kristoffer wanted to come up for a coffee, but he had declined, politely, excusing himself with an early morning business meeting. There had been a glint in his eyes, like he was finding her funny. His kiss on her cheek had been warm but fleeting, the scent of his aftershave lingering in the air as he walked away.

It was unlikely that he would be asking her out again. To her surprise, she was sad about that.

256

A man had already been to install the intruder alarm, as Kristoffer had promised. One tiny camera was mounted high up above her front door, and another inside the flat in the corner of the living room ceiling.

Gustav didn't appear to have noticed that anything had changed. 'I mean, there was the call with her boyfriend,' he said. 'What do you think he told her?'

'Don't know. It would have had to be pretty bad.'

'Like, dumping her?'

'Maybe. If she'd never had a boyfriend before that would have been a blow.'

'If we could find him, we could ask.'

'Agnete said no one ever found out who he was. Not sure how we'd track him down.'

'We could ask Susanne Brande.'

'Sure. Let's go see her right away.'

'Why not?'

'She's the CEO of a listed company, Gustav. We can't just turn up.'

'Yes, we can. We'll go to her office, wait outside and walk up to her when she leaves for the day.'

Jensen hoisted herself up onto her elbows. Gustav was right, of course, but why was he so fired up? Was Karoline tugging at his conscience about what had happened in Aalborg?

The two of them had printed out photos of Susanne Brande and Morten Rastrup and stuck them to the wall in the flat. You could read for twenty-four hours and still not get through the amount of online material on Susanne Brande. Only child of Victor and Bitten Brande. Lost her mother when she was fourteen, graduated from the University of Copenhagen with a law degree, joined her father's business and worked her way to the top, taking over as chief executive when Victor retired. The old man had died last September.

Rastrup on the other hand had only rarely appeared in the media and then always by Susanne's side.

257

'They were there that night, so they must know something,' said Gustav.

'But why does Karoline's photo turn up now, so many years later?'

Gustav didn't reply.

Jensen rolled onto her back, recoiling at the throbbing in her head. What were she and Gustav even doing now? They had found Irene Valborg's necklace and Regitse had paid them. Frank Buhl, *Dagbladet*'s crime reporter had already covered the murder. And the tragic case of a schoolgirl jumping in front of a train twenty-five years ago? Margrethe wouldn't buy it unless they were able to put more meat on the bones of the story, and exactly how were they going to do that?

'We need to work it out. Why not ten years ago? Or twenty? Irene Valborg was murdered in March. What set that off?' she said.

Gustav sat bolt upright on the sofa. 'Victor Brande died.'

'Yeah, last year, more than six months before Irene.'

Gustav jumped to his feet. 'Come on, we have to do something.'

'Please don't shout,' said Jensen, covering her eyes with one hand. 'I am not feeling too good. And I still fail to see what Karoline had to do with Irene, or Henrik's other cases.'

'That's what we have to find out,' said Gustav. 'A few months after Karoline died, Irene bought herself an expensive diamond necklace. We know she didn't inherit, so where did she get the money from? Could she have had a job?'

'Regitse would have told us.'

'Perhaps she saved up over many years?'

'She and Ove were hard up, and she didn't have any income of her own.'

'Maybe she sold something and bought the necklace with the proceeds?'

'Again, no. As Ove's solicitor, Brøgger would have known

258

about it, if she had,' said Jensen. 'But whatever it was, we know that something happened to make Irene scared that the necklace would be taken from her, and that she herself was in danger.'

'We also know that Irene's house is less than a mile from Ordrup station where Karoline killed herself,' said Gustav. 'And that a quarter of a century later, Irene is brutally murdered, and someone puts a photo of Karoline near her body.'

He got up suddenly and began to snatch the colourful post-its off the wall one by one. 'Take some more painkillers, have a cold shower, we have to start again from scratch. We must find Karoline's sister, and her mum.'

Jensen stared at him in disbelief. 'What's got into you? A few weeks ago, you couldn't as much as pretend to be interested, but now it's like someone put a rocket up you. You haven't forgotten that you're going back to high school soon?'

'If we can get a good story out of this, then Margrethe might change her mind,' he said, without looking at her.

'Good luck with that, Gustav,' laughed Jensen, but as she got up in search of paracetamol and a cold flannel for her forehead, she couldn't help but feel a tingle of excitement.

61

Monday 18:14

Henrik put the phone down and stared at the screen. He had remembered correctly. Ulla Olsen's daughter had confirmed that on three different occasions before she moved into the care home her mother had been found sitting on a bench at Ordrup station, rocking back and forth in a state of extreme distress. On reflection, this hadn't been as random as Anette had first suggested. For four years, while she was still living in the marital home in Ballerup, twice weekly Ulla had taken the S-train back and forth to a villa in Ordrup where she had looked after the cleaning and ironing for a wealthy company director who lived on his own. The villa happened to be located just a few streets away from where the Valborgs lived. Then in 1997, not long after Karoline's suicide, Ulla had got divorced, handed in her resignation and moved into an apartment in Bispebjerg that she had bought with her own money.

Henrik composed a message to Lisbeth and Mark.

My office. Now. Cancel your evening plans.

He had already spoken to Regitse Lindegaard, who had been released by Laurits Tønder after a friend had provided an alibi that ruled her out as a suspect. After ten minutes of drunken abuse, Regitse had finally confirmed that her mother had also now and again taken the S-train between Ordrup and central Copenhagen, usually to go out with her husband after work. 'And fucking awful evenings they must have been for Dad, because she never stopped moaning about the restaurants he chose or the cheap seats he'd pick in the theatre,' Regitse had hissed.

Henrik walked over to the whiteboard to which he had fixed photographs of the three victims with magnets. 'Ordrup station', he wrote in the middle of the board. He then drew lines from there to the photos of Ulla and Irene, leaving a question mark next to the photo of Vagn Holdved. Whatever the connection between the three victims and the small commuter station north of the city, the answer had to be found in the cardboard box he had brought with him from the basement of the local police station.

There was a knock on the door. Mark skipped in excitedly, followed more hesitantly by Lisbeth. Henrik checked both ends of the corridor outside his office, before shutting the door behind them. 'You'll both want to hear this.'

Mark followed him to the whiteboard, but Lisbeth stayed by the door, anxiously clutching her lanyard. 'Henrik, you're not supposed to be returning to investigating,' she said. 'Wiese was very clear—'

'And very nice to see you, too, Lisbeth,' said Henrik.

'The rules are there for a reason.'

'Yes, you're right, of course. Though it happens to be handy for Wiese to have me filling in forms for the next few months while he poaches the members of my team one by one.'

Lisbeth shot Mark an angry look.

'I thought he already knew,' said Mark, blushing.

'Congratulations, by the way,' said Henrik. 'Organised crime no less.'

'It isn't formal yet.'

'But you've accepted?'

'Verbally.'

She tried to stare him out but ended up looking down at her trainers.

'Look, Lisbeth, I know I've been a twat. I had some trouble at home which is all sorted now, but anyway it's no excuse for the way I behaved. You know, I know, and Mark here knows that I will never win Boss of the Year. I lose my temper, say things I shouldn't.'

'Never listen, even when people are trying to help,' said Lisbeth.

'That too. But we've been good together, the three of us, haven't we? We've been through a lot, achieved a lot. Can you mention even one case I've failed on?'

They did exist, those cases, Henrik reminded himself, but all of them were before Lisbeth and Mark had joined his team. Thankfully.

'There is a first time for everything,' she said.

This isn't Lisbeth talking, he thought. *It's Wiese briefing against me.*

'You do know Wiese doesn't like me, don't you? And do you know why?' he said.

'I have a feeling you're about to tell me.'

'Because Wiese wants to control people, turn them into biddable mini-mes who ask for his permission before so much as taking a piss. He'd sell his granny to get to the top.'

'I think he's a breath of fresh air actually. They say Monsen might take early retirement and that Wiese's going to replace him.'

'Nonsense. Wiese has none of Monsen's calibre.'

'It's not Monsen's decision, though, is it?'

Henrik shook his head slowly at Lisbeth. What had happened to her? How could he have lost her trust so utterly?

Mark stepped in between them, appealing to Lisbeth with his hands up. 'Let's just hear what Henrik has to say.'

Henrik pointed to the whiteboard, though Lisbeth's obstinacy had dampened the triumph he had felt minutes earlier. 'We've got a connection now between two of our victims and Ordrup S-train station where Karoline Kokkedal killed herself. Both travelled through there regularly and might conceivably have met on those occasions.'

Lisbeth frowned. 'But what's that got to do with anything? And what about Vagn Holdved?'

'We don't know the answers to those questions yet,' said Henrik, pointing to the cardboard box with the files on Karoline's death. 'But when we've been through that box, I'll bet you anything we will.'

Mark pulled out a file. He riffled through the photos inside, whistling softly.

'You really want us to read everything tonight?' said Lisbeth, but Henrik could tell she was intrigued. She wanted to see what Mark was looking at.

'Yep,' said Henrik. 'Every word. Unless you want to check first with Wiese that he is OK with that?'

62

Monday 22:21

Now that he had returned to work, Henrik had begun to answer his phone again. That was at least something, Jensen thought, even if he was as rude as ever. 'I can't talk,' he said. 'Unless it's important.'

'It's important.'

'Then you've got exactly one minute.'

'Last time I got fifteen minutes. What will it be next time, fifteen seconds?'

If she hadn't needed any information from him, she would have ended the call there. But, as ever with Henrik, she would have to play a game of *quid pro quo*. He was at work. She could hear people talking in the background and his voice was the one he used when he was being overheard.

Impatient.

Aloof.

It hadn't taken him long to return to his old ways after his little mid-life crisis.

'Have you found the sister?' Jensen said.

'No,' Henrik said. 'I am not officially back on the case yet, but I will be as of tomorrow.'

'The mother then, Pia Kokkedal?'

'Nope.'

'Then I'm going to try and find her.'

'You can't.'

'Henrik, we've been over this a million times. Denmark is a free country.'

'No, I mean you really can't, because she's gone. Died of cirrhosis of the liver at Riget in January this year. Goodbye Jensen.'

After the call, she sat for a long while and stared at her phone. Karoline's mother had died just weeks before Irene had been killed in her home. How were those two events connected?

She walked over to the kitchen sink. Earlier that evening, a florist had delivered a huge, cellophane-wrapped bouquet of long-stemmed pink roses. Jensen had filled the kitchen sink with water and left them there. Their scent was all over the flat. Something about them was making her nervous.

Her phone buzzed with a text message.

Kristoffer.

You like?

They were from you?

You have other admirers?

I thought we were done.

Not at all. You're a charming drunk, Jensen. Can I see you again?

When?

I'm downstairs with a bottle of Bollinger. You busy right now?

63

Tuesday 00:49

'Fuck me,' said Henrik. 'They were all there that night. All three of them. And now they are dead.' He was standing in front of the whiteboard, staring at it with his hands clasped to his scalp from which coarse brown hair had begun to sprout itchingly at the back and sides, adding ten years to his age. He felt sticky with stale sweat and frying fat from the burgers and chips he and Lisbeth and Mark had wolfed down an hour ago.

According to her statement, Ulla Olsen had seen Karoline Kokkedal, Susanne Brande and Morten Rastrup enter the station at about 18:45. Ulla, still compos mentis back then, had described the three as 'loud and obnoxious', especially Brande and Rastrup. Irene had said that the three teenagers had been 'larking about drunkenly'. Vagn, who had been on his way home from the Ordrup branch of Den Danske Bank which he managed, had added a kindly 'as young people do'. After a few minutes, Karoline had run across to the other side of the platform, pursued by the other two. Vagn, Ulla and Irene all agreed that she had appeared upset. Shortly after, she had jumped off the platform as the S-train pulled into the station.

The driver had never returned to work. His statement to the police had been rambling and incoherent. Henrik could imagine the scenario, having interviewed a handful of train drivers in similar circumstances in his time.

Five witnesses, including Susanne Brande and Morten Rastrup. An open and shut case. The coroner had wrapped it up in record time.

'So Vagn, Ulla and Irene were there. It's twenty-five years ago, and now someone kills them?' said Lisbeth.

'Who?' said Mark.

'Why now?' said Lisbeth.

Henrik shrugged. They would have to be methodical, gather the evidence, work it out.

There was a tape, a great big bulky thing that they had been unable to watch. The footage was from the platform camera, but the report noted that the recording was inconclusive in nature. 'Get hold of a VHS player,' Henrik said to Mark. 'Maybe something was missed.'

The door to his office flew open. A young man with a black beard and headphones, wearing the uniform of the cleaning company and holding a roll of bin liners, looked at the three of them for a few seconds, before mumbling an apology and slamming the door shut.

For a fleeting moment Henrik envied the man. Who would be a police officer, reading dusty papers in the early hours when you could mop floors for a far more certain outcome while leisurely listening to music?

This job isn't normal, he thought.

Mark was rubbing his face, keeping his eyes closed as he spoke. 'What if it's got nothing to do with Karoline?' he said. 'What if the three of them found themselves at Ordrup together for some other reason and that's why someone killed them?'

'We have to find out if they knew each other,' said Lisbeth.

267

'No,' Henrik said. 'Her photos were left by the three bodies for a reason.'

'Not very demonstrably, if they wanted to send us a message,' said Lisbeth.

'It wasn't for us,' said Henrik, realising the truth of the words as soon he had said them. 'It wasn't a message. It was a personal tribute, a ritual.'

'What now?' said Lisbeth, sighing deeply. Mark was resting his forehead on a pile of papers, hands down by his sides. He looked fast asleep.

Henrik thought of what Jensen had told him, annoyed to realise she had been one step in front of him all along. 'There was a twin sister, Rikke Kokkedal. She is known to us, I believe. We need to find her,' said Henrik.

Lisbeth yawned.

'Let's go home and get some sleep,' Henrik said. 'Back on it in the morning. Lotte and Laurits won't be happy, but I'll speak to Wiese about combining the three investigations, and then it's time to have a word with Susanne Brande and Morten Rastrup.'

64

'Yes, I remember. Liver failure is a brutal way to go. She was in a great deal of pain when she was brought in, vomiting blood and everything.'

Once intensive-care nurse Katrine Skytte had been reassured that she wouldn't be quoted for anything, she was chatty and forthcoming. A redhead with a garland of tattooed roses snaking up one arm and disappearing under the short sleeve of her white tunic, she was lively and energetic despite having just come off an eight-hour night shift.

They were in the staff room on the seventh floor of the national hospital, clustered around a small table next to a sink above which someone had pinned up a notice, 'Clean Up Your Own Shit'. Gustav was in a pensive mood, mindful perhaps of the days he had spent at Riget in January, his face swollen and bruised.

'Pia had no one,' said Katrine. 'That's alcoholism for you. I should know, my dad drank himself to death. In the end, everyone despises you. Not because of the drinking, but because of the lying and deceit that goes with it.'

'Probably nowhere near as much as you despise yourself,' said Jensen into her mug.

The coffee was from the thermos on the table, lukewarm and bitter. Jensen guessed it had been made at the same time as the open sandwich on the plate next to it, ryebread topped with a slice of cheese that was sweating and curling up at the corners. The smell of it was making her stomach turn.

She had been woken by birdsong, spreadeagled across her bed with her face down. On the floor was an empty bottle of champagne and two glasses with a red residue at the bottom. An empty bottle of red wine had rolled along the uneven floorboards into a corner under the eaves. Kristoffer had gone. She vaguely remembered him mumbling something about meeting the minister for industry. The bedclothes smelled of the expensive aftershave he wore.

The sex had been surprisingly energetic. No fumbling hesitation, and they had both wanted it. Though she had spent half an hour in the shower, there was still a phantom scent of him on her skin, a sense of every nerve ending being alive and tingling.

'Where did she live?' said Gustav.

'Vesterbro, I think. God only knows what kind of a pigsty her flat must have been. Her clothes stank when she came in. I took it all off, washed her. Her skin was yellow. Blood everywhere. It's not pretty sometimes, dying.'

Jensen swallowed back bile. It felt wrong to be here, taking advantage of Katrine's talkative nature, but not wrong enough to end the conversation.

'I asked her if I could call anyone for her, but she said no.'

Gustav leaned forward in his seat. He was jittery with impatience, his right leg bobbing up and down. Jensen suppressed an urge to reach out and put a hand on it. She didn't want Katrine to lose focus.

'Did she talk about Karoline?' said Gustav.

'Who?'

'Her daughter. Killed herself at sixteen.'

'No, sorry.'

'There was another daughter as well, Rikke?'

Katrine shook her head. 'She definitely never mentioned any children.'

Jensen's heart sank. She checked her phone, but there had been no new messages from Henrik since she last looked a few minutes ago. She was exhausted and hungover, longing for sleep. 'So, she didn't say anything at all out of the ordinary while she was here, and nothing happened?'

'Oh, I didn't say that.'

'Excuse me?'

'On the Thursday night during my shift, towards the morning, before she died on the Monday, she rang for me. Asked if she could borrow my mobile phone.'

'Who did she call?' said Gustav.

'I don't know, but—'

The door swung open, and a man and a woman in nursing uniforms entered the kitchen. 'You still here, Katrine?'

'Shit,' she said, checking her phone and getting up with a scramble. 'Shit, shit, shit, I'm late. Got to take my daughter to nursery.'

'Wait, you were about to say something?' said Jensen.

They followed Katrine into a smaller room with lockers and watched as she shrugged on her padded coat and re-tied her red hair into a ponytail. She sat down on a bench and took off her white clogs, replacing them with short black zip-up boots. 'Oh yeah, so after she died, I remembered the phone call, and I thought perhaps that person would like to know what had happened, you know? So, I rang the number, but just got this really rude person on the line. He refused to tell me who he was, so it sort of ended there.'

'And that's it?'

'Yes. Except for that guy who came and stank up the place the day before she died.'

'What guy?' said Jensen.

'Guy in a dirty parka, must have been one of her drinking buddies. It got rowdy. We had to call security to shift him off the ward in the end, but thankfully he left of his own accord.'

'Could that have been the man Pia called when she borrowed your mobile?'

'I don't think so. The guy on the phone sounded more ... official.'

'What do you mean, it got rowdy?' said Gustav.

'There was shouting. Pia became agitated.'

'Do you still have the number she called?' said Gustav.

Katrine paused and glanced at the door. 'Shut that, will you?' she said.

She waited until Gustav had done as she had asked before reaching inside her locker. 'I know I shouldn't have done it. But who was I to give it to? When Pia died, I couldn't just throw it away, as if she didn't matter or something. I had to wrap it in a plastic bag, it stank that much. Just rubbish in there, except there's a piece of paper with the phone number on it. Looks like it's been there for years.'

She pulled out a yellow and black Netto bag and handed it to Jensen. 'Take it, you'll be doing me a favour. And if you find out who it was that she called, just tell them Pia slipped away peacefully. That's what everyone wants to hear. And now I really must go.'

She ran for the door.

Jensen got out her phone to text Katrine's name to Henrik. It should be easy for him to find the identity of Pia's visitor.

'Did she really?' Jensen shouted after her. 'Go peacefully?'

Katrine stopped. 'In my years of nursing I have never seen anyone of whom that was less true.'

65

The head office of Brande PLC was a superyacht on land, a complicated structure of glass and metal that reflected the sun-soaked waters of Copenhagen harbour like a giant diamond. Henrik and Lisbeth had entered the atrium lobby craning their necks and counting the staggered floors towering above them. Drifting across the black tiles were young people in jeans and trainers who would not have looked out of place on a student campus. As Henrik had travelled up in the lift with Lisbeth, he had felt old and staid, wishing he hadn't swapped his boots for his smart black shoes.

'We abandoned formal dress ages ago,' said Brande, welcoming them into her office which appeared to be suspended above the water. 'We find that young people approach work quite differently to us older generations.'

Henrik had seen her in the papers loads of times. Everyone had. She was a media darling, a businesswoman who was forever winning awards or handing them out, shaking hands with the great and the good, but he wasn't prepared for how stunning she was in real life. Wearing a floaty red dress, her straight, strawberry-blonde hair shining like gold, she was the sort of woman it was impossible to take your eyes off. If he hadn't looked her up on Wikipedia and noticed that the two of them were around the same age, he would have put her in her early thirties.

He and Lisbeth sat down in the cowhide swivel chairs pointed out to them by Brande and gratefully accepted the offer of coffee.

Lisbeth had already arrived by the time Henrik had got to work that morning. 'You weren't wrong. Rikke Kokkedal *is* known to us,' she had said as he walked through the door.

'For what?'

'Where do you want me to start? Theft, burglary, assault, GBH, prostitution, public disorder. Burned down the home of her foster parents in 1997.'

Henrik whistled softly. 'She's inside?'

'No, but she was in Horserød Prison until about eighteen months ago.'

'Let's get her in,' Henrik had said, feeling his mood lift. Now they were getting somewhere.

'Of course. It's just ... no one knows where she is,' Lisbeth had replied. 'She was given a flat after her last release but hasn't been there for over a year, I am told.'

When Mark had arrived, Henrik had told him to go to Riget and speak to Katrine Skytte. He was annoyed that Jensen had spoken to the nurse already, annoyed that once more she was ahead of him. 'Karoline's mother had a visitor before she died, apparently. Find out who the guy was. Speak to security, get any CCTV you can lay your hands on,' he had told Mark.

Lisbeth looked as awkward in the smart surroundings at Brande PLC as Henrik felt. He could sense her hostility towards Susanne Brande.

'I suppose I should have expected to hear from you,' Brande said. 'Of course, I did read about the murders in the news, and should have clocked who they were, but I never thought . . . I mean, to be honest it was all such a long time ago that I guess . . . I've never been any good with names. And you really think this is connected to what happened to Karoline?'

Henrik was about to answer when the door slid open, admitting a large man in jeans and a hoodie, and an enviable mane of blond hair. He looked like a nightclub bouncer.

'I asked Morten, our COO, to join us. He was there that night too and might remember something,' said Brande.

'Rastrup,' said the man, shaking hands.

'COO?' said Henrik.

'Chief Operating Officer,' said Rastrup, looking him straight in the eye, and Henrik wondered exactly what kind of operations they were talking about.

Rastrup looked tense and jittery, his eyes vaguely staring. Cocaine, Henrik guessed. There was hardly a corner of society that wasn't touched by the stuff. Henrik had known several colleagues who had succumbed.

'Karoline, Morten and I were friends at high school,' said Brande. 'But you know that, of course.'

'Friends? You sure about that?' Henrik felt Lisbeth bristling beside him. 'As I understand it, Karoline wasn't exactly one of the "it" girls. How come you all ended up going out together that evening?' she said, opening the questioning, in circumvention of Henrik's unwritten rule of him always going first.

Brande blinked, glancing at Rastrup who was looking aggressively at Henrik. 'People make assumptions about me, because of who my father was, because we were rich.'

'Oh yeah? We heard that you two had been bullying Karoline,' said Lisbeth.

'Who said that?' said Rastrup.

'So you're not denying it?' said Lisbeth.

'It's OK, Morten,' said Brande, turning to Lisbeth with a disarming smile. 'I never claimed to be an angel when I was

275

young, but my stance against bullying is well known. You might have read my autobiography, *Growing Up*?'

'Never heard of it,' said Lisbeth, deadpan. 'But what do you mean by not being an angel?'

Brande glanced at Rastrup again. 'We were young, there was a lot of drinking. We might have made people uncomfortable from time to time, but Karoline wanted to hang out with us. She was cool.'

'According to a statement from her mother, given at the time, she was so happy to be going out with you that she'd been preparing for days what to wear, how to do her hair,' said Lisbeth.

Brande lowered her head and nodded. 'Makes what happened even sadder, doesn't it?'

Henrik put a hand on Lisbeth's arm, before she got a chance to speak again. 'After the incident, you said Karoline had been upset that evening because of a boy,' he said. 'Can you give us his name?'

'We didn't know him,' said Brande.

'So what made you so sure?' Lisbeth snapped.

'She phoned him from Morten's place. She'd hoped they were going to meet up in Copenhagen later that night, after the party, but instead he broke up with her. She was distraught. Honestly, the whole episode was just so awful.'

Episode. Like it had been a faux pas at a cocktail party, thought Henrik. Lisbeth must have had the same thought. He felt her recoil beside him.

'Of course, we had no idea the evening was going to end so tragically,' Brande said. 'It was a terrible shock.'

'You tried to talk her out of it?' said Henrik.

'Of course, but it all happened so fast. One minute we were standing there waiting for the train into town and the next, Karoline had run across to the other platform.'

Henrik met Rastrup's intense stare. 'You couldn't stop her from jumping?'

276

'We were drunk,' said Brande. 'And she was determined. Before we knew it, it had happened, and she was dead.'

Lisbeth shook her head.

Rastrup suddenly snapped and jumped out of his chair. 'What is this? Are you accusing us of something?'

'Morten,' said Brande, trying to calm him down. 'No one is accusing anybody of anything.' She looked at Lisbeth. 'It was awful. Have you ever witnessed something so bad that you wish you could go back and stop it from happening?'

'This isn't about me,' said Lisbeth, staring back.

Brande smiled, the sunlight sparkling in her golden hair.

'Your boss is right,' said Henrik to Rastrup. 'We are merely trying to find out why the other three people who saw Karoline jump are now dead. Got any ideas?'

'We don't,' said Brande, putting a hand on Morten's arm. 'Honestly, we've been racking our brains.'

Henrik wondered if she was sleeping with Rastrup. There was an energy between the two of them, a kind of over-familiarity, though he thought he had read somewhere that she was married and had children.

('Not that it stopped you!' said his wife in his head.)

'We wish we could help,' said Brande. 'Have you thought . . . Maybe this is about something else entirely? A coincidence?'

She obviously didn't know about the photos. Henrik wanted it to stay that way. The last thing he needed was for that piece of information to make its way into the press.

'We are pursuing a number of different leads,' said Henrik, before Lisbeth could get her answer in. He made a move to get up. 'Thank you both for your time. And if you think of anything, anything at all, here is my card.'

On the way out he stopped to look at a portrait on the white wall behind Brande's giant desk. It was of the hideous, modern kind that looked like it had been painted by one of his children.

'My father,' said Brande. 'Victor. We lost him last September.

Founded this company at home in his boyhood bedroom while studying to become a civil engineer. German measles had left him mildly deaf.'

'He must have been very proud of you, taking on the running of the company,' said Henrik.

Brande laughed, perfect teeth flashing in her perfect face. 'I am not denying I was Daddy's girl, but he wasn't the sort of man who handed out compliments, not even to his own daughter. Hard to please.'

Henrik reckoned Victor probably had been. Even through the random swirls of rainbow-coloured paint, you could tell that the man had been a shark.

66

'And you're positive it was a man's voice?' said Jensen, sinking her teeth into a roast pork bánh mì.

'One hundred percent,' said Gustav with his mouth full of baguette.

'Young? Old?'

'Neither. I asked his name, and that's when he ended the call, but it was definitely him Pia Kokkedal called from the hospital. Katrine was right, he was rude as hell.'

Jensen closed her eyes and turned her face into the sun. She had already texted the number to Henrik, irritated to be so dependent on him for information. He had not yet responded about Pia's visitor. 'Could we ask Fie to find out who the number belongs to?' she said.

Fie had hacked into Carsten Vangede's secret drive. Tracking a mobile phone number would be a piece of cake by comparison.

'Already did,' said Gustav, checking his phone. 'No answer yet.'

They were sitting in the sharp April sunlight outside a Vietnamese takeaway in Nørrebro, with people filing past on their bicycles. Jensen was enjoying the sun's warmth on her body. Between her and Gustav on the bench covered in red, flowery cushions lay the only known possessions of Pia Kokkedal, such as they were, held in a greasy cloth bag of an indeterminable colour.

'Pia used to have a life. Hope, dreams. What happened to her?' said Gustav.

'You heard what Agnete said. Her life fell apart after Karoline killed herself.'

They had already been to Pia's old flat in Mjølnerparken, a housing estate that featured prominently on Copenhagen's list of ghettos, now known formally as 'parallel communities'. But the woman who opened the door with a toddler on her hip said she didn't know Pia and that she and her boyfriend had just moved in. Presumably, the council had cleared the flat and got rid of Pia's stuff.

'Burnt it, more like,' Gustav had said.

In Pia's rank-smelling bag, they had found a faux-leather wallet that had once been pink but was now brown, sticky with some unknown substance. It contained her national security card, twenty-six kroner and fifty ører in cash, a threadbare strip of paper with the number she had called from the hospital and a dog-eared, faded photo of two teenage girls, seated at a dining table with plates of spaghetti in front of them. They had identical faces and were smiling broadly.

Karoline and Rikke.

Gustav and Jensen watched a man cycling past the restaurant on a cargo bike, with a woman and two dogs in the front. The dogs were panting in the sunshine, pink tongues lolling.

'What are you thinking?' said Jensen.

Gustav was looking disappointed. 'I am thinking that I thought it was Rikke who Pia phoned from the hospital.'

'Maybe the man who answered the phone was Rikke's boyfriend.'

'Don't think so.'

'Pia's boyfriend then.'

'Didn't sound old enough.'

'Older women can have younger boyfriends.'

'Not an old drunk like Pia.'

Gustav stuffed the last of his baguette into his mouth and crumpled up the paper bag, shooting it into the bin with admirable precision. 'What shall we do now?' he said.

'Wait,' said Jensen, getting up to head back into the Vietnamese restaurant to fetch them two cold beers. 'Either Henrik will tell us who it is, or Fie will. I know who my money's on.'

67

Henrik read Jensen's message and forwarded the phone number of Pia's mystery contact to Mark before deleting it. His wife shot him a curious glace. 'What was that?'

'Nothing,' said Henrik.

Nothing and no one. That was what Jensen had to be from now on. Just someone he used to know.

Easier said than done.

'What's going on?' his wife said.

She was working from home and had greeted him with a frown as he had turned up with lunch from Ole & Steen, still suspicious whenever his behaviour strayed from its usual pattern of benign neglect. 'Why do you ask?'

Answering a question with a question was juvenile but gave him time to deflect his wife's offensive.

'There is something up with you, I can tell.'

'It's work. That's why I am here. Did you say Susanne Brande once came to your school? I met her the other day, intriguing woman.'

His wife sent him a dirty look.

282

'Not like that!' cried Henrik. 'I *can* meet a woman without wondering what she looks like naked, you know.'

Another dirty look, but his wife let it drop. 'What's Susanne Brande got to do with work?'

He looked at her in the meaningful way that meant *I can't discuss my cases with you.* 'What did you make of her?' he said, with his mouth full of salmon sandwich.

'The kids loved her, the girls especially. She had them in the palm of her hand. They all lined up for selfies afterwards. The form teachers read her book with their classes. What was it called again?' she said.

'*Growing Up*,' said Henrik. 'Do you have a bullying problem at your school?'

'Any head who says they don't is lying, but we're no worse than others. Zero tolerance, of course, but that's only the stuff we get to hear about. Victims aren't always forthcoming.'

'You didn't answer my question about what *you* made of Brande.'

'She seemed genuine.'

'But?'

'We had a year-two pupil who had tried to take his own life. After Susanne Brande came to give her talk, I wrote to her and asked if she'd meet with him. I thought it would really help. She never responded.'

'You can hardly blame her for that. She probably gets lots of emails.'

'Funny that she responded to me immediately when I thanked her for coming to the school. Asked me to post a testimony about her book on Instagram.'

'And did you?'

'Didn't feel like it when she didn't respond to my request. Being a reformed bully is one thing, quite another is building a personal brand around it.'

Henrik's wife was smart. Far smarter than him. But was it

283

possible that she was slightly jealous of Susanne Brande, the beautiful and successful woman who was never out of the glossy magazines?

'I mean what about all the kids who are *being* bullied? I don't see her doing anything to help them,' said his wife.

Henrik shrugged. 'Isn't that what going around visiting high schools is all about?'

'Not when the person she helps the most is herself. Think of the book sales, the chat shows, the after-dinner speeches.'

'Whoa, shouldn't you be cutting her some slack for at least trying to do something?'

His wife dropped her half-eaten sandwich on her plate and looked at him with a cynical smile. 'I see what's going on here. You are smitten with her.'

Henrik thought about it.

Did she have a point?

Brande had been there when Karoline had jumped and that made her a person of interest. He failed to see how someone like her, living her life in the glare of publicity, could possibly have had any involvement in the three murder cases, but she had definitely been cagey when he and Lisbeth had talked to her.

Usually, that meant someone was lying.

About something.

He just had to find out what.

68

'How can you eat that so soon after lunch?' said Jensen, watching Gustav tuck into a chocolate-covered marshmallow whip sprinkled with desiccated coconut at Ole & Steen in Torvegade. They were seated on bar stools by the window, looking out at the sun-drenched canal.

'Beer makes me hungry,' said Gustav.

Jensen flicked open her laptop. There was still no reply from Henrik, but Fie, their hacker friend in Roskilde, had already come good with the name and address of the person Pia had called from her bedside.

Gorm Thomasen.

They had ducked into the nearest café with wi-fi. 'It's got to be this guy, here,' said Jensen. 'He is a social worker with Copenhagen district council.'

'Pia's social worker?' said Gustav, licking the marzipan disc at the bottom of his marshmallow.

'Possibly,' said Jensen.

The man in the picture looked to be in his forties. He had very short blond, almost white, hair and multiple piercings in one ear.

'So Pia is dying and calls her social worker? Why would she do that?'

'I don't know.' It was a mystery, but it had to hold the answer to what had happened to Irene Valborg. Pia had died and a few weeks later someone had killed the old woman and placed Karoline's photo next to her body.

From his Instagram, they were able to piece together that Gorm had a boyfriend called Pelle, a sister with three children and a mother who had recently been unwell. There were lots of pictures from his flat, a recent trip to Berlin, and him and Pelle and their friends, partying.

'I am not sure what all this tells us aside from the fact that Gorm needs to be more careful with the information he is putting online,' said Jensen.

'Keep going,' said Gustav.

Jensen flicked through the photos at speed.

'Wait,' shouted Gustav. 'Go back.'

'What?'

'Further back. Stop. That one. Isn't that . . .?'

A reluctant subject. A woman with short, greying hair, in a green coat, towing a shaggy dog. The face was both familiar and unfamiliar: rough, lined, a tattoo under one eye. The Instagram post was over a year old. It said 'Ran into a special friend today' with six heart emojis.

Jensen pulled out the photo from Pia's wallet. 'Rikke,' she said. 'That's Karoline's sister.'

69

'Gather round, boys and girls,' Henrik shouted. While he and Lisbeth had been out, the investigation had moved into a larger room now bustling with activity, a dozen or more detectives brooding over their laptops. As he spoke, people got on their feet and approached him by the whiteboard, mumbling to each other.

Henrik knew there would be no one left in the building who hadn't heard the story of his meltdown in Dyrehaven, but he was relieved to sense that people were still willing to listen to him.

'We've established a connection between Irene Valborg, Vagn Holdved and Ulla Olsen,' he said, pointing to the photos of the three victims fixed to the board. 'We now know that all of them were present on Friday the thirteenth of September 1996 just before seven o'clock in the evening when Karoline Kokkedal, aged sixteen, jumped in front of a train. She was on her way to a party at the time with two friends from school, Susanne Brande and Morten Rastrup.'

'*The* Susanne Brande?' said Lotte Nielsen.

More mumbling among the detectives.

'The one and the same,' said Henrik, raising his voice. 'And Rastrup is now COO of Brande PLC.'

'CO what?' said Laurits Tønder.

'Chief Operating Officer,' said Henrik in his best school English, ignoring the ripple of laughter from the back of the room. 'Now, someone left photos of Karoline next to the bodies. We think the photos are from the 1990s and were taken from an album. What motive could anyone possibly have for doing that?'

He looked around at the earnest and alert faces of his colleagues. Men and women who had got up that morning and come into work to do their best to catch the bad guys. For all its back-stabbing politics and manoeuvring, policing was sometimes as simple as that. It was everything he loved about his job.

'I want to know everything there is to know about our three victims.' He pointed to Irene's photo. 'This lady had no money to her name, and her husband struggled to pay the mortgage on their Klampenborg mansion, yet in early 1997 she bought a necklace so expensive that she had to get a safe made for it. And what about the others? We know that Ulla Olsen, a cleaner with an unemployed husband, was able to buy her own flat outright in 1997. How did she manage it? And what about Vagn, a bank manager and gambler? Any old debts knocking around? Check through anything you can lay your hands on. Lisbeth, I know you have been trying to track down the old bank statements. Let's push harder for those.'

Lisbeth nodded. 'On it.'

'Wait a minute,' said Laurits Tønder. 'What exactly are you saying happened?'

Henrik stood tall, hands at his waist. 'I am not saying anything. We're merely turning every stone. Which means we also need to look for other connections between our three victims. Is there any evidence that they knew each other before, or had ever been in contact?'

A couple of detectives put up their hands, receiving a nod from Henrik in acknowledgement.

'Read through the case notes again, all of them. I want to know what we have missed,' he said. 'And Lotte, I want you to check out Rastrup. Find everything you can. I don't trust the man.'

He felt Lisbeth glance up at him curiously. 'A cokehead,' she said. 'Doesn't mean he has something to hide, and we've no previous on him. What about Brande, though?'

Henrik thought of what his wife had said. Was Brande's anti-bullying campaigning a mere PR stunt with no substance? Possibly, but so what? Brande had seemed tense, but who wouldn't be under the circumstances? 'Check them both out,' he said. 'Including their movements in the past few weeks.'

The assembled officers and detectives had decided the meeting was over and begun to chat amongst themselves. Henrik clapped his hands loudly, startling them. 'Back to work, I want results. Today.'

He walked over to the corner of the room where Mark was inserting a brick-sized cassette into an antique video player. 'That the CCTV tape from Ordrup station?'

Mark nodded, and he, Lisbeth and Henrik huddled around the screen. Henrik immediately realised why the recording had been no good to the original investigation. The quality was terrible, as though the film had been taken under water.

'There was a note in the files saying that the camera on the south-going side had malfunctioned,' said Mark, pressing the fast-forward button while keeping an eye on the time stamp. 'But we should be able to see Karoline in a moment.'

Henrik folded his arms across his chest and looked at the screen. When Karoline turned up, she did so fast and was soon joined by Brande and Rastrup, their bodies merging into a grainy mess. It was not possible to tell exactly what happened. One minute the track was empty, the next a human figure was on it. Then the figure was replaced by a train. The difference between life and death, in three frames.

They stood for a while in silence, each in their own thoughts.

'Right,' said Henrik, breaking the silence. 'Any luck finding Rikke Kokkedal?'

'No,' said Mark. 'But we—'

'Fuck's sake, how hard can it be?'

'I spoke to the people where she stayed when she first came out of prison.'

'And?'

'They said she left because they wouldn't let her keep a dog there.'

'What, she'd rather be homeless than part from her dog?'

'That's what they said.'

'Find her!'

'Oh, and that number you gave me? The person Karoline's mum called before she died?'

'Yes?'

'Gorm Thomasen.'

'Let's get him in.'

Henrik stood for a bit and looked at the room, satisfied with the hum of activity he had created.

His phone pinged. Jensen. A picture with a message.

The person Pia phoned from hospital knows Rikke!

Henrik looked up, sensing a shadow by his side.

Wiese.

Not happy.

Not happy at all.

'Step into my office for a moment.'

'Sure, I'll just . . .'

'And that was now, Jungersen.'

70

'You can't just go barging in, questioning people like that.'

'People like what?' said Henrik innocently.

'Public figures, in a public place.'

'We were in an office with the door closed, and no one was being questioned. Susanne Brande was helping us with our inquiries, *voluntarily*. In fact, she was charming. In no way did I accuse her of wrongdoing.'

Wiese was staring angrily at Henrik over the rim of his reading glasses. 'That's not how her lawyer sees it. Henrik, for Christ's sake, you've got to stop making up the rules as you go along.'

Henrik felt his face turn bright red. 'I can't believe they called you to *complain*. I bet this is all down to Rastrup. Bloke never stopped scowling at me from the moment he came in the room.'

'They did more than complain. They sent me a recording of the interview, and you're very clearly heard referring to the 1996 incident.'

'Because it's relevant to our murder investigation,' Henrik shouted. 'That *incident* as you call it, when a sixteen-year-old

291

girl was crushed to a pulp, had three witnesses, all now residing in the stainless-steel hotel at the Forensics Institute.'

Wiese winced, closing his eyes. 'But that doesn't mean you can go ahead and accuse—'

'Who says I am accusing anyone? I was just asking a few questions.'

'Yes, and the point is they're not having it. They asked that if their involvement is required for your investigation in the future, it is handled discreetly and with a good deal more respect.'

'So that's how it works now, is it? If you're rich and famous, you get to call the police and tell us to lay off?'

'Don't be so bloody melodramatic. And just so you know, if it were up to me, you wouldn't be leading this investigation in the first place.'

'Then we can all be grateful it isn't.'

'It was Monsen, your old pal, who intervened on your behalf. The Brøndby mafia strikes again,' said Wiese. 'Anyway, I hear you've got nothing.'

Henrik didn't rise to the bait. 'Funny, I was about to say the same to you.'

He got to his feet and headed for the door. Before he got there, he stopped and turned. 'Do you know what? I wasn't going to go back and ask Brande and Rastrup any more questions, but now I think I will.'

Wiese stared at him. 'What?'

'If they're this worried about a couple of cops asking questions about something that happened a quarter of a century ago, it must mean they have *something* to hide.'

71

Tuesday 19:31

The atrium lobby at Brande PLC was dark and deserted when Henrik and Lisbeth arrived unannounced. The smart reception- ist had been replaced by a well-upholstered security guard who refused to let them in, police badge or no police badge.

'We're conducting a *murder* investigation, and Susanne Brande may hold vital information. Call her now, or you'll be in so much trouble you'll wish you hadn't been born,' said Henrik.

'It's OK, Carsten, send them up,' said a voice from above. Susanne Brande was leaning over the balustrade three floors up, her long strawberry-blonde hair framing her face like a silk scarf. In other circumstances her pose might have been sexy, but the expression on her face quickly disabused Henrik of such thoughts. She looked alarmed, close to panic.

'I'm so glad you're here,' she said when Henrik and Lisbeth stepped out of the lift.

'What's wrong?' said Henrik. 'Where's Rastrup?'

'Wait,' said Susanne, pulling them into her office and shutting the door, though there wasn't a single other human in sight. She pressed a button and the glass walls turned opaque. Henrik

293

noticed the office was messy. He could almost smell the fear on Susanne, something sharp and bitter under her perfume.

'It's Morten,' she said. 'It was him who pushed Karoline in front of that train all those years ago. She didn't jump, there was no boy, no call.'

'Wait, what?' said Henrik.

The words tumbled out of Brande. 'He always went too far, even back then. I tried to stop him.'

Henrik closed his eyes and held up a hand. 'Wait a minute, why didn't you tell us sooner?'

'I wanted to ...'

'You were afraid of him?' said Henrik, and Brande nodded. 'He said he'd take me down with him. That it would be my word against his.'

'Come on,' said Lisbeth, nodding at the paint-splatter portrait of old man Brande behind Brande's desk. 'The daughter of the mighty Victor Brande, afraid?'

'Dad was the one who persuaded me,' said Brande. 'He was a very astute man.'

'So you and Rastrup and your dad decided it would be better to cover up what really happened?' said Lisbeth.

'I agonised over it. It wasn't an easy decision. But I thought ...'

'Thought what?' said Lisbeth.

'That it wouldn't bring Karoline back anyway.'

Lisbeth shook her head. 'Unbelievable.'

Henrik put a hand on her arm. 'What about the witnesses?'

'I guess it would have been difficult for them to see exactly what was going on, given they were a little way away from us.'

'No doubt in *your* mind, though,' said Lisbeth.

'Morten probably looked them up, threatened them to keep quiet. He knew some bad people back then, still does,' said Brande. Her eyes were brimming with tears. 'To be honest, it's such a relief to tell you. All these years of knowing and being frightened of what Morten might say, what he might do.'

Henrik had seen this reaction many times, as people had unburdened themselves to him and his colleagues. Once they began to talk, there was no stopping them. 'Why are you telling us this now?' he said.

'Because Morten was acting really strangely after you left. He threatened me. I think there is something going on. I'm afraid now that maybe he is the one behind those awful murders—'

'Where is he now?' said Henrik.

Susanne's eyes were large and wide. She whispered her reply. 'He was still in his office about fifteen minutes ago.'

'And where is that?' said Henrik, nodding at Lisbeth as she called for reinforcements.

'Just down the hall, three doors along on the right.'

Henrik and Lisbeth exchanged a glance, both unbuttoning their service guns at the same time. 'Lock the door after us,' said Henrik to Susanne. 'Don't leave this room.'

Lisbeth went first, secured the hallway, then signalled for Henrik to join her. The two offices closest to Brande were empty, the door to the third was closed. Henrik pressed the door handle. Lisbeth nodded to him that she had him covered.

'POLICE!' shouted Henrik, bursting into the room.

Empty. The computer was still on, showing a screensaver of the Brande PLC logo. There was a blue blazer over the back of the chair.

They ran back out into the hallway, towards the lifts, leaning over the glass balustrade just in time to see Rastrup leg it across the black-tiled expanse.

'STOP! POLICE!' shouted Henrik, but Rastrup paid no heed.

Henrik turned to see Lisbeth push open the door to the stairs. He ran for the lift. By the time he reached the lobby, Rastrup was gone, and Lisbeth was already making her way out of the revolving door and setting off in pursuit.

Rastrup was sprinting up the cobbled street, with glass-fronted office buildings to his right, and to his left the harbour with gleaming white motorboats bobbing up and down like teeth gnashing in the dark.

Rastrup was fast, but Lisbeth was faster and closing on him. Where the hell were the reinforcements she had called for?

There was everything wrong with the situation. For starters, it was just the two of them and they weren't wearing bullet-proof vests. They were dealing with a potential murderer who might well be armed. In under a minute, Rastrup would reach the main road where there would be more people and cars and all sorts of hazards. They needed to stop him, but if he was provoked into defending himself, then Lisbeth's life was at risk. He watched in horror as she caught up with Rastrup and rugby-tackled him to the ground.

'No, Lisbeth, let him go,' he shouted.

But Lisbeth didn't hear him. She and Rastrup rolled around on the cobbles. Then Rastrup had her on her back and punched her hard, once, twice, before getting up and running away, leaving Lisbeth behind motionless.

72

'I told you, I am fine, just drop me at the metro.'

Lisbeth looked at Henrik angrily, with the dirty towel from his sports bag pressed to her bleeding nose. Her right eye was closing. It would be black in the morning.

'No chance,' said Henrik. 'I want to make sure you get home and stay there.'

The imbecilic patrol unit had arrived five minutes after the incident, the two officers apologetic and flustered. 'Took a wrong turn, boss. Roadworks.'

'Fucking amateur hour,' Henrik had shouted at them. 'Get your arses back in the car and retrieve our suspect. He just assaulted a police officer.'

'It's nothing,' Lisbeth had said, refusing to be taken to hospital. 'I am just so angry with myself.'

'Don't be. You acted on instinct.'

'I should have got my punch in first. Fucking bastard took me by surprise.'

'He looks to me like the sort of man who spends hours in the gym,' said Henrik.

('Takes one to know one,' said his wife in his head.)

'All the same,' said Lisbeth. 'I shouldn't have let him get away.'

Henrik's mobile phone buzzed in its holder on the dashboard. Mark.

We got him.

Good.

'Left here,' said Lisbeth, as they passed the darkened park around Utterslev Mose, a single runner with a miner's lamp just visible through the trees.

Henrik was grateful for the chance to speak to Lisbeth for a few moments alone. 'About earlier,' he said. 'What I said about Wiese and organised crime. I didn't mean it. That is, I *did*, but I understand if you want to make a move. If I was in your shoes, I'd probably feel the same.'

Lisbeth dropped the towel. Her face was smeared with blood. 'You would?'

'Sure. You want a promotion, I get it.'

'Turn right here,' said Lisbeth.

'I think you could go all the way.'

'Even to your giddy heights, you mean?'

'Further still,' said Henrik. 'You're exactly the sort of talent the force needs. Sharp. Modern. Inclusive. Not a dinosaur like yours truly.'

'You're not so bad. Taught me a lot, especially what not to do.'

Henrik laughed. 'A compliment indeed.'

'It's the red house on the left,' said Lisbeth, pointing. 'The one with the white car outside.'

'Nice. I wouldn't have taken you for a villa and Volvo sort of girl.'

'On *my* salary? Not a chance,' said Lisbeth.

'Oh?'

'I'll be fine from here,' she said, as he parked outside the red house.

Seconds later the front door opened, and a tall brunette with long legs emerged, squinting at Henrik's car. You could tell she was beside herself with worry by the way she was wringing her hands.

'Oh,' said Henrik.

'It's Julie's house, her car. She's got a proper job, unlike mine.'

'But you are . . .?'

'We are what?'

'A couple?'

'It would seem so,' said Lisbeth flatly, opening the passenger door. She seemed embarrassed about Julie's presence, as if she couldn't get away and inside the house fast enough.

'Lisbeth,' said Henrik. 'Tell me to mind my own business . . .'

'Mind your own business,' she said, getting out of the car, but he could tell she was interested. She turned to face him with her bleeding nose and swollen eye, one arm draped over the open car door.

'If you really want to learn from my mistakes, there is really only one lesson of any importance.'

'Which is what?'

'Look after the ones you love.'

73

'I'll do the talking,' said Henrik, as he and Mark took the stairs down to the interview room.

'Take it easy though, boss,' said Mark, running to keep up. He was rewarded with an angry stare. Wiese had already given Henrik much the same warning, and with none of Mark's genuine concern for his blood pressure.

Wiese had made clear that what had happened to Lisbeth, and Henrik's role in it, would be investigated thoroughly, and that he was merely being granted a stay of execution as the investigation was now at a critical stage. In this respect, Wiese was no different from Monsen. Nothing counted as much as results. All the top brass just wanted cases solved and criminals convicted as fast as possible, and they could count on Henrik to deliver. As he opened the door to the interview room, he told himself as much.

Rastrup had declined having a lawyer present. Why, Henrik couldn't fathom. Not only was he the chief suspect in three murder cases, he had also been found in possession of large amounts of cocaine. Assaulting a police officer to boot had

300

placed him so far up shit creek that he would need all the legal help he could get to paddle back down.

As soon as they walked into the interview room, Rastrup wasted no time proclaiming his innocence. 'I haven't done anything,' he said.

'Punching a police officer? Resisting arrest? I don't think you'll be able to find a judge who'd agree with you. You assaulted a colleague of ours. We take that sort of thing personally.'

Rastrup shook his head miserably, his passive-aggression from their earlier visit all but gone. 'I didn't mean to. I was under pressure, I lashed out.'

'Well, you lashed out at the wrong person,' said Henrik. 'Why did you run? Doesn't look like the action of an innocent man, does it?'

'Susanne told me that she was going to say I did it, that no one would believe my word against hers,' said Rastrup.

'You pushed Karoline in front of that train. Then you bullied Susanne into staying quiet about it for years.'

Morten laughed bitterly. 'Good old Susanne. Always gets her strike in first.'

'You're denying it?'

'Yes. Susanne was a bully. Still is. She is the one who pushed Karoline. I've been lying for her all these years, cleaning up her mess.'

'Sure. And I am Donald Duck,' said Henrik, arms folded across his chest.

'What's the point?' said Rastrup. He leaned forward, his face in his hands.

Mark looked up from his typing and glanced quickly at Henrik to ask for permission to take over the questioning. This was granted with a faint nod.

'Tell us what happened,' said Mark.

'She had it all planned.'

'What?' said Mark.

301

'She wanted to kill someone. She'd been going on about it for ages.'

'Why?'

Rastrup shrugged. 'Said she wanted to know what it felt like. I thought it was a game she was playing. We worked out that the easiest would be to push someone in front of a train. She picked Karoline. Made her think the three of us were friends. Karoline came around to my flat, and we poured a lot of vodka in her. We'd told her she was coming to a party and that we would have to take the S-train from Ordrup.'

'And all that was Brande's idea, was it?' said Henrik.

'Yes,' said Rastrup. 'We were drunk when we got to the station, and that's when Susanne told Karoline that there wasn't a party. Karoline began to cry. She ran across the platform to the other side of the platform.'

'And then you pushed her,' said Henrik.

'No. Susanne did. It was a shock. I never thought she'd actually go through with it.'

'Come on, big strong boy like you couldn't stop a girl like Susanne?'

'I'd been at the vodka too.'

'Bet you had.'

Rastrup turned away. The man was close to giving up. No more fight left in him.

'You pushed Karoline and then bullied your friend Brande and the three witnesses into keeping their mouths shut. Were they threatening to break their silence? Is that why you killed them?' Henrik said.

'I never touched them.'

'You certainly had the means, and the motive.'

'I never touched them,' repeated Rastrup. 'They were nothing to me. Because it wasn't me who pushed Karoline, it was Susanne. It was always her. Like I told you, I tried, but when Susanne gets an idea into her head, no one can stop her.'

Henrik sat back, folded his arms across his chest.

'Why are you smiling?' said Rastrup.

'Just enjoying the show,' said Henrik. 'You can keep lying all night long, if you like. Me and Mark here have all the time in the world.'

'You don't understand what Susanne is like. Her dad was just the same. Masters of the universe who think nothing of destroying people.'

'People like you, you mean? Son of a rich diplomat?'

'My father was an arsehole.'

'From what I hear, you had your own flat at sixteen. Can't have been that bad.'

'Dumped me in Copenhagen and went around the world with his women. Died when I was twenty-six, left me nothing. Susanne and her dad picked me up, gave me a job, money, but there was a price. There is always a price with people like them. When you came to the office earlier today, Susanne knew the game was finally up, so she made sure I'd take the bullet for her.'

'Do you want to know what I think?' said Henrik, leaning across the table.

Rastrup looked at him warily. 'Not particularly, no.'

'I think your cute little story is rather convenient. We already know what really happened. Susanne told us.'

Rastrup laughed sarcastically but didn't quite pull it off. 'That's what people like Susanne do. They make stuff up, and people swallow it.'

'Whereas you're as pure as the driven snow.'

'I didn't say that.'

'Well, I don't believe a word of your sob story,' said Henrik.

Rastrup tried another laugh, even less successfully than the first. 'This is a joke,' he said. 'A total, fucking joke. I knew you wouldn't listen. I might as well have saved my breath.'

'Pretty much yeah, if all that comes out of your mouth is lies.'

Henrik signalled to the officers standing by the door that they could take Rastrup away.

'Let's try again tomorrow,' said Henrik. 'A night in custody might help to jog your memory, but don't expect a warm welcome. There is nothing police officers hate more than to see one of their own hurt.'

74

'Ah, Miss Jensen, you beat me to it.'

Jensen, leaning on her bicycle, turned to find that Ernst Brøgger, AKA Deep Throat, had crept up behind her. They were alone on the octagonal Amalienborg Castle Square. It was too early for the tourists who would still be turning over in bed or tucking into Danish pastries at their hotel buffets.

Behind Jensen and Brøgger was the verdigris statue of King Frederik V on his horse, looking towards the dome of the Marble Church. In front of them, across the water, the modern opera house with its giant cantilever roof was just about visible, like a spaceship in the morning mist.

The two of them stood for a while, looking at the royal guards who were marching back and forth between their red-pencil guardhouses in their bearskin hats and blue trousers.

'She is not at home, you know,' said Brøgger, nodding at Queen Margrethe's wing, the Christian IX palace.

'Oh?'

'She is in Aarhus for Easter, at Marselisborg Castle.'

305

'Right,' said Jensen. 'And the Queen told you this personally, of course.'

'Have I not told you I know everyone?' Brøgger laughed. He opened his camel overcoat and pulled out a copy of *Dagbladet* from his inside pocket, pointing to the photo of the monarch on the front page. 'Says so in the newspaper you used to work for. Speaking of which, isn't it about time you got yourself back there?'

Jensen ignored the question. 'Any particular reason why you asked me to meet you here?'

'Oh, no reason. Only, I stop here most days on the way to my office.'

'Which is where exactly?'

'Oh, very nearby,' said Brøgger, rocking back and forth on the balls of his feet, leather-gloved hands clasped at his back.

Still insisting on keeping a low profile.

'I always wanted to be a royal guard, but I was one centimetre too short. Do you know you have to be at least 175 centimetres tall in your bare feet to be accepted?'

'I didn't, but thanks for telling me.'

Brøgger laughed again, a low, warm humming sound. 'So young and so sarcastic. But seriously, I like to walk past here as often as I can, to remind myself.'

'Of what?'

'Where I come from. Denmark is a tiny kingdom, Jensen, a mere speck on the surface of the planet, as this little palace with its little soldiers and guard houses shows. But it is mine. I have been all over this Earth in my time, but this is where I belong. And like those proud royal guards in their bearskins, I would do anything in my power to protect it.' Brøgger paused, lost in thought. Then he turned to Jensen, as if suddenly remembering she was there. 'Anyway, I believe you wanted to talk to me about something.'

'It's Carsten Vangede,' she said. 'I haven't had a chance to tell you this, but before he killed himself, he sent me a USB stick with a message.'

Now she had Brøgger's full attention. 'Saying what?'

'"In case something happens to me".'

'What was on the USB?'

'Financial stuff, invoices, spreadsheets, that sort of thing. Mainly.'

'Mainly? Does that mean there was something else?'

'Yes. There was an encrypted folder, but Gustav and I managed to get into it.'

'And?'

'It was very peculiar, just an address. Nothing online about who it belongs to or what it might have had to do with Vangede, except we think he was conducting his own piece of investigation into the fake accountant who defrauded him.'

'Could be anything,' said Brøgger.

'Then why encrypt it? And why send it to me?'

'Tell me, what was the address?'

Jensen beckoned him closer, though the royal guards were too far away to hear. If Carsten Vangede had gone to so much trouble to keep the address secret, she wasn't going to blow it by being careless. She whispered it into Brøgger's ear.

Brøgger recoiled with a jolt as though she had shouted. He stared at her as if looking for answers on her face and failing to find any. 'Have you told anyone what you just told me?'

She shook her head. 'No one, but—'

'Don't. Whatever you do, keep it to yourself and stay away.'

'Why?'

'I can't tell you why, but Jensen ...' He grabbed her arm. 'Promise me you'll do as I say. I asked you to look into Carsten Vangede's death and you have, and I am thankful for that.'

'So you know who the address belongs to?'

He didn't reply. 'And the USB stick, I want you to destroy it, and any evidence that Vangede sent it to you.'

'Why?'

'Jensen, this is not a trivial matter.'

'I went there you know, on Sunday.'

Brøgger looked at her in alarm. 'Did anyone see you?'

'I don't know, but there were these cameras by the entrance pointing at me. And, on Sunday night, someone broke into my flat. Do you think it might have been them, whoever they are?'

'Did they take anything?'

'No, that's what was so weird about it,' said Jensen, deciding not to mention that she had left the USB stick in her underwear drawer. 'Do you really think I am in danger?'

'I think you are being watched.'

'By whom?'

Once more, Brøgger ignored her question. 'Listen to me, Jensen. Forget the address and the USB and Vangede's note. Do nothing to attract attention. There must be some other story you can work on.'

'Sure, I am trying to find out why someone would want to kill Regitse's mother, miserly old woman that she was, but—'

'Stick with that. And change your locks.'

'My landlord has fitted an alarm and a webcam.'

'Good,' said Brøgger distractedly. 'And now I must go. Let me know where you get to ... with err ... Irene.'

He marched towards Bredgade in a great hurry, with his arms swinging by his side like the royal guard he never was. Watching him disappear into the mist, Jensen felt the deepest sense of dread.

75

The minute he stepped through the doors to the office, Henrik knew something was badly wrong. It felt like the whole building was vibrating and humming with a thousand whispered conversations.

'Wiese wants you,' said the receptionist, avoiding his gaze.

Monsen was already there when Henrik stepped through the doorway to Wiese's office. The big man was standing with his back to the window, blocking out the light.

'What is this?' said Henrik. 'Will someone please tell me what's going on?'

Wiese closed the door, a solemn expression on his face. 'We just heard. Morten Rastrup has killed himself in custody.'

'What? How is that even possible?'

'Managed to strangle himself with a blanket,' said Monsen.

'Fuck.'

'That's right,' said Monsen.

Henrik put his hands on his head and stared at the two of them in disbelief. 'I don't understand. Did anything happen last night? Did he say something? Was there a note?'

'Nothing,' said Monsen. 'Rastrup asked for painkillers shortly before midnight. The nurse who attended said he was displaying withdrawal symptoms from drug abuse. He was given paracetamol.'

Like a sticking plaster on a perforated artery, thought Henrik.

He felt Monsen's hot, heavy hand on his shoulder. 'Looks like we have our man,' he said. 'Well done, Jungersen.'

'Is the DNA test back? On the hairs we found at Irene Valborg's house?'

'Not yet. We're chasing,' said Wiese.

'And Rastrup's alibi? Anything on his devices?'

'The team's going through them, but I think we can assume ... I spoke to Susanne Brande just now. I think it's fair to say that we—'

Monsen held up a hand to stop Wiese, who immediately shut up. 'One moment ... Henrik, we know this is not how anyone would have wanted things to turn out, but don't go blaming yourself now.'

There was a knock on the door and Lisbeth entered without waiting for a response, her left eye and half of her face covered in a theatrical bruise.

'What are you doing here?' said Wiese. 'You should be at home resting. I told you—'

'Sorry for barging in,' said Lisbeth, panting with exertion. 'But you've got to see this.' She picked up the remote from Wiese's desk and pointed it at the TV screen mounted on the wall next to the conference table.

Henrik, Monsen and Wiese watched as Susanne Brande appeared in her red dress outside Brande PLC, flanked by a small group of serious-looking men and women who couldn't look more like lawyers if the word had been tattooed on their foreheads. Henrik spotted *Dagbladet*'s crime reporter Frank Bull in the throng of journalists who were holding out their phones to record Brande's every word.

310

'It is with huge sadness that I ...' She faltered and looked for a moment as if her legs were going to buckle under her. One of the lawyers took her arm and mumbled something into her ear, but she shook her head and steadied herself. '... that I announce the death of Morten Rastrup, our COO, in police custody last night. Morten was detained yesterday following new information passed on to the police by me, relating to an incident at Ordrup S-train station in 1996, in which a sixteen-year-old girl was tragically struck by a train. It is with shock and incomprehension that I report to you that Morten was also subject to a police investigation into his suspected involvement in a series of murders on the three witnesses to the 1996 incident. I ...'

She faltered again, this time looking at the sky as if she were searching for the right words. 'I wrote in my autobiography *Growing Up* about the person I used to be and never made any secret about the shame I feel. Yesterday, I told the police that it was Morten who pushed the girl, our dear school friend Karoline Kokkedal. She did not kill herself. I was forced by Morten to keep this terrible truth a secret for all these years. I would like to reassure you that I am cooperating fully with the police in this tragic matter which will hopefully shortly be drawn to a close. Until such time, I will be stepping back from my duties as CEO as agreed with the board. No further statement will be made by me until the police investigation has been concluded. Thank you.'

Susanne turned and disappeared through the sliding doors, a waif of red and gold, stooped and humble, with the cameras snapping furiously and reporters shouting questions for which no answers came.

'Brave woman,' said Wiese. 'There's far too little accountability in public life these days.'

Lisbeth stared at him, mouth gaping. 'Brave? She just admitted publicly to lying for years.'

311

'But now she is standing up and dealing with the fallout. I think it takes guts to do that.'

'I am sure her army of lawyers will help her wriggle free of the consequences,' said Lisbeth.

Wiese's phone pinged. 'Brande says that she has new evidence to share with us,' he said, reading from his screen.

'What sort of evidence?' said Henrik, frowning.

'You can ask her yourself. She is on her way in,' said Wiese.

'I'll call the Commissioner,' said Monsen.

Henrik held up a hand. 'I think that's a bit premature.'

'Let me worry about that,' said Monsen, smiling and patting him on the shoulder on his way out.

'What is it?' said Lisbeth when Monsen had left and Henrik had made no move to get up.

Henrik didn't know.

Something.

A feeling of disappointment?

Don't be so bloody absurd, he told himself. *You felt all along that the man was guilty as hell, and he has just proved your point.*

But in a way Rastrup had evaded justice by taking his own life. It was like a match that had been called off before the first whistle. An anti-climax. Henrik rubbed his face in his hands. 'Let's see what Brande has,' he said.

'We'll go through everything again,' said Lisbeth.

'No,' said Wiese. 'Not you. You're going home to rest.'

'Not necessary,' said Lisbeth. 'I am completely fine. Damage nowhere near as bad as it looks, and I want to see this through to the end. Like you said, Henrik, we're a team.'

Getting up, Henrik smiled broadly at Wiese. 'Looks like your protégé just voted with her feet.'

76

'Hey, are you going to buy that sandwich?' the teenage girl behind the counter in the corner shop shouted at Jensen.

'What?'

'You've been standing there for fifteen minutes with that sandwich in your hand.'

'Have I?'

'Yes. Are you going to buy it or what?'

'Sure, hang on.'

Jensen scrolled down to finish reading the coverage of Susanne Brande's press conference. 'Butter wouldn't melt,' she mumbled to herself.

'Excuse me?' piped up the girl from behind the counter.

'Not you,' said Jensen. She waved her phone. 'Just ... it's work.'

She approached the counter, grabbing a sparkling mineral water from the fridge on the way. The girl scanned the items aggressively.

Jensen's phone pinged. She tapped absentmindedly on the message and found herself looking at a black-and-white video.

It was a few seconds before she realised what it was.

Her own flat.

With the tiny sofa and her washing on the laundry rack. A hooded person was moving across the room, looking at the wall above the sofa where she and Gustav had put their post-it notes.

What the hell?

'Sorry. Got to run,' she said, rushing for the door.

'What the fuck?' said the girl behind the counter. 'Hey. HEY!!!'

Jensen sprinted along Torvegade, darting in and out of the crowds, down her street and up the stairs, her lungs on fire.

The front door was open. She briefly registered a presence in a black hoodie. 'WHO ARE YOU?' she shouted, gasping for air.

There was an ear-piercing scream.

Only one person screamed like that.

'Gustav?'

'Shit, Jensen, why do you always creep up on me?'

'How did you get in?'

'Did you see the news? Rastrup's topped himself.'

'Don't change the subject.'

'Your door was open. I thought you were home.'

Jensen ran up the spiral steps to the mezzanine and tore open her underwear drawer.

It was gone.

'Did you take it?' she shouted.

'Take what?' said Gustav.

'Vangede's USB stick.'

'I don't know what you're talking about.'

'You watched me hide it upstairs. What are you up to?'

'I am not up to anything. Why won't you believe me?' Gustav said.

'Er . . . let me think. Because you lied to me about what really happened in Aalborg?'

314

Gustav stared at her. For a moment, the only sound was the traffic in the street down below and the whirring of her fridge.

When Gustav spoke again, his voice was dark, calm and devastating. 'I never lied to you. I just didn't tell you what happened. There's a difference.'

'Well, I know now, so you can drop the pretence.'

'How?'

'Your dad told me everything.'

'My dad?'

'Yes. Why did you do it, Gustav?'

'Dad doesn't know anything.'

'Your former headmaster Ole Loft would disagree. He more or less confirmed your dad's version of events.'

'He doesn't know anything either.'

'I don't think he was proud to admit what happened at his high school that night.'

'So?'

'So why lie about it?' said Jensen. 'Gustav, look at me. There must have been a reason for you to do something like that. Your dad said you were depressed, about your mother. Is that it? Why can't you just tell me?'

'You wouldn't understand.'

'Try me.'

'No. Let go of me. You don't have to know everything, Jensen.'

'Gustav, don't go, please . . .'

But his feet were already thundering down the stairwell. Ten seconds later the street door slammed so hard it felt like the whole building shook.

You don't have to know everything.

But I do, Gustav, I really, really do.

77

Wednesday 09:36

'You won't believe this, boss,' said Mark, once more running to keep up with Henrik on their way to the interview room.

'Go on.'

'You know those bank accounts you asked us to look into? How Irene Valborg got the money for her diamond necklace, and all that?'

'Say it.'

'Well, you know stuff's not digitised that far back. We had to access the paper archives, and it's hard to—'

'Now or never,' Henrik snapped.

'Irene had a massive transfer of money into her personal bank account in December 1996.'

'From whom?'

'That's the thing. We couldn't tell at first, because it was from a company no longer registered. So we had to go back into the company registry to find out who owned it, and there was this other company behind it, based in Luxembourg.'

'WHO?'

'Victor Brande.'

316

Henrik stopped on the stairs and stared at Mark.

'And there's more,' said Mark. If he had had a tail, it would be wagging. 'Ulla Olsen and Vagn Holdved each had a large pay-out from the same account around the same time. But the weird thing is, they got different amounts.'

'They did?'

'Irene had by far the most. Then Ulla, then Vagn. We know that Irene bought the necklace, and Ulla bought her flat, and we assume that Vagn paid off some gambling debt or another.'

That bastard Victor Brande, the man with the shark eyes. He had found out what each of the witnesses most wanted and given them the money for it. 'Were there any subsequent payments?'

'None that we've been able to find, but I guess once the three of them had been persuaded to lie to the coroner, they were on the hook for perjury, so they wouldn't have had much leverage.'

'And old man Brande would have made damn sure they knew they'd all go down in flames if they changed their story,' said Henrik to himself.

He nodded to the uniformed officer who stepped aside to let them into the interview room, then did a double take when he saw Susanne Brande. She had changed out of her red dress in favour of a pair of black jeans and a solemn black roll-neck jumper. Her blonde hair was scraped back sternly from her face in a tight bun. She looked up at Henrik and Mark like a frightened deer, eyes ringed with red.

Henrik recognised her lawyer from a couple of other cases involving rich people who found themselves in a spot of trouble. He started the tape recorder with the usual preamble, but to his surprise, before he could get his first question in, the lawyer began to speak.

'First of all, I'd like to reassure you that my client wishes to cooperate fully with your enquiries.'

Henrik turned his gaze to Brande. 'So I gather from your

little TV appearance earlier. It would have been good if you had thought to—'

'Secondly, my client would like to offer new evidence in this tragic case.' The lawyer reached inside a folder and handed Henrik a printed sheet.

'What's this?'

'It's a copy of a statement from a bank account controlled solely by Morten Rastrup,' said Brande.

The lawyer pointed to an item underlined in red pen. 'It's a payment of twenty thousand kroner made last year.'

'I can see that, but who's it for?'

The lawyer pulled out a second sheet from the Bank.

Henrik looked at the name on the page without comprehending.

Pia Kokkedal.

What?

'Where did you get this?'

'From Morten's accountant.'

'Are there any others like this?'

'No. It was a one-off, as far as we know, but there might have been cash payments,' said the lawyer.

'There is only one explanation. Pia must have found out what Morten did to her daughter somehow,' said Brande. 'And Morten paid her to go away.'

As blood money went, it was a pittance. Twenty-thousand kroner to not make a fuss about the killing of her own daughter. But Pia had been an alcoholic and desperate. 'This only means that Rastrup paid Pia. It doesn't mean that he killed the witnesses. Besides, how do I know that he wasn't simply acting on your orders?' said Henrik.

'Because we came straight here with this. If Morten had acted on my behalf, do you think I would have volunteered the information?' There was a sudden sharpness in Brande's voice, a hint of impatience. Her blue eyes were sparkling

318

provocatively at Henrik. Then she looked away. 'Forgive me. I haven't slept.'

'Bet you haven't,' said Henrik.

'What's that supposed to mean?' said the lawyer with a frown.

Henrik leaned back, made himself comfortable. 'It means that your client finds herself in an awful mess.' He paused, looked straight at Brande. 'Were you aware that your father transferred large sums of money to the three witnesses just a few weeks after Karoline Kokkedal died?'

He paused, but Brande was still looking down at her hands, her expression unchanged. 'Yes. He would have done anything to protect his precious firm,' she said, the last two words pronounced with bitterness.

'Still, would have been cheaper to just dump your pal Rastrup in it, wouldn't it?'

Brande laughed bitterly. 'My father abhorred scandal. I told you already it was him who persuaded me not to tell on Morten. He threw money at everything. My dog died when I was ten years old, and he bought me a pony. When I had my first heartbreak at eighteen, he gave me an open-top sports car. Never told me he loved me but would get his wallet out at the drop of a hat.'

'Poor little rich girl,' said Henrik.

'Mock me if you like,' said Brande. 'It's all in my book. I suggest you read it.'

'So your father and Rastrup colluded to persuade the witnesses to change their testimony and forced you to go along with them?'

'Yes.'

'Yet, later, when you did your "growing up" and had your Road to Damascus moment, you still didn't come clean.'

'What good would that have been? Karoline was still dead, and my father was ageing by then. It wouldn't have served any purpose, except to send him into an early grave.'

As he deserved, Henrik thought.

319

'Look,' said the lawyer. 'My client has already admitted to withholding the truth about what happened that evening and is prepared to take the consequences. What more do you want? Her head on a spike on City Hall Square?'

Henrik ignored the man and kept his gaze on Brande. 'Did your father threaten the witnesses to stay quiet, after he gave them the money?'

'Look here,' said the lawyer, raising his voice. 'My client is willing to make any documents relating to Morten Rastrup available to you. I sincerely hope that in return you will make clear that she is above suspicion in any way.'

'Oh, I wouldn't put it like that,' said Henrik. 'Your client lied to the coroner, leaving a grieving family to believe that Karoline had killed herself. That's not just perjury, that's being an accomplice to murder.'

The lawyer opened his mouth to speak, but Brande silenced him. 'You're right,' she said. 'I think I managed to persuade myself that none of it was real. And whenever I brought it up, Morten would get so aggressive. Him and my father, they ...' She shook her head, her eyes closed.

'And, when your father died? Did the witnesses come after you?'

'Not me. But I'm guessing that Morten ... One of them must have told Pia what really happened. He paid her off, but he probably realised that he couldn't keep the truth contained for ever. I suppose that's why he did it.'

'Did what?'

'Why, killed them. To stop them from talking.'

Henrik had had the same thought. After Victor Brande died, Irene must have seen her main chance to blackmail Rastrup. Her brain tumours had perhaps played a part, making her braver, but Rastrup had responded by threatening to kill her and take her diamonds, so Irene had got herself an Alsatian and an alarm system and decided to stay indoors.

320

Later, for whatever reason, Rastrup would have decided a bunch of old people weren't worth the risk, so he killed Irene and Vagn Holdved and made a fatal assault on Ulla Olsen.

Who had told Pia Kokkedal? Irene, out of spite, when Rastrup had refused to give in to her demands? Perhaps that was how she had first approached Rastrup. 'If you don't pay up, I am going to tell Karoline's mother.'

It all fitted.

Except for the photos.

Where would Morten have got hold of them? And what were they supposed to mean? Were they some sort of warning or trophy?

Henrik was surprised to hear Brande begin to cry. Big, heaving sobs. The lawyer began to gather his papers. The sharing was over.

'Interview terminated at 09:51,' Henrik said, stopping the recording.

When he and Mark left the room, Lisbeth was waiting in the corridor, waving a piece of paper. 'The hairs that were found at Irene Valborg's house, the ones forensics couldn't account for? They've just confirmed they were Rastrup's. We're going through his IT, but we now know for sure that he had been to Irene's property.'

Wiese came up behind her, smiling. 'We're there,' he said. 'Well done, Jungersen.'

He stuck out his hand.

Henrik looked at it absentmindedly and walked off.

They weren't there, Wiese was wrong. He could feel it in his bones.

78

Wednesday 20:19

'Margrethe, thank God,' said Jensen, dropping her food shopping on the kitchen counter in her Christianshavn flat. 'Is Gustav with you?'

'Why?'

'He's not answering his phone. I've been trying all day. Could you put him on for me, please?'

'No. Gustav expressly told me that he doesn't want to speak to you.' Jensen could hear Margrethe taking a swig from a glass. Red wine, she imagined. Margrethe was fond of the stuff. 'Now, it's been a shitty week, even by recent standards, so if you don't mind . . .'

'I spoke to your brother.'

'I heard.'

'He told me what happened in Aalborg. There was this school party, and Gustav—'

'I know.'

'What?'

'Jensen, we've *had* this conversation.'

'It doesn't bother you?'

'And to think I once thought you were a good journalist. Goodbye, Jensen.'

Jensen stared at her phone. She had to know. If only she could find out who the boys were, she would get the truth out of them. It had been naïve to think that any of the kids at the high school would volunteer information.

'Who do I know in Aalborg?' she said out loud.

There was one person.

A famously lazy man and a womaniser to boot.

A politician whose career she had made, along with her own, when he had given her a scoop so big that *Dagbladet* had bought her story. Esben Nørregaard was elected in Aalborg as a member of parliament for the ruling party.

She tapped on his number.

He answered almost immediately, traffic noise in the background. 'Jensen, where the hell have you been hiding?'

'Not now, Esben, I must—'

'I'm on my way home from Borgen, but it's not too late for a drink. Much to discuss. The champagne bar at D'Angleterre in ten minutes?'

Jensen imagined Esben in the passenger seat of his black car, shooting through Copenhagen to his home in Klampenborg with his giant of a Syrian driver at the wheel. 'How's Aziz?' she said. 'Send him my regards, will you?'

'I see what you did there.'

'Esben, I need your help.'

She told him the whole story. About Gustav, and as much as she knew about the two boys. 'Please, Esben. There's got to be someone you know in Aalborg who will tell me what really happened?'

'Seems you know it already. Come on, Jensen, you of all people know how brutal kids can be.'

They had often talked about Jensen's own miserable youth in North Jutland.

323

'No,' she said. 'Not Gustav.'

'Bullies come in all shapes and sizes.'

'Esben, I beg you.'

He sighed. 'I'll see what I can do.'

'Thank you. I promise, if you help me with this, then I *will* have that drink with you.'

Any day now.

She put her food away. In the end, she didn't feel like having the sushi she had bought for supper and opened a Carlsberg instead. The bottle shook in her hand. Gustav had said that her front door had been open already when he turned up. What if he had been telling the truth? And more to the point, why hadn't she had an alert when the door had been forced?

She rang Kristoffer but there was no answer. He had mentioned taking some Norwegians out for dinner, and she had told him she wanted an early night.

Come on, Jensen.

Brøgger had acted strangely. Was her life really in danger? In this cosy attic flat, in the middle of Copenhagen?

She pushed the sofa in front of the door and grabbed the biggest of the kitchen knives she had bought at IKEA. Then she climbed upstairs and lay down on the bed, fully clothed, blinking into the dark.

79

'I want you to think very carefully about what you say next,' said Henrik, speaking with exaggerated slowness. 'This is a murder investigation. If we find out you've been lying to us, the consequences for you will be swift and severe, so I ask you again. Where is Rikke?'

The thin blond man opposite him stared back obstinately. With his fine features and vaguely pointy ears, he looked like an angry elf.

'I told you a million times. I don't know. She never tells me, and I don't have a number for her. She just checks in now and again, to let me know she's OK. Or if she needs to see a doctor or her dog needs the vet.'

'All part of the service?' said Henrik.

Gorm Thomasen stared back at him angrily. 'I've been trying to get her off the streets for months now. She won't even talk about it if she can't have her dog with her.'

Lisbeth intervened. 'You said Pia asked you to get in touch with Rikke. Had that ever happened before?'

'No. I only met Pia once. At the court case where Rikke was convicted for arson.'

'Her foster parents' home?' said Lisbeth. 'Do you know why she set fire to it?'

'You need to ask Rikke that, but let's just say it wasn't a happy place for her.'

'Were Rikke and Pia on speaking terms back then?'

'No, Rikke refused to have anything to do with her mother, but I guess Pia must have kept my phone number all these years.'

'And you say you're no longer Rikke's case worker?'

'Not officially. More like friends these days.'

Henrik looked at Gorm, frowning. 'A somewhat unusual friendship, isn't it?'

'Not at all,' said Gorm, glaring back at him. 'I like Rikke. She was just dealt a shitty hand by life.'

'Did you ever talk about Karoline?'

'No. I only know about her twin sister from reading her file. It wasn't something we chatted about.'

'Tell us about the dog,' said Lisbeth. 'When did Rikke get it?'

'You'll be familiar with her criminal record,' said Gorm.

'Visible from space,' Henrik said.

'She's been clean since she left Horserød the year before last.'

'A miracle,' said Henrik.

Gorm looked at Lisbeth. 'Are you going to let this clown carry on like this?' To Henrik, he said, 'You don't have the faintest clue what Rikke is like.'

'No,' said Lisbeth. 'You're right. We don't know anything about Rikke. But you were saying, about her dog?'

'I think it saved her. She got Charlie when he was just a puppy, bought him off some guy she met. The two became inseparable.'

'That's nice.' Lisbeth smiled encouragingly. 'So Pia calls you from hospital and tells you that she doesn't have long to live and wants to see Rikke. Did she say why?'

Gorm shrugged. 'I suppose she wanted to apologise.'

'What for?' said Henrik.

'Leaving Rikke to fend for herself. She was sixteen when she was sent to live with the foster family.'

'Rikke was difficult, and Pia was grieving.'

'So was Rikke. Her twin sister had just died.'

Lisbeth consulted her notepad. Henrik knew that she was trying to pull the interview back to their investigation, but Henrik doubted if the angry elf really knew anything.

'So Pia rings you on the Thursday and you say you'll pass the message on to Rikke next time she calls in, which she did three days later,' said Lisbeth.

'Lucky,' said Henrik.

'Coincidence,' said Gorm.

'Rikke listens to you but doesn't say what she intends to do.'

'Right. She ended the call very quickly. She does that sometimes.'

'And you really don't know if she went to Riget and saw Pia, and you don't know where she is right now?' said Lisbeth.

Gorm shook his head.

'OK,' said Lisbeth.

Henrik looked up at the ceiling of the interview room, trying to think. They knew Pia Kokkedal had received at least one visit in hospital, but that person had been a man.

He rose to his feet, wondering if Mark had made any progress with security at Riget. Gorm Thomasen had told them nothing at all. Lisbeth could see him out, he thought as he headed for the door.

'Great, thanks, no really, the pleasure's all mine,' said Gorm behind him.

327

80

Thursday 08:42

'Are you . . . Jensen?'

There was no caller ID. 'Who is this?' said Jensen, closing her eyes and rolling back in bed. She had slept badly, worrying about Gustav and everything he wasn't telling her.

'My dad said you're after information.' The voice was young, male and scared, with an Aalborg accent.

'Yes, right, I am.' Jensen sat up in bed, wincing as her thigh brushed against the cold steel of the kitchen knife. She must have fallen asleep holding it. 'What's your name?'

'Dad says I don't have to tell you that. It was him who made me do this. Apparently, he owes Esben Nørregaard a favour.'

Esben. Networker supreme. Man of favours. You scratch my back, I scratch yours.

'How do you know Gustav Skov?' said Jensen.

'We were in the same class, but we weren't friends or anything. Gustav didn't—'

'Have friends?'

'No.'

328

'Look, I just want to know what happened, why he did that thing, at the high-school party last year.'

'It's . . . promise you won't quote me or write about this?'

'I promise.'

There was a long pause, before the boy spoke again, almost in a whisper. Jensen could hear music in the background. 'There was this girl Gustav liked in our parallel class. A pretty girl.'

'What was her name?'

'Josefine,' said the boy after a long hesitation.

'Were they going out?'

'Going out?'

'Well dating, or whatever you call it. Were they together?'

'No, nothing like that . . . It was just, like, you could tell. He would blush whenever they spoke. She was nice to him.'

'Was?'

'She left.'

'Why?'

'Something happened. They found out that he liked her.'

'They who?'

'Those boys . . . the ones, he . . . you know. I am *not* giving you their names. If you try and make me, I'll stop talking.'

'I promise I won't. What are they like?'

'One of them has a half-brother who's in a biker gang. They threaten everybody with getting beaten up. If you're not in their crowd, and if they happen to notice you, they can make your life very bad.'

'Sounds like you're speaking from experience?'

'I know how to make myself invisible, but Gustav was different. His Copenhagen accent, you know. He stood out, wouldn't shut up.'

That's our Gustav all right, thought Jensen.

'Anyway, so they found out about the girl, and there was this video going around, like a porn film, with their faces superimposed.'

329

'Gustav and Josefine?'

'Yes, and they made out that Gustav put the video together himself. It went around the whole school.'

'Did the teachers find out what was going on?'

'Fat chance. If you tell on those boys, you're as good as dead. Anyway, Josefine stopped talking to him and Gustav got ostracised even more than before.'

'And what did Gustav do?'

'Nothing. He didn't even try and defend himself. Not until that night when he did ... that ... that thing.'

'How did you know it was him?'

'Everyone knew. There was this show and Gustav had asked to perform a solo act, but when it was his turn, the curtain went up and there was this death metal music playing really loudly and ... well, you know the rest.'

'He must have planned it for a long time.'

'I've got to go now.'

'Wait,' said Jensen. 'One more question. I know Gustav was expelled, but nothing more happened. Why didn't the two boys pursue it any further?'

'I suppose they were embarrassed that they'd allowed someone like Gustav to do something like that to them. And everyone was scared to talk about it, even the teachers, so it was like it never happened. But let me put it this way – I wouldn't come back to Aalborg anytime soon, if I were Gustav.'

The boy ended the call.

'Oh Gustav,' said Jensen to her phone, thinking about what he had told her about playing music in his headphones, how it helped him to stay calm.

She felt proud of him. No wonder he didn't want to go back to school, or that Margrethe had been protective of him. It was obvious now why Karoline Kokkedal's story had got him so fired up.

She composed a text.

She went down to the kitchen and stood by the sink drinking three glasses of water while she looked out at the yellow and red courtyard and the people coming and going behind the windows of the other flats. Normal people, with normal jobs and safe homes.

The Susanne Brande story was all over *Dagbladet*, most of the articles written by Frank Buhl. Apparently, the police had new evidence pointing at Morten Rastrup. It was now thought that Morten had killed Irene Valborg and two others who had witnessed him pushing Karoline in front of the train twenty-five years ago.

Irene had bought her expensive necklace with the money she had been paid by Susanne's father to keep quiet, but when Victor Brande had died, the old woman hadn't been able to resist the temptation to try blackmailing Morten.

There was no mention of the photos of Karoline, nothing to suggest why Morten might have left them by the victims, or how he had got hold of them in the first place.

'This is wrong,' Jensen said to the empty flat.

The person who left the photos really cared about Karoline and wanted her to be remembered. Morten couldn't have cared less, but the police said they could prove that he had been to Irene's house and, bizarrely, that he had transferred money to Pia Kokkedal.

Why? Had Pia too been blackmailing Morten? What had she and Gustav missed?

Jensen still had Pia's greasy cloth bag, wrapped in the black-and-yellow Netto bag. She gagged at the smell as she emptied the contents out on the floor. Scraps of a life. She emptied the old receipts out of the pink wallet along with the handful of coins, and the piece of paper with Gorm Thomasen's number and the photo of Karoline and Rikke, before the Kokkedals' lives had imploded. She ran her fingers inside the pocket of Pia's wallet and the zip-up compartment. Nothing. She looked at the other items. A comb with several teeth missing. Chewing gum. A tub of hand cream with the contents spilling from the side. A plastic pouch of tobacco. One glove. A letter from social services. An earring with a green feather.

She looked again. Tobacco, but no cigarette papers or a lighter or matches.

Odd.

She felt the plastic pouch. There was definitely something in it.

It wasn't tobacco.

It was a letter of thin, light-blue paper. Soft and torn. Opened and refolded a hundred times, with fastidious cursive handwriting in blue ink.

The message was anonymous and brief.

I saw Susanne Brande push your daughter in front of the train.
If you don't believe me, ask her yourself.

Jensen rummaged in her bag for the envelope Irene had used to tape the diamonds to the inside of the chimney. The handwriting was identical.

After receiving the letter, Pia must have gone to see Susanne and been sent packing with enough money in her pocket to drink herself to death. But before she had breathed her last, Pia had been struck by guilt and shame. She had used Gorm Thomasen to contact the daughter she hadn't seen or spoken to for years and told her the real reason she had lost her mother and father and beloved twin sister.

Oh God.

Rikke.

Jensen grabbed her coat and ran for the door.

332

81

'I have news,' said Mark, joining Henrik and Lisbeth in Henrik's office.

'Good news?' said Henrik.

'Bad, I'm afraid. You know we were checking out Morten Rastrup's alibi?'

'Don't tell me, he had one.'

'He did,' said Mark. 'We're not sure about Irene, but he was definitely in London on business when Vagn was killed, and on the night Ulla was attacked, several witnesses saw him at a reception at Borgen. Doesn't mean he had nothing to do with it, of course.'

'What, you think he had an accomplice?' said Lisbeth.

Henrik thought about what Goldschmidt at the Forensic Institute had said. Whoever the killer was, they had been either very strong or very angry. Angry people made mistakes.

If Rastrup had had an accomplice, it would have been some sort of hired muscle who would have finished the job on Ulla Olsen there and then.

'I knew it,' said Henrik. 'It didn't feel right.'

'I guess we're going to have to tell Wiese and Monsen,' said Mark.

'Not yet,' said Henrik. 'I need to think.'

With his sloping shoulders, Rastrup had been the very image of a beaten man. Henrik had assumed it was because the truth had caught up with him at last. Now that didn't fit. And in any case, it had been a little too convenient for Susanne Brande to point fingers at the dead, hadn't it?

Rastrup's laptop and phone had revealed an aggressive vocabulary and criminal contacts (Brande had been right on that score) but no evidence that he had interfered with the witnesses. Yet, he had definitely been to Irene's house, or they wouldn't have found his hairs there.

Henrik walked over to the window and looked out on the street. 'What about Susanne Brande?' said Lisbeth. 'Have we checked her alibi?'

'Still working on it,' said Mark.

'What if Rastrup told the truth and it was Brande who pushed Karoline?' said Lisbeth. She looked at Henrik. 'Don't you think . . .'

'Don't I think what?'

'That you might have been a little blinded by her? I mean, she is an attractive woman, and she knows it.'

'Are you saying you have new evidence to suggest she was involved in our murders?' said Henrik, sharply.

'I'm saying that you don't get to be someone in her position by being open to coercion and bullying by your father and school friend, yet this is what she is now asking us to believe. It doesn't stack up. If you ask me, that woman would be capable of anything, let alone killing three elderly people.'

Lisbeth was right: they would have to quiz Brande again, and a lot harder. But how could she possibly have got hold of the photos of Karoline, and what motive would she have had for leaving them by the bodies?

334

'I meant to ask, Mark,' said Henrik. 'Where did you get to with security at Riget? Did you find out who it was who visited Pia?'

'No,' said Mark. 'They only confirmed what the nurse had said. She had called them to the ward, but the guy had scarpered by the time they got there, and the nurses had been busy trying to stabilise Pia.'

'CCTV?'

Mark pulled out his phone and showed Henrik and Lisbeth a grainy image of a figure in a hooded coat. 'Could be a woman,' said Henrik. 'Did you ask the nurse to describe him to you?'

'She didn't see the face.'

'His voice then?'

'Couldn't hear because Pia was shouting and screaming.'

'Yet, she was sure it was a man?'

'That's what she said.' Mark's voice trailed off. He sat down, enlarging the CCTV image with his thumb and index finger and scratching his head.

Henrik turned to the window again. Karoline had been born when photo albums were still a thing. When you would take a roll of film to a shop and pick up the prints days later, hoping for at least a couple of shots that weren't out of focus or ruined by red eye, then patiently glue them into an album. He remembered his mother doing that, a hundred years ago in another life.

Henrik hadn't even owned a camera by the time his first child was born. He had taken plenty of photos of all three kids on his mobile phone, but never printed any of them. Instead, the evidence of their childhood resided precariously as ones and zeros on various hard drives and devices, which seemed to Henrik a poor substitute.

For Karoline, the photos had stopped abruptly in September 1996. There had been no high-school graduation photo, no first car, no wedding or first child. None of those landmarks had come to pass for Karoline, while Brande and Rastrup had had their fill of everything life had to offer.

And the rest.

Henrik had a sudden thought. He went across to the white-board and took down the three photos. 'Who could have been in possession of photos like these?'

'Pia,' said Mark.

'But she couldn't have done it,' said Henrik.

'The nurse at Riget said she didn't see any photos in Pia's belongings when she was admitted,' said Lisbeth. 'So that only leaves one option.'

'Rikke,' said Henrik. 'The twin sister no one knows the whereabouts of.'

Of course.

Jesus, Jungersen, you blind fool.

Later, he would not be able to explain to himself why he had thought of Jensen in that moment. The way she moved in his life was a mystery to him, but something had made him look at his phone, and the messages he had felt buzzing in his back pocket for the past hour. As usual, she was way ahead of him.

Brande is in danger.

And

Henrik, are you dead?? Wake up!!

'Mark, what was it that vet said, out at the dog place in Hvidovre?'

'Emilie?'

'Yes. She said she assumed someone from the dog shelter had called us and offered to take Samson. Did you ever find out who it was?

'Yes. Or rather no. It wasn't anyone from the shelter. I know because I went back and spoke to each and every one of the staff and volunteers. So I checked with the call centre and they said the person would only give their first name.'

'Which was?'

'Wait one moment. I am sure I took it down. Some pretty ordinary Danish name. What was it?' Mark thumbed through his notebook. 'Shit.' He looked up at Henrik, eyes wide open. 'It was Rikke.'

Rikke Kokkedal loved dogs. Less so people. Killing Irene, a woman who had taken money to lie about Karoline's murder, had posed no difficulty, but Rikke hadn't been able to bring herself to abandon Irene's Alsatian without food, nor see the creature put down at the discovery of Irene's body.

Henrik understood where she was coming from.

But Rikke had made an error.

And now only one person was still alive who had been present on 13 September 1996 when Karoline's body had connected with the S-train at Ordrup.

Lisbeth's phone began to ring. She checked the screen and put the caller on speaker. 'Gorm? What do you—'

'I just got home and I think something may be up with Rikke.'

'Why?'

'Because her dog is here, Charlie. Tied to a post outside my house, with a blanket and a bowl of water.'

'Fuck,' said Henrik, rushing for the door. 'Get hold of Brande. Tell her to lock herself inside her office. I'm heading there now.'

'I'm coming with you,' said Lisbeth, buttoning her gun into its holster, and following Henrik out of the door.

337

82

Jensen dropped her bicycle outside the sliding doors and ran
into the cavernous reception area of Brande PLC, sensing people
stopping and staring.

'Jensen, what the hell?' said a familiar voice.

Henrik was standing by the reception desk next to a well-
built blonde woman wearing a police lanyard. She was pushing
her badge into the face of the receptionist who was typing
frantically into a mobile phone.

'Susanne Brande is in danger. We need to find her,' Jensen
cried.

'Who the hell are *you*?' said Henrik's colleague, squaring up
to her.

'Lisbeth, it's OK,' said Henrik, turning to Jensen with his
hands up. 'We're handling it. Go home. Now!'

'Brande is safe?'

'I *said* we're handling it.'

The three of them watched open-mouthed as Gustav came
bounding in through the sliding doors. 'Where is she?' he
shouted.

338

Everyone spoke at once.

'For fuck's sake,' said Gustav. 'We've no time for this.'

He ran for the lifts, followed by Henrik, Lisbeth and Jensen. The four of them jumped over the barriers. Behind them the receptionist called for security in a loud falsetto.

'Where is Susanne Brande?' shouted Jensen at alarmed members of staff as the lift doors slid open.

'This way,' said Lisbeth and began to run.

A young man with brown hair in a middle parting looked up at them in horror as they entered a giant glass-walled office overlooking the harbour.

'We need to speak to Susanne Brande,' said Gustav.

'You can't,' said the young man, his eyes wide. 'She left.'

'Left for where?'

'I can't tell you that.'

Henrik pulled the man's shirt, so their faces almost touched. 'Someone's coming for your boss, so if you want to save her life, you tell us where she has gone, or you might be an accessory to murder.'

'She got me to order a taxi for her.'

'Where to?'

'I thought it was really odd. She never takes the S-train, and Nordhavn station is only just up the road.'

'WHERE?'

'Ordrup station.'

'Let's take your car,' shouted Jensen at Henrik.

83

Thursday 11:06

Henrik's car screeched to a halt by Ordrup station and the four of them ran down the cobbled subway and up the steps to the white station building with the globe lamps crowding the ceiling. Jensen ran for the door to the platform, spotting a flash of blonde hair through the glass. 'She's here!'

Susanne Brande was standing at the far end of the north-going platform with her back to them. She had a bag over one shoulder and both hands in the air in front of her as if she was pushing at an invisible wall as she walked forward.

A few people were waiting for the Copenhagen train, craning their necks at the sudden commotion. Some were filming on their phones. Lisbeth shouted and waved at them. 'Police, this way. Now!'

Susanne Brande turned around in alarm. 'Leave us,' she screamed, but was quickly distracted.

Jensen signalled to Gustav, and they used the moment to run up the far side of the waiting hall in the middle of the platform. Henrik set off after them, cursing loudly, as he reached for his gun.

'I have the money you asked for,' said Susanne.

At first, Jensen couldn't see who she was talking to. Then Rikke Kokkedal stepped into view, wearing a red baseball cap, her face screwed up in aggression. Jensen recognised her from the photo on Gorm Thomasen's Instagram. Rikke had the same genetic material as Karoline, but there was nothing left now of the schoolgirl who had smiled sweetly at the camera in her high-school photograph.

Before she could stop him, Gustav ran forward and took up position between Rikke and Susanne, waving his hands.

'Gustav, no!' Jensen shouted. 'Don't.'

'It's OK,' shouted Gustav to Rikke. 'Everything is going to be OK. It's over now. We know what she did to Karoline. You don't need to say anything. It's over.'

No one had reckoned with Rikke, just like nobody had reckoned with Gustav.

For almost twenty-five years, Rikke had believed that Karoline had jumped in front of a train. There had been no one to blame for the total collapse of her family, the vanishing of everything she had known. But all that had changed when Pia had called her from her deathbed at Riget, ashamed and remorseful, telling Rikke about Irene's letter, wanting her to know the real reason her family had been blown apart.

Rikke ignored Gustav and shouted at Susanne. 'I don't want your money.'

'But you said ... I thought we had agreed on a sum,' said Susanne. 'You want more? That's no problem, let me just—'

'You think you can pay everybody.'

'What?'

'You killed my sister.'

'No, I did not, it was Morten who pushed her, I swear to God.'

'When will you stop lying?' said Rikke. 'I know everything.'

'I didn't mean to do it. I was a different person then, a bad

341

person. I have regretted it ever since. Not a day has gone by when I haven't thought about it—'

She didn't get to say any more. In a flash, Rikke had pushed past Gustav and grabbed Susanne around the throat. Her golden hair framed her terrified face like a halo as Rikke pulled her backwards towards the far end of the platform.

'No,' shouted Gustav, running after them, trying to pull Susanne away from Rikke by grabbing onto her legs. 'Don't do it, Rikke. You might think it's going to help, but it won't. It won't bring your sister back. It will still feel as bad afterwards. It will never be fair.'

'Let go of me,' yelled Susanne. 'I'll pay you. I'll give you anything you want.'

There was a tussle that seemed to go on in slow motion, a jumble of limbs, with glimpses of blonde hair and red baseball cap. Then, Jensen heard the tracks humming as the S-train approached. 'No. Gustav!'

'Stop,' shouted Henrik. 'Or I'll shoot.'

But Jensen saw that he couldn't get a clear sight on Rikke.

'STOP,' she and Henrik both shouted as the train came into view, like thunder, brakes screaming.

A body separated from the melee and landed on the tracks. There was a pink cloud as unyielding steel connected with soft human flesh.

84

Thursday 13:37

They wouldn't let him in at first. In the doorway, Minna
Hansen was hiding behind the bulky form of her husband
who had troubled himself to get out of his armchair for once.
'*You* were rude to us last time,' said Kent Hansen, jabbing his
finger at Henrik. 'You're not coming in until you tell me what
you want.'

'All right then,' said Henrik, putting on what his mother
would have called his outdoor voice. 'We can discuss your wife's
theft here in the stairwell if you don't mind your neighbours
hearing?'

The door was opened wide. Henrik stepped inside the narrow
hallway. There was no offer of coffee this time, no invitation
to come into the lounge and sit down. Minna hovered like a
frightened bird. Kent puffed up his considerable belly. 'Coming
here, making accusations.'

'Drop it,' said Henrik. 'I know she took the watch. I take it
that it was your idea?'

Minna collapsed onto her knees, sobbing uncontrollably. 'I

told you,' she screamed, slamming her hands into the hallway rug. 'I told you this would happen.'

'Be quiet,' shouted Kent. 'You have evidence, do you?' he said, looking Henrik straight in the eye.

The nerve of the man.

'Tell you what,' Henrik said, getting out his phone. 'Let me call for reinforcements, some nice friendly uniformed officers and sirens as well, why not. Then all three of us can have a nice little chat about evidence down at the station.'

Minna composed herself and got up off the floor. 'Don't Minna, he's bluffing. He doesn't have any proof,' shouted Kent. 'Come back here!'

'I've had enough,' Minna sobbed, disappearing into the lounge. 'I can't take any more of this pressure.' She returned with her handbag and reached inside, pulling out Ove Valborg's gold watch and handing it over. 'How did you work it out?' she said, sniffling.

'I didn't. It was just an educated guess.'

'It was Kent's idea. She owed me compensation, he said. For the way she'd treated me. I shouldn't have gone along with it. I've felt awful about it ever since. I tried to go back to the house to put it back, but she'd changed the locks.'

'You stupid woman,' said Kent, shaking his head.

'He said we'd sell it.'

Henrik laughed into Kent's face. 'You'd be lucky to get a couple of hundred kroner for this piece of crap.' He turned to leave.

'Where are you going?' said Mrs Hansen. She looked as though she was expecting to be handcuffed and jailed.

'Back to the office. Ove's watch magically just turned up. I will let his daughter know.'

'What, you're not going to press charges?' said Kent Hansen.

Henrik made a show of looking around. 'For what? You know of a crime that's been committed? No? I didn't think so. But I tell you what, you'd better start treating your missus with some respect, or you will be hearing from me. Have you got that?'

('You bloody hypocrite,' said his wife in his head.)

85

'I kept your office just as it was,' said Margrethe to Jensen
as she led her and Gustav up the stairs of the old newspaper
building.

No one left to pass it on to, more like, thought Jensen. Another
three reporters had recently been sacked and *Dagbladet* was now
being written by a skeleton crew. Margrethe was facing the fight
of her life to save the newspaper.

As they passed Henning Würtzen's office, the old man shuffled
to the door, gnarled white hands trembling by his side. 'The
heroine returns,' he chuckled. 'Knew you couldn't keep away.'

'I never could stand that Brande woman,' said Margrethe,
turning on the lights in Jensen's office and looking around the
room as if seeing it for the first time.

Gustav slipped past her deftly and plumped down on his old
desk chair, spinning it around like a lunatic. Jensen shook her
head at him.

'Always struck me as phony, all that anti-bullying *mea culpa*
bollocks,' said Margrethe. 'The woman is a nasty piece of work.
Shame the sister bottled it at the end.'

346

At first, Jensen hadn't even noticed. The only thing on her mind had been to make sure Gustav was all right. He had sobbed inconsolably onto her shoulder as Henrik had led Susanne Brande off the platform.

Susanne had been swearing at Henrik, biting his arm as she tried to twist free of his grip.

Rikke Kokkedal, finally faced with the woman who killed her sister, had instead decided to take her own life. Or perhaps that had always been her intention. Rastrup and the other three witnesses were dead, but Brande, who was responsible for it all, would live. She would be going to prison, and her carefully built public persona was in tatters, but she would live.

'Perhaps Rikke knew deep down that you can never win against people like her,' said Jensen.

Afterwards, they had found two photos taped to the dark-green door to the station building. They were pictures of Karoline from the night she died. One of her in the Kokkedals' kitchen, leaning against the counter and eating a slice of rye bread with salami, and another taken in her bedroom. She was smiling broadly in the photos, looking straight into the lens.

One photo for Susanne Brande. One for Morten Rastrup.

Karoline *in memoriam*.

In Rikke's rucksack, abandoned on the platform, they had found a photo album, the pages worn from turning, with five photos ripped out of it.

'Come on,' said Margrethe, clapping her hands. 'The front page won't write itself. You've got precisely two hours.' She turned to leave, then added, 'You know, Jensen, I once told you I wasn't going to beg, but I really would like you to come back. I've been talking to the board. We've got one year to turn *Dagbladet* around, and we're going to have to take some pretty bold steps to make it. You won't get another chance to be part

347

of something this big and exciting in Danish journalism ever again. What do you say?'

Jensen didn't have to think about it for long. 'On one condition – Gustav stays too.'

Margrethe smiled. 'I thought you might say that. I already told the high school at Østerbro that he won't be taking up the place they offered him.' She turned to Gustav. 'We'll talk again in the summer, but you got your wish. For now. I'll talk your father around.'

Gustav fist-pumped on his swivel chair.

When Margrethe had left, her purposeful footsteps disappearing down the corridor, Jensen sat at her desk and opened her laptop, then closed it again. 'I never got a chance to apologise.'

'For what?'

'Calling you a liar, about what happened in Aalborg.'

'I don't want to talk about it,' said Gustav, without meeting her eye. 'If you ever mention it again, I—'

'OK,' said Jensen holding up her hands. 'I get it.'

Gustav dragged deeply on a vape and breathed out a cloud of liquorice steam.

'No more roll-ups?' said Jensen.

'Nah, smoking sucks.'

They smiled at each other.

'Tell me, was my front door really open when you came around yesterday?' said Jensen.

'Yes. Why?'

'Because that makes it twice that someone's been in my flat. It's like they just want me to know that they can do it whenever they want.'

She looked out of the windows at the red rooftops of Copenhagen and the bright blue sky. Soon, it would be summer, her favourite season in the city.

'We have to find out who *they* are. Could they be the people from that mansion in Vedbæk?'

She looked at Gustav. *Or are they your little friends from Aalborg, seeking revenge?* she thought.

'Will you be staying in the flat?' Gustav said.

'Nowhere else to go.' This wasn't strictly speaking true. Kristoffer had suggested that she move in with him in his flat in Nordhavn, but she couldn't, could she? A man she had only just met and knew hardly anything about?

They were halfway through writing their feature when her phone pinged with incoming mail.

David Goldschmidt.

> Dear No One,
>
> I looked at that case you mentioned. All I will say is that it *might* not have been suicide. I am not saying I can prove that it was murder. I am saying that I can't prove that it wasn't. You may be onto something.
>
> David

'Shit,' said Jensen.

Stay away, she heard Brøgger say in the mist at Amalienborg Square, as serious as she had ever seen him. Had he not realised that his warning would only make her more determined to discover the truth?

'What is it?' said Gustav.

'Carsten Vangede might not have hanged himself.'

'What?'

'Vangede was trying to tell us something, something that probably got him killed, and now all we have is the Vedbæk address. What if there was something for us to find in all his spreadsheets and invoices? With the memory stick gone, we'll never know what it was.'

'Not necessarily true,' said Gustav.

'What?'

'I might have accidentally made a copy.' He grinned widely and opened his grubby boy's palm to reveal another USB.

86

Friday 9:34

When Henrik pulled up in front of Jensen's apartment building in Christianshavn, he felt, for the first time in months, that all was well with the world. The sun was shining on Copenhagen, wiping away the memory of the long, drab winter along with his spectacular marital balls-up. The canals, the depository of many a dark secret, were shiny and inviting, cutting shimmeringly through the streets. A girl cycled by his car, sitting upright on an old-fashioned bicycle, her skirt and long hair billowing out behind her. There was endless possibility in the air, excitement, hope even.

He had found himself driving to Christianshavn after his daily training session, a detour to the office at Teglholmen where he could just imagine the reception waiting for him: Monsen would be triumphant that his man had come good, Wiese contemplative, his protection of Susanne Brande having turned out to be a spectacular error of judgement. Though he was loath to admit it, Henrik could hardly blame the man for that, having been taken in by the woman himself. Lisbeth had been right. He had given Brande too easy a ride for far too long. Still, the truth had come out in the end, and that was all that mattered.

Case closed.

To Henrik's mind, the only thing missing to make the morning perfect was having his old team back together. Would Lisbeth be making the move into organised crime? So far, she was making him wait. This was a well-established pattern with the women of his life.

('Too bloody right,' said his wife in his head.)

He had been about to text Jensen several times, but in the end had settled for a neutral message to both her and Gustav with the simple word '*Tak*' (thank you).

Neither of them had answered, which hurt a bit, even though he knew there must be no contact with Jensen from now on. As he had thought more about it, he had concluded that *if* he were to see Jensen, briefly, to thank her in person, it would not be wrong, but merely a professional recognition of the crucial role she had played in solving the case and bringing Susanne Brande to justice. There could be no official acknowledgement of that role, of course, no admission that Jensen existed in his life. Not if he was going to be the father he wanted to be to his three children, the husband his wife deserved.

The sun was beating down on his car. He put on his shades, rolled down the window and rested his elbow on it. The scent of spring wafted through the air, along with the smell of beer and cigarettes from the drunks on Christianshavn Square.

He had woken up thinking about Samson, Irene Valborg's Alsatian, and what would become of it now. Could he take Samson himself? His wife would go berserk if he came home with a dog, but the kids would soon talk her round. The more he thought about it, the more it seemed like it was meant to be.

'You can't,' Emilie, the vet at the animal home, had said when he had rung her. 'Samson's gone already.'

'What do you mean?'

'You know that old lady who owned it? The one who was murdered?'

'Irene Valborg?'

'Yes, her. Her daughter came and picked Samson up this morning.'

Henrik had seen dogs bring people back to life before. A dog had given Rikke comfort, but Regitse had struck him as someone who cared only about herself. Still, you could hardly blame the woman for having turned out unloving, with Irene for a mother. Perhaps now the old woman was gone, and she had lost everything, she would be able to start again, properly. Perhaps she really did have a heart after all.

The front door to Jensen's block of flats hadn't opened once while he had been sitting in his car, Henrik realised to his disappointment.

What were you expecting, a red carpet and a fanfare?

She might not even be in, he thought. Or perhaps she had returned to London for good this time. Or worse, something had happened to her. He removed his sunglasses and rolled the window back up, leaning over the steering wheel. Suddenly he wanted to see Jensen very badly. A quick five minutes, ring the doorbell, see if everything was all right, then make his excuses and leave. No one would know. It would be as if it never happened.

He almost knocked over a cyclist opening his car door, earning himself a mouthful of ripe Copenhagen abuse. He began trotting towards the front door, then ducked and backtracked to his car when the door flew open.

Jensen.

Jensen and a man.

His hand on the small of her back.

What?

Jensen did not have boyfriends. She wasn't the type. He had no right to feel that way, but this had always been all right with Henrik.

The man by her side was tall and looked like he used to carry a few spare kilos. Slowly, it dawned on Henrik who it was. 'Kristoffer Bro,' he said to himself.

Of all the men Jensen could have chosen, she had gone with the most dishonest man in Copenhagen.

He looked on, not knowing whether to run after them, or get in his car and drive away, when Kristoffer Bro turned, looked straight at him over one shoulder and winked.

Acknowledgements

I finished my first Jensen novel, and started this second one, during Covid lockdown, unable to visit Denmark from my home in London. I am grateful to my Danish friends and family for answering my countless questions from afar, and to Lars Jung, special consultant in the Danish police, for sharing so generously of his knowledge. Any mistake in this work of fiction is entirely my own. I am indebted to my first readers, Jules Walkden, Philippa Green, Helen Pike, Nick Aldworth and Jeremy Osborne, for their love and support. Thank you, as ever, to Kate and Sarah Beal of Muswell Press for believing in me; to Laura McFarlane and Catherine Best for their astute editing; and to Frederik Walkden for the map which accompanies this book. Finally, I would like to thank Copenhagen, my beloved city of birth, without which there would be no Jensen and, ultimately, no me.

DENMARK

1. Amalienborg Castle
2. Bakken
3. Bellevue Beach
4. Bredgade
5. Christiansborg (Borgen)
6. Christianshavn Canal
7. Church of Our Saviour
8. Dyrehaven
9. Forensic Institute
10. Frederiksberg Gardens
11. Gentofte Church
12. Kløvermarken
13. Knud Rasmussen statue
14. Købmagergade
15. Lakes
16. Marble Church
17. Opera House
18. Ordrup Station
19. Potato Rows
20. Riget
21. Nordhavn
22. Sankt Peders Stræde
23. Strandvejen
24. Teglholmen
25. Torvegade
26. Utterslev Mose
27. Østerbro

AALBORG

RANDERS

AARHUS

GILLELEJE

ROSKILDE

STOREBÆLT

SVENDBORG